In *Confessions to a Stranger*, Danielle Grandinetti weaves a tale that is at once mysterious, suspenseful, romantic, and inspiring ... Filled with truths that made me ponder my own life, this novel is a lovely start to what is sure to be a wonderful series!

—Heidi Chiavaroli,
Carol Award-Winning Author of *The Orchard House*

Danielle Grandinetti has crafted a wonderful tale of suspense and romance that will keep you on the edge of your seat. With well-drawn characters authentic to the era, a gripping plot, and a strong message of hope, *Confessions to a Stranger* is a read I recommend!

—Misty M. Beller,
USA Today bestselling author of the Sisters of the Rockies

A Strike to the Heart is a compelling story. From the very first page, I was immersed into the thrilling action and remained gripped with intrigue until the satisfying ending. The romance escalated right along with the winding plot, creating a layered mystery that is sure to delight readers.

—Rachel Scott McDaniel,
Award-winning author of *The Mobster's Daughter*

Riveting from the first scene, *As Silent as the Night* offers a unique, edge-of-your-seat Christmas read ... A beautiful, gripping, and romantically suspenseful Christmas story you wouldn't be able to put down if you tried.

RELYING ON THE ENEMY

Relying on the Enemy

Danielle Grandinetti

Hearth Spot Press

To my fellow mothers

"A mother's love for her child is like nothing else in the world. It knows no law, no pity, it dares all things and crushes down remorselessly all that stands in its path."
Agatha Christie

As for you, you meant evil against
me, but God meant it for good.
Genesis 50:20a, KJV

CHAPTER ONE

Wednesday, January 14, 1931
Crow's Nest, Wisconsin

Marian Ward battled the wind and her disgust as she pushed out of the door to the Lightning Bug, where the less reputable fishermen drank the winter away regardless of Prohibition. Never would she have considered asking for a job—and still not get one—at such a place, but she was desperate. If she couldn't find a job, couldn't heat their home, her little girls ... she shuddered, and not because of the icy wind that ripped across a sluggish Lake Michigan only to slam into her threadbare coat.

Where else could she look for work? The Lightning Bug was the last place in Crow's Nest for her to try, and without money to buy gas for the old truck, how could she drive to Hawk's River to look for a job? Were there any open positions left? Just one, at a place willing to hire a woman instead of a man. A woman with children, even if she was a widow. As times became leaner, those types of jobs became even more scarce. And how she needed one.

Tears pricked her eyes as she turned her back to the deserted lake and ducked into the alley beside the Lightning Bug. Walking home along Main Street would provide a better buffer to the wind. It hadn't snowed since the new year, making January bleak and gray. What little sunlight peeked through the overcast sky vanished in the narrow space between the buildings. However, she refused to give in to despair. Her girls, and her ill mother-in-law, depended on her. She would do anything for them.

"If you breathe a word of this ..." A hushed voice came from around the back of The Lightning Bug. Marian froze before she reached the corner and pressed against the wooden side of the building.

"I know, I know," came a second voice. Marian couldn't place either, though both were male. "You'll gut me like a fish."

"It's not a joke," the first voice growled. "If Wilson finds out, we'll both be dead."

Marian clasped a hand over her mouth to contain a gasp. Did he mean Buck Wilson, the head of the Crow's Nest Conglomerate, would ... *kill* ... them?

"Do you follow?" the first voice said. The click of a gun's hammer was unmistakable. She knew because her father had taught her to shoot. Growing up in the logging camps, he insisted she know how to defend herself.

"Get that out of my face. Of course, I understand what's at stake."

Marian's hands shook. The best way to defend herself now—and keep her girls safe—was to slip away and pretend she hadn't heard a word of this exchange. If the men knew, would they come after her? Threaten her children? Her heart pounded in her chest, but she forced herself to take one quiet step at a time, carefully backing out of the alley the way she'd entered it. Halfway to the opening on the wharf, she turned and quickened her pace.

"Hey, you!" The shout came from behind. "Stop!"

Marian ran. Steps pounded behind her as she dashed onto the boardwalk. *Think, think.* How could she blend in when there were so few people?

"Stop, you!"

She ran past The Lightning Bug, then ducked into the alley between the next two buildings, shedding her coat and hat and pitching them into a trash can at the back of the building. She turned the corner onto Main Street, scanning which building would give her the best chance at hiding. There. The milliner. It was only two doors down.

In an instant, she'd dashed inside, and held the bell above the door still to keep it from clanging.

"What's the matter?" Samantha Martins came out from behind the desk. The young single woman had secured an apprenticeship position here this past summer. "Where's your coat?"

Marian grabbed the young woman's shoulders. "I've been in here an hour trying on hats."

Bewildered brown eyes stared back at her.

Marian shook her gently. "Okay?"

"Yeah, yeah, of course." Samantha nodded, the ends of her bobbed black hair swinging. She spun from Marian's grasp and snagged two hats. She handed one off to Marian before grabbing three more. "Put that on and look in the mirror."

Marian obeyed. The baby blue hat washed out her pale face, highlighting the two pink dots on cheeks more hollow than they'd been a year ago. Her lips stood out redder than usual, too. At least the wide brim hid her windblown brown hair.

"That is not your color." Samantha rested her elbows on the wooden counter between them, in her hands a tan beret. "Want to tell me what's—"

The shop door flung open, the bell jangling like Marian's nerves. She spun, her hand pressed to her throat, not having to act an ounce.

Samantha sashayed around the counter. "You gentleman looking to buy a hat for the special woman in your life?" Her voice was a casual purr that caused Marian's nerves to settle and her mother's instinct to rise. Samantha's mother passed away when the girl was a child, leaving her in the care of her widowed grandmother. Did Mrs. Martins know her granddaughter could flirt like a flapper? Marian was of a mind to take the girl by the elbow and escort her straight home.

The taller of the men removed his bowler. "We're looking for a woman in a long wool coat. Brown. Faded." His voice immediately identified him as the first speaker from the alley, the one with the gun.

With trembling fingers, Marian reached for a black veiled cap similar to what she'd worn that first year after Zachariah died. If only he were here to protect her now. She set the hat at an angle to keep from drawing attention to herself.

"No one wearing a brown coat has come into the store at all today." Samantha's statement pulled Marian from her memories. "Isn't that right, Mrs.—"

"Certainly no one else has entered the store as long as I've been here." Marian interrupted Samantha before the young woman could give away Marian's last name. She didn't recognize either man, and had no interest in giving them any help if they looked for her later. She would not put her children in danger.

"There you have it." Samantha flashed a most flirtatious smile and batted her eyes. "You sure you won't buy something for your lady?"

The shorter one opened his mouth, but the taller one spun him by the shoulder. "Parker, leave it."

Mr. Parker shoved through the door. "I'm not a dog, Hayes. And I ain't—" The door closed behind the pair.

"Whoa, you need to sit down, Mrs. Ward." Samantha leapt to Marian's side before Marian's knees buckled. Samantha tugged her to a pair of upholstered chairs off to the side of the desk. "Who were those men? I've never seen them before. And why are you scared of them? Don't tell me you aren't."

Marian pressed her hands to her legs, willing them to stop shaking. "Just some bad men."

"They looked all right." Samantha gazed at the door.

Marian caught the young woman's hand in her own. "Promise me you won't go near them. Do you hear me?"

Samantha frowned as she turned back to Marian. "You sound like my uncle. Are they Conglomerate people?"

"Sounding like your uncle—and you listening to him—is not a bad thing, Samantha." Marian caressed Samantha's shoulder as she would one of her own girls. "He is looking out for you, just like your brother and grandmother do. Because they love you."

Samantha laughed. "How often have you told Nettie and Essie the same thing?"

Marian bristled at hearing her girls' names flung at her like that.

"No offense intended, Mrs. Ward, but I'm not your daughter."

"You're right. I have no place giving you maternal advice. But Samantha, those two, they're dangerous. Can you trust me on that? If your uncle were in town, I'd go straight to him about those two, if that tells you anything."

Unfortunately, Detective Michael O'Connor was not in Crow's Nest. Over Christmas, his nephews, Samantha's older brothers, ran into trouble at the lumber camp where Marian's parents still worked. Of course, that pulled Detective O'Connor out of town, even if it was out of his jurisdiction, and he hadn't yet returned. Not that she blamed him, seeing that she knew he was getting her mama's cooking. But the mustached older man was the only police officer in Crow's Nest she'd trust with what she overheard. Not only was he already investigating the Conglomerate, but his boss, Chief Sebastian, wasn't someone she'd tell anything of importance. Not after the way he treated her brother-in-law this past fall. That was a whole other story. But it meant all the men she trusted were out of town for the foreseeable future.

"I know just what you need." Once again, Samantha pulled Marian from her tumbling thoughts. "My grandmother would love to have you for tea. You can borrow my coat and I'll loan you a hat—not that blue one—and you can stop by and pay her a visit. You know she's lonely with the boys gone. Though she spends most of her time with Mrs. Whittlebush now that your brother-in-law whisked her niece off to Montana. They walk to each other's homes every other day no matter the temperature. Unless it's raining, of course."

Marian forced a smile. She was happy for Silas and Cora. Honestly, she was! But after Zachariah died, Silas had returned home and focused all his attention on providing for his mother, Marian, and the girls. Now Cora, as his wife, took first place in his life, as she should. It made Marian miss Zachariah all the more.

They were married for eight wonderful years after meeting one winter when he came to work at the Alaric lumber camp where she lived and worked beside her parents. She missed him terribly, but no longer accidentally set a place for him at the table, or looked for him to return from the fields as the sun drifted toward the western horizon.

The weight of providing for the family pressed heavily. Silas had returned West to send money home, but first he had to provide for his wife, then for his mother and Cora's great-aunt, both widowed and aging. While Mrs. Whittlebush worked as a seamstress, she had fewer and fewer jobs these days, and Marian's mother-in-law … her health was declining, and her medicine costly. What Silas couldn't send, Marian had to make up. With no job and no prospects.

"Come." Samantha tugged her to her feet as the bell towers of the two churches on either end of town chimed three o'clock. Mercy! Where had the time gone?

Marian gathered herself, and her purse. "I appreciate everything, but the girls will be racing home from school momentarily."

Samantha tugged the blue hat from her head and replaced it with a tighter fitting wool hat. "It's a brand new style from last year. A madcap, it's called. You can borrow it. Drop it off tomorrow at Grandma's, along with my coat."

"Thank you, Samantha, but I can't take them." Marian couldn't help pulling the young woman in for a hug, then holding her at arm's length. "Think about what I said?"

"Of course." But her wink said she'd do whatever she wanted, anyway. Including sending her with the hat. Marian refused the coat.

Similarly, Marian couldn't force Samantha to follow wisdom, but she thanked her for the borrowed hat, then hurried home. She would circle back to the alley where she tossed her coat and hat tonight, after the girls and her mother-in-law were asleep. Hopefully, Parker and Hayes would be long gone by then, or drunk inside The Lightning Bug—rather a blessing not to be hired at the place, even if she needed the work—either way, as long as they didn't see her, she'd be happy. She could wash her coat and it would be as good as new. Well, not new. Clean.

South along Main Street brought her swiftly to her husband's family's property. None too soon, as the cold seemed to seep into her bones. The property sat at the end of the wharf along Lake Michigan. She loved it here. The white farmhouse. The large barn she and her mother-in-law turned into a curiosity shop. She hadn't made a sale since Christmas, though, and since her mother-in-law's health turned this past fall they had purchased nothing new. Still, someday the business would revive. Wouldn't it?

"Mother?" she called as she entered the house, cold air following her inside. Obviously her mother-in-law hadn't gotten out of bed while Marian was gone or she wouldn't have let the stove's fire go out. It was their only means of heat now that Marian had canceled the gas and electric that ran the furnace. Her husband had been so proud of that appliance. He'd wanted to get her an electric oven, too, but his mother wouldn't hear of it, and since they lived with her, Elaine Ward got the final say. Now Marian was glad for the wood stove, though how she'd replenish the wood supply once it ran out, she didn't quite know. Fortunately, Silas left her well-stocked before he left.

"In here." Elaine sat propped up in bed, a book in her lap. Her eyes appeared the clearest they had in days. "How was your trip into town, dear?"

"Very good." Marian hated lying, but Elaine's memory had taken a hit this fall. Sometimes she thought her late husband and Zachariah were both still alive. It broke Marian's heart to remind her. Marian certainly wouldn't worry her over a couple of ruffians.

The back door banged open. "Mama!" Nettie's voice preceded the girls' appearance at the door to Elaine's downstairs room. They hugged her legs just long enough for Marian to lay a kiss on top of their heads. After her scare, she wanted much longer snuggles.

"Hi, Grandma!" Essie, Marian's six-year-old, clambered up onto the bed to plant a kiss on Elaine's wrinkled cheek. "Read me a story?"

"Of course, sweetie." Elaine patted the bed on her other side. "Nettie?"

"Here, Mama, catch." Nettie, a precocious eight, practically tossed her bundle of school books at Marian before climbing up beside her grandmother.

Marian smiled at the picture—the two girls with their brown braids and Elaine with her curly gray head all bent over the girls' favorite fairy tale. Marian was glad it was one of Elaine's good days. The girls didn't quite know how to manage when Elaine had one of her spells. If only Zachariah was here to help them know what to do. Marian was a capable woman, but she didn't realize how much she missed having a man around until Silas left with Cora.

A shiver reminded her she needed to restart the stove. Leaving the girls with their grandmother, Marian returned to the kitchen. She carefully placed the borrowed hat on a top shelf. No need to risk the girls mistakenly ruining it and then having to pay for it.

No sooner had she gotten the fire stoked and the kettle refilled than a knock came at the door. The hairs on the back of her neck rose and her heart picked up speed. Had the two men followed her home? Did she hide or face the problem head on?

"Who's at the door, Mama?" Nettie's shout provided only one option. No cowering for her.

Marian grabbed her broom, the closest weapon at hand, and flung open the kitchen door. Only to find no one there.

Had he gone to the wrong house?

Gilbert Cox shuffled his feet, his breath a white cloud as he stood on the Ward's front porch. He pulled his gray fedora from his head, running fingers through his black hair, belatedly remembering he'd used pomade to hold his curls at bay. He was most comfortable in a flat cap and rarely tamed his curls. But today, he needed to dress his best. Which meant donning his church suit and pulling the fedora from where it had been stashed in his closet.

Taking a fortifying breath, he knocked again. This time, footsteps bounded his way. *Finally.* Yet with that knowledge, his gut churned at what he needed to do. The reason he was here.

The door flew open, but instead of the adult he expected, a child appeared. In fact, she appeared to barely be of school age.

He bent at the waist to see her at eye level. "Hello, Miss. Is Mr. or Mrs. Ward at home?"

The girl cocked her head, her brown braids swinging and her nose turning pink in the cold. "There's no Mister—"

"Essie!" A woman swept in, wearing a worn cotton dress. She tucked the child behind her skirts and gripped a broom with two hands as if he were a mouse she meant to shoo away. Perhaps he was, at that. "What do you want?"

"Mrs. Ward, I presume?" He rotated the brim of his hat in his hands. He had to set her at ease or he'd never get the chance to say what he came to.

She merely raised an eyebrow, but Essie peeked out from behind her mother's skirt, her brilliant blue eyes staring wide at him. He was tempted to wink, but figured her mother wouldn't approve.

"Who is it, Mama?" Another child, a little older than Essie came to her mother's other side. She wore a wrinkled frock, though it appeared cleaner than the other little girl's frilly dress.

The woman barred the child's way with the bristle end of the broom. "Stay inside, Nettie. You too, Essie. It's too cold for both of you to be standing out here." It was cold for her, too, but Gilbert wouldn't suggest entering her home without an invitation. And he doubted one of those would ever be issued toward him.

"Who is he, Mama?" This from Essie, who used her mother's focus on her sister to slip closer. Gilbert tightened his grip on his hat to keep from kneeling to talk with the little one. He enjoyed children, cherished their innocence and openness, wished he'd become a schoolteacher instead of an accountant. Some day he even wanted a house full of them, maybe adopt a couple, too. For now, he contented himself with helping at a local orphanage as often as he could manage.

"Essie! Both of you. Go read with Grandma and stay inside. You hear?" Mrs. Ward tugged both children into the house, her movements furtive and her voice high with tension. Was she scared? Of him? She closed the door, leaving her alone with him not two feet away on the porch. "Can I help you?"

She wrapped her arms closely around herself, her knuckles white on the hand that kept the broom crossed against her body like a shield. A devoted mother, putting herself in between perceived danger and her children, no matter her own comfort, feelings, or safety. He needed to get through this quickly so she could warm up inside and be free of him.

Gilbert raised his hands. "I come in peace, Mrs. Ward. Actually, I came to offer an apology. More than that, if I am to be honest. I came to beg your forgiveness."

That got her attention. Her expressive brown eyes widened and her grip on the broom lessened. A gust blew in from around the house. She ducked her chin against it and shivered.

He couldn't let her freeze just to ease his conscience. "I can wait while you get your coat, or here's mine." He tossed his hat onto the porch swing behind him and shrugged out of the wool coat his mother got him a few Christmases ago. Before his father lost everything.

"I'm fine." But her teeth chattered. "Say what you came to say, sir."

He risked closing the distance. She eyed him as he set the coat around her shoulders, the scent of cinnamon wafting between them, but she didn't stop him. He retreated a step, though not out of broom range, despite the risk of her using it on him when he gave her his name. He cleared his throat. "I'm Gilbert, ma'am. Gilbert Cox. Robert Cox is my father."

It took only a moment for the name to sink in. He knew because her face—a rather pretty one, if he might be so bold—washed pale, then turned a brilliant shade of red. "How dare you come here after what your father did to us? Have you come to swindle us some more? Or take—"

"Mrs. Ward. I came to make restitution."

"You ..." She blinked. "What?"

Gilbert breathed a smidgeon easier, slightly more confident that he wouldn't be run off with the broom. Though that could change at a moment's notice. "I came to make amends for all the harm my father caused you last fall."

The broom now rested at her side, his coat nearly closed in front for how large it was over her slender frame. "I'm not sure what to say, Mr. Cox."

"Perhaps you might gather all the offended parties, so I must only do this once?" It was both an excuse to move her into a warmer area and a vain hope that he wouldn't need to humble himself multiple times. But he would, if he must. His conscience couldn't rest without doing what he could to repair the damage his father had done.

"I'm afraid the most injured parties are no longer here." She was a striking woman, standing before him, ready to defend her household against him, but even more so now that she'd softened. He could see the capable wife, the warm mother, that she must be.

"Your husband, then, is … Silas, right?"

She smiled a most brilliant, incredible smile, and something caught in his chest. He shut it down immediately. He was here to ask forgiveness because the Lord convicted his heart, not notice another man's wife. *Lord, have mercy, please!*

"Silas is my brother-in-law. He and his wife, Cora, were the ones your father kidnapped and held at gunpoint."

Gilbert lowered his gaze, shame outweighing any strange relief to learn that Silas wasn't her husband.

"My mother-in-law was nearly denied medical care by your father, so I don't believe it would do her good to be reminded."

He hadn't heard that part of the story, and it brought his chin up. "I'm so sorry. I didn't know." What his father had done to these people, all in the name of greed, Gilbert couldn't stomach it. He turned away again as tears pricked his eyes.

"Mr. Cox?" Her hand rested on his arm. "Are you quite all right?"

He gave a humorless laugh. "How can you ask me that? You should use that broom on me after what my father did to you and your family."

Her lips pursed. "Well, seeing that I'm the only one left to whom you might grovel, I give you permission to proceed."

"Your husband?" The last thing he needed was a jealous husband to arrive with a shotgun—the woman already wore Gilbert's coat—not that he deserved anything less after the attraction that had flared at her smile.

"I'm a widow, Mr. Cox. As is my mother-in-law." The words hit him in the gut, doing anything but letting him off the hook.

"That makes what my father did so much worse. The Bible says the Lord defends the fatherless and the widow. They are to be protected, not harmed. What my father did was reprehensible." He'd felt compelled to pay restitution for his father's sins, but this situation was even worse than he thought.

Her head tilted, so much like her daughter's had earlier. "Help me understand, sir. Why are you the one here asking forgiveness? It is not you who has wronged us. Why would you willingly invite guilt and shame for something you haven't done?"

How could he explain while standing on her front porch in the cold something that he wrestled with for months? He stuffed his numbing fingers into his pockets for warmth. "Because my conscience couldn't sit by without presenting myself to your family. I'm not asking for your trust or anything other than your forgiveness. And ..."

"And?" A tiny smile peeked out, the kind that all mothers seem to have mastered. The one where she's caught a child not telling the whole truth. Indeed, there was more to Gilbert's visit. The forgiveness request was his doorway to ask the very thing he hoped would finally assuage his guilt.

"My boss sent me to the Hawk's River area to visit clients. I'll be here for another ten days." Two weeks, total. It had just taken Gilbert a few days to work up the nerve to come here. "What I really want to know is whether there is anything I can do to make amends. Work I could accomplish around the place to pay back what my father did. Learning, now, that you are a widow, I cannot leave without doing something for you."

A newer Ford bounced along the drive behind him, parking in the gravel area before the barn where Gilbert had parked his own car. Mrs. Ward glanced from the new car, out of which a man in an impeccable suit emerged, to Gilbert, and back to the new man again. Gilbert didn't miss the way the color had drained from her face or the shake of her hand as she renewed her clutch on the broom handle.

"I do believe you can begin paying your debt right this moment." She closed his coat over her shoulders with a tight grip on the lapels, an action that caused an odd feeling in his stomach he'd worry about later. It would also be a message to this other man. One Gilbert was surprised Mrs. Ward would be willing to say. "Just follow my lead."

She marched toward the newcomer. Whoever he was, she feared him enough that she'd rely on the son of the man who ruined her family rather than begging this other man to run Gilbert off. Was that the real reason she'd sent her girls back inside when he knocked at the door? Had she been expecting this man? His father had caused her enough harm. There was no way he'd allow someone else to inflict any more.

CHAPTER TWO

"**M**rs. Ward, I was hoping I might have a word." The newcomer flashed a charming smile. Gilbert watched closely, attempting to understand the dynamics at play. Was the man a threat? An unwelcome caller? His muscles tightened. What would he do if that man resorted to violence? Gilbert had a strong belief in peace, and Jesus' command to *turn the other cheek*. He'd never considered how he'd do that and still physically protect someone.

"What can I help you with, Mr. Wilson?" Mrs. Ward faced off with the man, much as she had with Gilbert when he first arrived. His respect for her rose even more.

Wilson cut his gaze to Gilbert, who stayed behind and to Mrs. Ward's left, flexing his knees to ease his tension and keep the blood moving. His suit jacket didn't provide quite the warmth he needed against the January wind, but he wouldn't let on. Could Mrs. Ward feel his presence? Could she trust he had her back? It was the least he could do for her, though how he would act on it, he didn't know.

"Perhaps in private, Mrs. Ward." Wilson returned his penetrating gaze to Mrs. Ward.

She pulled the broom handle to her chest. "I'm sure what you can say can be said here."

Wilson frowned, the look marring the angles of his face. Gilbert had seen good-looking men like him plenty of times. Men who thought themselves better than others because of the amount of money their parents had. Honestly, Gilbert had no desire to make enemies of a man like that, nor did he wish to cause more trouble for Mrs. Ward.

"I can step beyond earshot, if it would make you more comfortable." Gilbert waved toward the barn. He'd give Mrs. Ward the option. Did she mind him hearing what Wilson had to say? If he stayed where he could see them, then he could still be available should she need him. *And just what do you think you can do for her?* The question had plagued him for months, though this was the first time he had a specific person in mind rather than the collective Ward family.

"I would appreciate that, Mister ..." Wilson held out a hand as he let his sentence hang, obviously hoping for the introduction.

"Gilbert Cox." He shook Buck's hand. "And you are?"

Buck did not let go, extending the greeting longer than appropriate. "Buck Wilson. Are you any relation to Robert Cox, formerly of Hawk's River?"

The man knew his father. Nothing good could come of that, no matter how they'd made their acquaintance.

Mrs. Ward stepped between them. "You know, let's step closer to the barn, Mr. Wilson, and you can tell me what you came to say." She hooked her arm in Wilson's to pull him away. It rubbed Gilbert wrong that she sought to protect Gilbert from something his father had obviously done. He was here to make amends, not make things worse.

"I'm his son." Gilbert called after them. Mrs. Ward cringed, but Gilbert wasn't sorry. Better to get the truth in the open, than let it fester, hidden away in the dark. He'd prefer Wilson target him than her, anyway.

Wilson spun, advanced on him. "And just what do you think you're doing here?"

Gilbert squared his shoulders. "Did he harm you, too?"

Wilson crossed his arms, appearing large and intimidating. Gilbert stifled a chuckle. Posturing didn't phase him. And if Wilson struck him, he'd take the blow and wouldn't fight back. That usually caused bullies to leave him alone.

"He harmed the Wards and Marian is under my protection." Wilson swung his arm toward her. *Marian*, he'd called her. "If you are here to hurt them, I—"

"I mean them no harm." His words were quiet, but he made sure there was a force behind them. Conviction.

"Wait." Mrs. Ward pushed Wilson's upper arm to turn him toward her. "Protection?" Wilson's countenance gentled. "Silas, before he left, secured a promise from me to look out for you. Mrs. Whittlebush and Mrs. Martins, too. All the widows he and David usually watch over."

Gilbert filed away the names to learn more about these people later. Ever since he'd left home, it was his mission to care for widows and orphans. If his father had harmed these widows, he'd add them to his list of people to whom he desired to pay restitution.

Mrs. Ward glanced back at the house. Was she looking for her girls? Gilbert was surprised they hadn't reappeared yet. The orphanage children rarely left him alone when he visited.

"Let's go inside and talk." Wilson gently touched her shoulder. He must have been thinking the same thing. Gilbert blew into his cupped hands, then reddened when Mrs. Ward noticed, and stuffed his hands in his pockets.

"You both need a warm cup of coffee, and the kettle should be boiling by now. Follow me, both of you." Mrs. Ward led the way back toward the house, the men following. Though Gilbert had to fight the urge to step a hair faster than Wilson, just to prove he could.

Right on cue, Nettie, the older girl, swung the door open and stuck her head outside. "Mama, Grandma fell asleep right in the middle of the story. I told Essie not to wake her, but she keeps trying. Grandma sure sleeps soundly, though."

Mrs. Ward's face washed pale. With one look at Wilson, she tossed the broom aside and flew into the house, Wilson right behind her. Left behind, Gilbert waffled. Whatever was going on inside sounded serious. Obviously Buck Wilson—whoever he was—understood the situation without explanation. Should Gilbert offer to help? Be there for Mrs. Ward? She had his coat, so he didn't want to just leave. Nor did he feel right about inviting himself into the house without her permission. Though he was getting colder by the minute.

Nettie stared at him. "Who are you?"

He squatted down to Nettie's level. "My name is Gil. You can call me Mr. Cox."

She cocked her head. "Like Anne's Gil?"

"Um ... I'm not sure." He could wait in his car, but that didn't sound like a suitable answer, either. He was worried about what had happened to the elder Mrs. Ward.

"Anne Shirley, you know." Nettie beckoned him inside and he followed, surprised not to find it all that much warmer in the front hall. Maybe the door had been opened too long.

Gilbert scanned the house, wanting to know more about where Marian Ward lived. Did she buy this house with her husband and then invite her mother-in-law to live with them? Yet his search had shown that Silas Ward lived here, too. Or had. What had Mrs. Ward said about him not being here anymore?

Nettie flung out her arms. "Anne of Green Gables. Don't you read stories?"

Gilbert laughed. "That Anne and Gilbert. Yes, I have read her story." Only a hundred times to the children at the orphanage. Some of the girls seemed to especially love the story, hoping they'd be taken to a home like Anne Shirley, and be able to leave the orphanage forever.

"Mama won't let me help wake Grandma." Essie trotted down the hall, arms crossed. "She yelled at me. Mama never yells."

If only he had medical knowledge, he could offer aid rather than be in the way. Then again, the pout on Essie's little face offered a way he could be of help. Once again, he crouched down to the girls' level. "Sometimes mamas don't mean to yell, but their voice gets away from them because they're worried about something."

"Do you think Mama is worried?" Nettie inched closer.

"She yelled at Mr. Wilson to call Dr. Thompson." Essie shrugged.

Gilbert's mind raced to scenarios, each worse than the next. He needed to keep the girls occupied until their mother could tell them what was happening. He could only pray the worst hadn't occurred. If his father had caused a medical condition that could lead to the death of these girls' grandmother... Gilbert already struggled to forgive his father. Now he wasn't sure he ever could.

"What do you girls say we read about Anne Shirley? Is the book nearby?"

"It's on the shelf." Nettie skipped into a room behind Gilbert that he guessed doubled as a front parlor. Its walls were lined with bookcases, and a sofa and two chairs sat on a large rug.

While Nettie pulled a worn book from a shelf, Gilbert went to sit on one of the upholstered chairs. Except Essie slipped her little hand into his first, and pulled him to the sofa. He sat, and she climbed up beside him. Nettie also clambered up next to him, resting her little head on his shoulder as he opened the book. His heart squeezed. This was a dream he had one day, reading to his own children while their mother listened nearby.

He banished the vision. How could he think that when the older Mrs. Ward might be fighting for her life? He cleared the emotion from his throat and read. "Mrs. Rachel Lynde lived where the Avonlea main road dipped down into a little hollow ...'"

Marian held her mother-in-law's hand, praying with all her might that Elaine would emerge from this episode. She didn't even pray that Zachariah's mother would emerge unscathed. All she wanted was for the dear woman to be alive. She checked Elaine's pulse again. Erratic, but present.

"Dr. Thompson is on his way." Buck returned to the room. She felt bad for nearly shouting at him to call the doctor, but panic had overtaken her when she saw Elaine slumped over and her little Essie trying to wake her. "Are you all right?"

She swiped at an errant tear. "This is the third episode since Silas and Cora left. Should I write them to return home?"

Buck clasped his hands in front of him. "You can tell them the truth and let them decide. I know Silas aims to provide for all of you."

Gone was the charming smile he'd greeted her with. Marian had never fallen for his charismatic ways. A snake oil salesman, Buck was. Hiding something, and after hearing those two—Hayes and Parker—talking about Buck maybe killing them... She trusted him even less than before.

But he couldn't know she knew that. And Silas did trust him. Why, she didn't understand.

Buck shifted. "What did Cox want?"

She realized then that she still wore the man's coat and that he hadn't followed them into the house. "Do you know where he is?"

"Reading to your daughters in the front room."

"Really?" Her girls were more curious than she'd like sometimes, but they didn't open up to just anyone and they'd never asked Buck to read with them. She needed to check on them. "Sit with Mother for a moment?"

"Of course." Buck caught her elbow as she moved toward the door. "Be careful around him, Marian. I wouldn't be honoring my promise to Silas if I kept silent."

"I appreciate that." But she didn't want to send Mr. Cox away. There was strength in numbers, and she was pretty sure Buck and Mr. Cox would not unite against her. Considering the animosity she felt between them, they would watch the other, keep one another in check.

Buck appeared to want to say more, but Marian slipped away. She supposed he was a good-looking man, but if she were to compare them, Mr. Cox, with that black hair fighting to curl against his collar, was more handsome. Not that she was interested. Zachariah was her one true love, and no man would ever live up to the down home country boy she had loved with her whole heart.

She heard Mr. Cox's animated voice before she reached the front room. "'I'm not expecting a girl,' said Matthew blankly. 'It's a boy I've come for.'"

Nettie giggled. "We're about to meet Anne."

"Shh." Essie hissed.

They'd made it into chapter two? Nettie rarely sat still long enough for more than a chapter, and was constantly wandering off. Essie, on the other hand, could read all day, unless she needed something from her mama. Marian peered around the door frame and her heart melted at the sight. Mr. Cox held the book well in front of him, elbows tucked close, leaving plenty of room for the girls to see the pictures without getting close to him if they didn't wish to do so. Her girls weren't overly affectionate with just anyone except her and their grandmother, certainly not strangers, but here they were, leaning against Mr. Cox as he read them their favorite story.

Marian cleared her throat, and three sets of eyes met hers.

Mr. Cox closed the book over his finger, but Marian motioned for him to stay. She needed to think. He was keeping her girls busy, away from the troubling scene of seeing their grandmother this way. It broke her heart that they had witnessed Elaine losing consciousness at all. Yet what did she know about this man other than that he was Robert Cox's son? It troubled her. What was the best way to protect her children in this situation? Who was the biggest threat to them? The sight of their grandmother? Buck, who could kill someone? Or this criminal's son who wanted forgiveness?

"Did Grandma wake up?" Essie leaned her head on Mr. Cox's shoulder. He inclined his head toward her littlest as she spoke, but met Marian's gaze, his asking an unspoken question. *Did Grandma live?*

"She is stirring, but hasn't woken yet." In other words, she was still alive, but not well. "Dr. Thompson will check on her."

Mr. Cox pressed his mouth closed, as if he wanted to tell her something, but wouldn't with little ears. She appreciated his deference. It made her want to pull him aside and lay out her problems. But his father had caused many of them.

"I wish Dr. Nick was still here." Nettie slouched on the sofa beside Mr. Cox. "He always knew how to help her."

Ah, Nick Matrone. Cora's friend, a good-looking Italian immigrant and doctor who lived in New York City. While he welcomed her correspondence regarding her mother-in-law, she felt awkward doing so since Dr. Thompson was the one treating Elaine. Marian ignored the curiosity that sparked in Mr. Cox's eyes. She'd consider contacting Dr. Matrone, depending on what Dr. Thompson said once he arrived.

An awkward silence fell. Marian cast about for an answer to what to do with her girls. Then she realized she still wore Mr. Cox's coat. Her skin heated. What must Buck think of her, wearing another man's coat? And that she'd forgotten she even wore it! She removed it faster than the girls wiggled out of their winter hats, gloves, and scarves. She caught Mr. Cox's amused expression. Her girls gawked at her, making her warm even more.

With shaky hands, she folded it over one of the upholstered chairs. "I'll just leave this here for you." Why did she miss its warmth and the citrusy scent it gave off?

At the other end of the house, a knock preceded the opening of the kitchen door. "Mrs. Ward? It's Dr. Thompson."

"I need to..." Marian pointed back toward her mother-in-law's room. What should she do about her girls?

"Go." Mr. Cox opened the book and her girls leaned in to see the pages. "I'll be here as long as you need."

There was a promise in his words that warmed her in a way she didn't understand. "Girls, call me if you need anything, okay?"

"We will!" Nettie bounced on the sofa. "Read, Mr. Cox. We need to meet Anne."

Mr. Cox winked at Marian, then picked up where he left off in the story. She hesitated, wanting to stay in this room where it felt safe and homey thanks to the mix of Mr. Cox's voice and the presence of her girls. Her mother-in-law needed her. Her girls needed her, though they seemed happy and content listening to Mr. Cox read.

"Marian?" Buck appeared in the doorway. He rested his hand against her back, an attempt to comfort, or was he sending a message to Mr. Cox? The former, Mr. Cox's coat had done better. And the latter she didn't appreciate. "Dr. Thompson is in with Elaine. Do you want me to stay here?"

"Please." She spun on her heel, unable to manage any more and needing to speak with Dr. Thompson. She filled in Dr. Thompson with all she knew about her mother-in-law, then stood aside as the doctor worked.

"It appears like another fit of apoplexy." Dr. Thompson tucked his stethoscope back into his bag. The older man shuffled toward the door. "Let's try putting her on a consistent dose of aspirin, but these episodes are getting worse. One of these times, she won't wake again."

Marian hugged herself. "I'll send Silas a telegraph right away."

Dr. Thompson stopped in front of her. Though he was shorter than her, his hooked nose gave her the impression he looked down at her. "I'm sorry, Mrs. Ward. I wish there was more I could do, but I can't even give you a specific time frame to tell Silas."

"Will she wake up this time?"

"Only time will tell." He headed for the kitchen. "And we won't know the extent of her faculties until then. I've seen some have an attack like this and be gone instantly. Other times, they have multiple attacks and each one leaves them weaker, and with less ability. She may lose her ability to speak or walk. We won't know until we see what happens."

Marian nodded, shoving her billowing emotions deep inside. First, she had to be practical. "What type of care does she need right now?"

"Water, tea, and broth." Dr. Thompson set his bag on the kitchen table and shrugged into his coat. "You'll need to go to the drugstore in Hawk's River for the aspirin."

"Don't worry, Marian," Buck materialized behind her, making her jump. "I'll pick it up and bring it over."

"That won't be necessary." They weren't that familiar with one another. The kitchen seemed to close in on her.

"Mrs. Ward?" Mr. Cox stepped into the kitchen. "Are there rules about snacks for your girls? I'm happy to butter toast or—"

"I appreciate everything all of you are doing." She threw up her hands. "Honestly, I do. But I need everyone to leave. Right now. Out. Please."

Dr. Thompson raised a gray eyebrow, Buck opened his mouth to speak, and Mr. Cox shoved his hands in his pockets.

"I mean it." She used her mother-voice, the one her girls knew meant business. "Out. All of you."

Buck visibly dug in his heels. "But you can't do it alone."

"He's right, Mrs. Ward," Dr. Thompson adjusted his spectacles. "Caring for your mother-in-law and the girls … You need help."

She knew that, but she was also at her wit's end. She wanted to scream and cry and would do no such thing in front of these men, which meant they needed to leave this moment.

"Gentlemen." Mr. Cox's commanding tone cut through the room. "Mrs. Ward might need help, however, she's the one who can decide when and where and the type of help she needs. Honestly, what good are we three to help her? We'll be underfoot. Let's leave her be."

Buck blustered, but Dr. Thompson mumbled his agreement. "Wise, man, sir. And you are?"

"Robert Cox's son." Buck spat the words, shifting away from Mr. Cox.

Dr. Thompson rubbed his chin. "I don't suppose we'll be leaving this house until you do, then."

"Oh, for pity's sake!" Marian shoved Buck toward Dr. Thompson and the door. "Leave the man be and go home. All of you."

"Mr. Gil?" Nettie ran up the hall, Essie trailing her. "Did Mama say you could stay for dinner?"

Marian—and Buck and Dr. Thompson—made to protest, but Mr. Cox dropped to one knee. "I can't stay tonight, Miss Nettie, but I have a favor you both can do for me."

"What is it?" Nettie asked, and Essie bobbed her chin.

"Can you be very good listeners to your mother? She's going to be busy tonight, so she'll need your help. And, when it's time for bed, give your mama a big hug and—"

"Mama, are you sad because Grandma is sick?" Essie took her hand and tears pricked Marian's eyes. "Don't be sad. Mr. Gil says that we can tell Jesus about it and He'll help us feel better."

"Oh, honey." She gathered her little girl into her arms. *Lord, I am overwhelmed and I need your peace.* She lifted her eyes and her gaze fell on the hat Samantha Martins had loaned her. Instantly, she knew how to solve everything.

"I think we should go." Mr. Cox stood with a smile to Nettie and a wink to Essie. "I left my wool coat in the other room, so I'll go out that way."

Marian herded Buck and Dr. Thompson through the kitchen door with much consternation on their part, then met Mr. Cox at the front door. "Around here, you can just come around back."

He shrugged into his coat. "Is that an invitation to take me up on my offer?"

Marian sighed and opened the door. She'd almost forgotten the reason he'd visited today. Somehow, he didn't feel like a perfect stranger any more and their conversation on the porch seemed like weeks ago.

"I'm serious about it, Mrs. Ward. Now more than ever. I'm not afraid of manual labor." He stepped outside and snagged his hat from the swing. "I'm in the area for another ten days. You can reach me at the parsonage next to the First Church of Hawk's River. The reverend and his wife are putting me up while I'm in town, seeing that my family's house is no longer ours."

Marian leaned against the doorframe, her girls beside her, and she realized Gilbert Cox had lost his childhood home because of his father's actions. He was a victim, too. Yet he felt some level of responsibility, enough to wish to make amends for his father's actions. The dichotomy intrigued her. If she didn't have her girls and her mother-in-law depending on her for their care, she might explore what made Mr. Cox offer to help her.

"I will keep that in mind, thank you." She attempted a smile. "And thank you for reading to the girls today."

"My pleasure, Mrs. Ward." Mr. Cox tipped his hat and walked away into the twilight. Marian closed the door against the cold.

"Will we see him again, Mama?" Nettie looked up at her. Marian caressed her eldest daughter's cheek, then tugged both girls into a hug. To be honest? Marian didn't know.

She kissed each head. "Let's put supper together for Grandma while I call Mrs. Martins and Mrs. Whittlebush to see if they'd like to join us. Doesn't that sound delightful?"

The girl's muted responses as she heard Mr. Cox's car drive away matched the same odd feeling in Marian's chest. She wanted the men to leave, but she might not have minded if Gilbert Cox had stayed.

CHAPTER THREE

Thursday, January 15

"Thank you for your time, Mr. Weber." Gilbert shook the hand of this Hawk's River store owner, grateful for the chance to introduce himself, not as the son of a greedy criminal, but as a dependable accountant for Burkes and Dudley.

"I appreciate your assurances that you are not your father." The middle-aged man stepped aside as a customer entered his shop. "I've worked with Burkes and Dudley for years, but also had a negative experience with your father."

"I trust his delinquent account has been satisfactorily settled?" Gilbert would wash through what little savings he had at this rate, but at least his conscience would be clear.

"Indeed. And I look forward to years more with your accounting firm."

Gilbert walked out of the store, noting the sky was as overcast as it was yesterday, and it dragged his spirits down. Just before Thanksgiving, when his work superiors had realized his filial relation to a financial criminal who had stolen from several of their clients, they presented

Gilbert with a choice. Either go on what amounted to a goodwill tour or lose his job. Though there was hope the economic downturn would be righted in the coming months, neither Gilbert nor Burkes and Dudley could afford to lose clients. And Burkes and Dudley certainly did not consider Gilbert special enough to risk losing business over.

So Gilbert spent the holidays praying over what to do. His mother urged him to follow his conscience, whether or not that meant keeping his job. Either way, the Lord would provide. What prompted him to agree to visit with all the Burkes and Dudley clients who had been negatively affected by his father, including those who were simply apprehensive about having a financial criminal's son with access to their accounting books, was the Ward family. The more he learned about what his father had done to them, the more he knew his time in Hawk's River had to center on making that situation right. And so as the new year rolled around, he arrived in Hawk's River.

Of course, yesterday's attempt to make things right with the Wards had been a failure. Bad timing. Or maybe his family just caused bad things to happen to the Wards. An image of Mrs. Ward—Marian—appeared in his mind. Her strength and frailty. The force of motherhood she wielded like a sword and yet she appeared as if a strong wind could blow her out to sea. He was drawn to the combination, which worried him. Kept him up last night, in all honesty. The desire to make restitution needed to remain his focus, not her expressive brown eyes.

Gilbert lowered his head against the stiff breeze. Though it was warmer here in Hawk's River than it had been at the Ward's property in Crow's Nest, the wind still found a way under his collar, chilling him. Should he visit the Wards again today or wait? He didn't want to be a nuisance when the elder Mrs. Ward was fighting for her life, but if he could help ...

"Mr. Cox?"

Gilbert halted and turned. Speaking of Marian Ward. She smiled at him from under a brown hat. Her brown coat shone in the overcast light, as if it had been recently cleaned. On closer inspection, he spotted the wear around the buttons, cuffs, and hem. Nevertheless, the bland color made her brown eyes shine. Or maybe that was the smile she gave him.

"It's a pleasure to see you," she said.

It was? He closed the distance, not sure how to greet her after yesterday. "I'm glad to see you, as well. How is your mother-in-law? And the girls?" Nettie and Essie stole a little piece of his heart with their acceptance of him.

"I'm here to pick up the aspirin Dr. Thompson believes will help." She waved at the drugstore where he had just been. "Elaine woke soon after you left yesterday, but is struggling to right her memories. Friends of hers are staying with her today. The girls are in school."

Gilbert was glad for the report. He stuffed his hands in his pockets, rocked on his toes. "How are you?"

Mrs. Ward glanced around. Was she as acutely aware of standing in a public space with the son of a criminal as he was of being one? "Might you escort me into the store, Mr. Cox?" Without waiting for his answer, she nearly dragged him into Mr. Weber's shop.

They paused just inside the door, and as his eyes adjusted to the dim interior, he realized her hand trembled on his arm. What caused such a reaction? He leaned close to her ear, an apple scent wafted around him. "Marian, what's going on?" Goodness gracious, he had just called her by her given name. Marian peered past him to something outside, then ducked, using him as a shield.

"Please pretend to be my ..." Her cheeks turned red. "I need your protection, Mr. Cox. Please?"

"Anything." He might not understand, but he didn't like her being afraid. Did it have to do with Buck Wilson from yesterday? Though she seemed fine with him after her mother-in-law's collapse. He wouldn't forget the skittishness she'd shown until a crisis demanded her attention. He couldn't be the cause if she turned to him now. They walked to the front counter together.

"Back so soon, Mr. Cox?" Mr. Weber greeted him, not hiding his curiosity at Gilbert's return with a beautiful woman on his arm. No words came to mind as Gilbert was still reeling from the last three minutes.

"He's helping me pick up aspirin for my ... mother." Mrs. Ward's hesitation spoke to her desire not to identify Elaine as her mother-in-law. By assumption, would Mr. Weber have thought Elaine to be Gilbert's mother? Did Mrs. Ward wish to pretend to be ... married? A surreptitious glance at her left hand showed she still wore her wedding band.

Mr. Weber set a rectangular tin on the counter. "There are twelve doses in here. That will be fifteen cents."

As Mrs. Ward removed her coin purse from her clutch, Gilbert's mind calculated the cost. This he could not only do in his sleep, but it helped settle his mind. Fifteen cents every twelve days, plus the twelve cents in gas to drive to Hawk's River and back. That was nearly thirty cents or sixty-eight cents every month. But if she bought two tins, that would save her seventeen percent over twenty-four days.

He whispered in her ear, the scent of apples again encircling him. "Buy two." What had she baked this morning? His stomach wanted to know.

Her long fingers paused over the coins in her purse. An instant and he'd counted them. Eighteen cents. She didn't have enough for two tins. How low was her gas tank? Did she have an income? A curiosity shop, wasn't it?

"I can't." Came her quiet reply.

He turned so that his mouth didn't face Mr. Weber. "Let me. Please?" There were many reasons he could use to convince her, but now wasn't the time or place. Would she allow him this without explanation?

"Okay, Mr. Cox. This once."

He jerked his gaze to hers, realized how close they stood, and his throat went completely dry. *What is happening?*

"May I get two tins?" Marian broke the moment by addressing Mr. Weber.

She seemed wholly unaffected, but Gilbert was whirling. He laid the required amount on the counter as the bell above the door rang, announcing a new customer. Marian tucked the tins into her purse, thanked Mr. Weber, and turned for the door, only to spin away and tuck her chin, her face perfectly white. Gilbert immediately wrapped his arm around her shoulders, and she leaned into him. Yes, he was not the cause of her fear.

Which meant whomever entered the store just now was. Gilbert glanced over his shoulder as he directed Marian away from the counter, deeper into the store. One tall, muscular man studied the shelves of shoelaces and another, similarly built but shorter than the other, picked up a can of polish. Their flat caps sat low over their faces, but their gazes pointed toward them.

Gilbert leaned close to Marian's ear. "Are these the men you're hiding from?"

She nodded, her grip on his arm tightening.

The men wove toward them, blocking the exit.

Gilbert's heart pounded. He hated violence. There had to be a way to protect Marian without fighting. He tugged her toward the back of the store. "Come on, let's see if we can find your mother a get well gift." He spoke loud enough for Mr. Weber to hear, the lie gritty on his tongue even as he prayed Mr. Weber had a back door out of this place. *Hypocrite*.

Behind them, Mr. Weber greeted the men, but they merely grunted. Gilbert quickened their pace, leading Marian through stands of ready-made clothing.

"They recognized my coat. I'm sure of it," she whispered. "I'm so sorry I got you into this."

"What is *this*, Marian?" No way out and the men's footsteps followed them. They were trapped, and no door provided a way of escape. He put Marian behind him as the two big thugs boxed them in.

"I'm so sorry." Marian trembled against his back.

"May I help you?" He rested his hands on his hips, hoping to appear as intimidating as the two fellows he faced. The sneer from the taller one said Gilbert hadn't impressed him.

"We need a word with the woman." The shorter one pointed to Marian.

Gilbert felt Marian shift behind him. He reached to hold her in place as he raised his chin to the men. "No."

"Okay." The larger man shrugged.

That worked?

The thought barely registered before a fist flew toward his nose. He turned in time for the hit to land squarely on his cheekbone. Pain shot through his head and his knees crumpled. He'd failed to help Marian in the one way she'd asked of him. He couldn't protect her.

Marian covered her mouth as Mr. Cox hit the ground. What had she done, getting him involved? And what were these men going to do to her next? If only she hadn't gone back for her coat last night while Mrs. Martins stayed with Elaine and the girls. If only she had another coat, she could have worn to replace this one.

Parker, the taller of the two, removed a six-shooter from a holster under his arm and spun the cylinder. "If you tell anyone about us, I'll do more than punch your boyfriend. I know who you are, Mrs. Ward, and the family who lives with you. Wilson hears about any of this and you'll be seeing me again. Understand?"

Marian's heart clogged her throat. The man wasn't just threatening her or Mr. Cox, he was threatening her girls.

Hayes tapped Parker's shoulder. "We need to go. The store owner is coming." Parker gave a nod as he stuffed his gun in its holster. He tipped his hat, and the pair disappeared into the shelves.

Marian allowed her shaky legs to lower her to the ground beside Mr. Cox. "Wake up. Gilbert, please."

Mr. Weber rounded the corner and froze. "What's happened here?"

"I'm fine." Mr. Cox pressed a hand to his face and tried to sit up. Marian slipped an arm under his shoulders. She needed to get him to a doctor, then she needed to see her girls. They should be safe in school, but she wouldn't let them walk home alone. Not until she was sure they were safe.

"Did she ... hit you?" Mr. Weber stared. *What?*

"Mercy, no!" Mr. Cox grabbed Marian's hand. His strength drew her in, and for a moment, she didn't need to be the strong one. Her forehead lowered of its own accord, gently resting on his shoulder.

"I don't like it." Mr. Weber growled. "I know your father was a criminal, but I honestly believed you when you assured me you weren't. Now this. I—"

"He protected me, sir." Marian wouldn't let Mr. Cox's brave defense be misinterpreted. "He's a hero, not a criminal."

Mr. Cox's hand tightened on hers. Did she truly think that of him? Compared to Parker and Hayes, yes, yes, she did.

"Well, I believe you should exit through the back. Follow me." Mr. Weber didn't wait to help Mr. Cox to his feet. Marian helped him stand. He wavered, but she braced him.

"I'm so sorry," she said as he gained his feet.

"We'll talk in a minute." Mr. Cox grimaced. That sounded ominous. "Help me back to my car. I'll take you somewhere safe."

Oh. She nodded, noticing the worry bracketing his eyes. They followed Mr. Weber to a side door—they'd turned the wrong way when circling the clothing—then Mr. Cox took her on a circuitous path to his car. Despite his woozy state, he drove a few blocks to the First Church of Hawk's River. Marian recalled him saying he was staying at the parsonage.

The brief drive allowed the situation to settle into her bones. Her body trembled. She folded her arms and sank into the car's seat. Was she really trusting Mr. Cox? Mr. Weber was right that he was the son of a criminal, yet he'd stood up to those men to protect her. He wanted her forgiveness. He'd been wonderful with her girls.

Mr. Cox parked the car. "I didn't know where else to go and those men won't follow us here. I trust Reverend Moller and his wife. They will have wise counsel on how to keep you safe." He ran a hand down his face, releasing a hiss as his fingers grazed his cheekbone. He'd taken a punch for her.

"Why did you let them hurt you, Mr. Cox?" She'd seen many men, including her late husband, throw many a punch to protect themselves or someone else. Growing up in the lumber camps, brawls were not welcome, but were also not uncommon as the winter months stretched long and the work, cold, and isolation wore on the men.

"Gil, please." He laughed in a self-conscious way. "I'm a pacifist and I didn't know how else to protect you other than putting myself in their way. It obviously didn't work very well if a single fist took me down. I heard their threat to you, Marian, and I can't let that go. You shouldn't have to face it alone."

She was already shaking her head. "I'm not pulling you deeper into this situation, *Gil*. Just because you helped me out here doesn't mean—"

"Stop." He faced her, eyes flashing. "You were terrified of them. And I know you were hiding from them yesterday, too. The broom gave you away. You have two little girls and a sick mother-in-law to think of, loved ones they threatened."

"Do not use my girls as a bargaining chip. That's what *they* did."

"I'm not bargaining, Marian." He flopped back against his seat. "I could have stopped my father. He was crooked, and I knew it, but he was only scamming other rich men who were scamming him right back. He wanted me to join the charade. It's why he sent me to school as an accountant. I refused, and he disowned me. So I left him to his criminal ways. I'd hoped he'd get what was coming to him. I didn't figure he'd hurt someone who didn't deserve it."

The explanation touched her. "That's why you came to the house yesterday."

He rolled his head to face her, showing his purple cheek. "Ever since he kicked me out, I've worked to be the opposite of him. I devoted my free time to volunteering at the orphanage near where I live. I do their books and spend time with the children."

"That's why you were so good to Nettie and Essie." It also explained how he read their favorite story with such a theatrical tone. He'd probably read dozens of stories hundreds of times.

"I save a little, but when I see a widow in need, I help. When I hear a woman threatened, I step in. Usually I can talk the situation down." He took her hand. "I'm sorry I couldn't do that this time. I—"

Someone tapped at the window behind her, and Marian yelped.

Gilbert leaned across her and opened the door. "Sorry, Reverend. We're coming in."

"I was beginning to wonder." A middle-aged man with graying temples bent at the waist to peer inside. His clerical collar declared his profession. "I'm Reverend Moller. My wife put the kettle on. Come inside."

Reverend Moller helped Marian out of the car in the time it took Gilbert to round it. As unsteady as she felt about the whole situation, she kept her hold on the reverend's arm as he escorted them to the parsonage. Gilbert trailed behind, which made her feel bad. She glanced over her shoulder and he gave her a lopsided smile. The pain in his eye—the one that wasn't swelling shut—caused guilt to rise.

"Come inside," a wisp of a woman beckoned them from the doorway. Her gaze bounced from Marian to Gilbert, as if not sure who needed her concern more. "I'll pour the tea and get you a bit of the meat I picked up from the butcher's today. Make yourselves comfortable."

"Don't go through any trouble on my account, ma'am," Gilbert called after her, but the woman merely waved a hand over her head and disappeared into the kitchen.

"Let me take your coats and things." Reverend Moller soon had Marian and Gilbert sitting together on the sofa in the front room. He took a chair opposite, leaving the rocker for his wife. A moment later, she bustled in. First, handing a small steak, partially wrapped in paper, to Gilbert for his eye, then pouring tea for each of them.

"Allow me to make introductions?" Gilbert removed the meat from his face for a moment, glancing at Marian with his good eye. Her stomach clenched. "Marian Ward, this is Reverend and Mrs. Moller. They've been instrumental in helping me learn about the Lord, especially when my father ... well. They were positive influences in my life before I had to leave home."

"And it is a delight to have him back under our roof, even for a short time." Mrs. Moller smiled at Gilbert almost as a mother would, then turned to Marian. "And how do you know Gilbert?"

What should Marian say to that?

Gilbert cleared his throat. "This is the woman I went to see in Crow's Nest. The one who my father attempted to swindle."

"And she's willing to be in your company?" Mrs. Moller squinted. "Or is she the cause of your eye? If that's the case, then I want my meat back."

"That isn't the Christian way, dear," Reverend Moller whispered loudly. Marian felt as if she watched a sports match, her gaze bouncing between the middle-aged couple.

"Maybe not, but a woman can defend herself." Mrs. Moller set her jaw. "Or we'd never have gotten the right to vote. I didn't march in '13 to take a step back two decades later."

"If you can't tell," Gilbert leaned closer to Marian, "Mrs. Moller is a suffragette, much to the reverend's dismay."

"It's not that I don't approve." Reverend Moller tugged at his collar. "It's the methodology that I cannot always condone."

Mrs. Moller opened her mouth, but Gilbert jumped in. "My black eye is from attempting to protect Mrs. Ward, which is why we've come here." Attempting, indeed. He'd gotten knocked out because of her.

Two sets of brows raised. Gilbert wrapped his fingers around Marian's, causing those two sets of brows to raise even higher. Marian couldn't pull away. She liked the comfort she drew from him. The feeling of not having to go it alone. It'd been two long years since she felt this way. But did it have to be with this man?

"You have a wedding band, Mrs. Ward." The censure Mrs. Moller pointed toward Gilbert was now aimed directly at Marian. She gulped at the force of it. Was she dishonoring Zachariah?

Gilbert tightened his grip. "Her husband passed a couple years ago. She has two adorable little girls, Nettie and Essie, as well as the care of her ailing mother-in-law. They are in danger, and I won't stand idly by."

Marian's heart swelled. Her brother-in-law had provided and protected, but it was out of duty, she knew that. Gilbert Cox's voice rang of something deeper, something personal. It touched her deeply.

Mrs. Moller's expression changed again, this time to utter respect. "I'm so sorry for your loss, Mrs. Ward. Forgive me. I might lecture our Gil, but I'm mighty protective of him, too."

"What's this about needing to protect Mrs. Ward?" Reverend Moller leaned forward in his chair, elbows on his knees, hands pressed together as if in prayer. "Tell us everything."

Gilbert nudged her to speak, but the threats Parker and Hayes had leveled tied her tongue. If she told this couple, would she put her children's lives in danger? She would do anything, anything to protect her precious ones. But having an ally in her fight would be most welcome.

Gilbert firmly believed his friends could help them, but he also understood Marian's reticence. After the blow, his ears might have been rushing, but he'd heard the man's threat and it sank in deep. He squeezed her icy hands. "I'll tell it," he said.

She shivered, but didn't stop him as he told about running into her today outside the drugstore, her suggestion at subterfuge, the men following them inside, and the blow to his cheek.

"But why did they threaten you?" Mrs. Moller wrung her hands. "How awful."

"I overheard them yesterday." Marian leaned into Gilbert, sending a wash of emotion through him. "Nothing specific, just that they didn't wish someone to find out about something. Rather cryptic, I know. They must have thought I heard more than I did because they chased me."

Gilbert flexed his jaw. That's why she'd been so scared yesterday. "How does Buck Wilson figure into it?" The men had mentioned the man after they walloped Gilbert today.

"I don't know. That's what I overheard, that Buck would kill them if he found out." She spoke so matter-of-factly.

Gilbert spun toward her. "That man was in your house, Marian."

She raised her chin. "And so were you. You both acted like territorial bears, so I figured you'd keep each other in line."

"Oh, I like you." Mrs. Moller spoke in an undertone. Her husband sent her a glare.

Gilbert ignored them both. "He was proprietary toward you, like he thought you two had something going. Do you?" As if it mattered.

Marian straightened her shoulders. "He's a flirt, Mr. Cox. I would no sooner think him a potential match than I would you."

Ouch.

"I'm sorry, that's not true." She pressed her free hand against her forehead. "Your father might have been a crook, but I find myself trusting you. Even before you took that punch. I don't understand why. I shouldn't. Your father nearly killed my brother-in-law and Cora. He nearly denied medical treatment to my mother-in-law. He ruined us financially. If I don't find a position soon, I won't be able to heat my home for the winter. My girls ..."

Gilbert set the steak beside his untouched teacup, the butcher paper protecting the table, his gaze straying to Reverend Moller for any quick glimpse of wisdom. Finding only compassion, Gilbert figured that was his best move, too. He turned to Marian, but was interrupted by the ringing of the telephone in the hall.

Mrs. Moller excused herself. Before Gilbert could try to express himself again, Mrs. Moller motioned for him. "It's someone from your company, from Burkes and Dudley. A Mr. Burkes, actually."

The boss himself was calling? This couldn't be good.

Gilbert entered the hall, picked up the ear cone, and leaned close to the telephone box. "Hello, sir."

"What's this I hear about an altercation at one of our client's place of business?" The man's voice boomed over the line.

How had he ...? "Sir, please allow me to explain. I was protecting someone, sir. A widow—"

"A woman who was thought to be your wife," Mr. Burkes interrupted. "Your reputation is already in tatters. Impropriety is unacceptable."

"That's not—"

"Mr. Weber fired our company, Cox. He fired you. And I will fire you if you don't make an honest woman of whoever it is you're corrupting. Do you hear me?"

"Sir—"

"Do. You. Hear. Me?"

"And if I choose not to comply, if she refuses to marry me?" Marian's words from not a few moments ago roared in Gilbert's ears. *I would no sooner think him a potential match than I would you.*

"Then you should begin looking for work at once. Work not in accounting because not only will I not give you a recommendation, I will make sure everyone in our business refuses to hire you. All doors will be closed to you. I probably should have fired you as soon as it became known that your father was a criminal. But you've been an exemplary employee until now. I thought you could fix this." His implication was clear: he didn't think so any more.

"And if I marry her, I keep my job?" Gilbert needed to know, even if he would never take this route. He couldn't ask Marian for a marriage of convenience just to save his job. He'd be no better than his father, using her for his own gain.

Mr. Burkes hesitated. "It depends on whether you can redeem yourself after this latest fiasco. We are an upstanding company and you are tainting it. Being married will make you more respectable. I hope. But one little misstep and you're done, Cox. Understand? And if you don't marry her, then you're through. That's a certainty."

"I'll need to speak with her. May I call you with my answer within the hour?" It was too short a time to make such a decision, but he knew his boss wouldn't wait any longer.

"She is there with you, at the church where you're staying?" The insinuation darkened Mr. Burkes' voice.

"She's visiting the reverend's wife." It was a partial truth to save Marian's reputation.

"Good. Then the reverend can marry you both at once. Call me before the top of the hour a married man or don't bother looking for work in accounting again. Are we clear?"

"Yes, sir," Gilbert said before realizing the phone line was dead.

CHAPTER FOUR

Gilbert leaned his head against the wall beside the phone box, his face aching. If he lost his job, he would lose his house and the ability to care for his mother. She was an outcast among society because of what her husband did, but before anyone knew about Robert Cox, she'd escaped him. She refused to tell Gilbert why she'd left her husband, and Gilbert respected her privacy. But she also depended on Gilbert. The way Marian's girls and mother-in-law depended on her.

What should he do? Marriage was a lifelong commitment, not a spur-of-the-moment decision to placate a boss who wouldn't listen to his side of the story. And for Marian, marrying Gilbert would be like marrying the enemy. He could never ask it of her.

"Gil?" Marian appeared beside him. "What did you mean that if you marry, you keep your job?"

He grimaced. "You heard?"

She nodded. "I'm assuming I was the subject of the conversation?"

He told her everything. She deserved to know what was at stake. Their reputations, his career, his mother … "I can't ask you to do this. It's selfish of me to even consider."

Her shoulders bowed. "I would whisk my children away from the dangers. With Elaine, I can't move her, especially now."

Of course not. Another reason this wouldn't work. His job was in Milwaukee. Though his mother would surely be willing to move to Crow's Nest to help Elaine. It would give her purpose, a way to correct what her husband had done to the Wards, just as Gilbert desired to do.

Marian fingered her wedding band. "I've had my chance at true love. I never planned to marry again because I had my chance at happiness, and I surely never thought I'd need to marry for convenience. But my girls' lives come before my own. I will do anything to protect them."

"Even marry the son of the man who ruined your family? How does that protect them?" Gilbert stared at her, realization hitting him. "Are you actually considering agreeing to this idea?"

She slid the ring from her finger. "You would keep your job, which means you could provide for us."

"You would be relying on the enemy, Marian." He couldn't let her do this. It was too drastic a solution. "I could barely keep you safe at the drugstore."

She laid the ring in her palm, running her finger over it. "I'm desperate, Gil. I cannot heat my home or afford medicine for my mother-in-law. And now my family is under threat. I need a provider, a protector. You need a wife." She shrugged as if it made every logical sense. On paper, perhaps it did, but this was marriage they were talking about.

He closed her hand over the ring, her fingers dry, cracked from work and winter. He couldn't let go as he should. "I cannot in good conscience allow you to do this. No. It's not right. I'll provide for you, protect you as best I can, but you do not have to marry me for me to do that for you." Even if it cost him his income.

She kept her gaze on their hands, twin pink dots appearing on her cheeks. "It is rather forward of me, I suppose. And I understand your reticence to marry a widow with a ready-made family. You deserve to marry for love, not necessity. I know what a love like that feels like, and I would never want to deprive that from you."

"That's not it, Marian."

She tugged away. "I thought we could help each other, but it was foolishness. Gil, you deserve a marriage of love. I'm sorry I brought this on you. Risking your job ... I thought I could help you fix it. I'm sorry. I'm so—"

"Stop." He clasped her upper arms, barely resisting the urge to draw her into an embrace. She wouldn't welcome such an action, but she raised her liquid gaze to his and his thoughts grew wings. This brave, beautiful woman would do anything to protect her family, even marry the son of the man who caused this pain. It put him to shame. If he were to be so unselfish, what choice would he make?

Yes, this situation would help him keep his job—maybe, his boss left him with no guarantees—but it would be of greater benefit to Marian. To be her protector, her provider, to redeem what his father had broken ... he deserved to sacrifice the type of marriage he always hoped to have. He'd never force Marian into the physical expectations of marriage, though he could hope she'd come to care for him one day.

Or he could walk away. Walk away from Marian and her problems, his job and their expectations, his father and the shadow he cast, even from prison.

Words from the book of Micah filtered into his mind like sunlight through the clouds. *He hath shewed thee, O man, what is good; and what doth the Lord require of thee, but to do justly, and to love mercy, and to walk humbly with thy God?*

That was his answer. Whether or not she agreed to marry him, no matter what it meant for his job ... Gilbert would protect Marian Ward and provide for her family. He might even prayerfully reconsider his stance against violence if it meant keeping her and her sweet little girls safe.

The clock chimed half past the hour. Only thirty more minutes to decide and, if that decision meant a wedding, to get married. He would leave the decision, and his future, in Marian's hands. He had his marching orders.

Marian listened to the grandfather clock complete its musical tones. The cheery notes conflicted with the complex emotion swirling in her chest. And then Gilbert dropped to one knee.

"The decision is entirely yours, Marian." He held out open hands. No ring or wildflowers as Zachariah had done when he proposed to her at the lumber camp so many years ago. "I would be honored to be your husband, your provider, your protector. Will you marry me?"

Words clogged in Marian's throat. Desperation battled doubt. She didn't know what to say, what the right answer would be, so she motioned for him to stand up, then tugged him back into the front room where she'd left Reverend Moller and his wife. Surely they could help point her in the way God would have for them.

The reverend stood when they entered. "No need to repeat anything. We heard everything."

Marian's cheeks heated, but she was grateful. They had little time if they were also to save Gilbert's job. She dropped his hand, but remained standing beside him. "What do we do?"

Reverend Moller glanced at his wife, who nodded, then back to Marian and Gilbert. "First let me ask ... Gilbert, why do you want to marry Marian?"

"To protect and provide." His answer was immediate, sure. It surprised Marian.

"Not for your job?" That was why this conversation started. It's how she'd help him in exchange for his provision and protection, exactly what he was offering. But that he thought of her needs first had her off kilter. Honestly, she hadn't expected that from Robert Cox's son ...

"It'll help that, of course, but I'm on thin ice with my boss right now and there is no guarantee I'll keep this job."

"Then how will you provide for us?" Panic set in. Marriage was a permanent decision.

"Then I'll find another job." He bent so she had no choice but to look at him, his expression so earnest she wanted to trust him. "I'll go wherever I have to in order to make sure you're provided for."

"But then you won't be here to protect us." Tears pricked her eyes as her gaze took in his bruised cheek. She shook her head. "This is foolishness."

"Would you gentlemen take the dishes to the kitchen, please?" Mrs. Moller's question was anything but. Her husband and Gilbert obeyed immediately, then the middle-aged woman drew Marian to the sofa and sat beside her. "You are a strong woman, Marian. I could tell from the first moment I met you. You've been forced to be everything for your children, your mother-in-law, and now your back is pinned to a wall."

Marian traced the flower pattern on the sofa fabric. "What if I make the wrong choice? What if I put my children in more danger?"

"From Gil?"

Marian thought back to how he was with the girls yesterday, how they warmed up to him immediately. She raised her gaze to Mrs. Moller. "What if he breaks their hearts?"

Mrs. Moller cocked her head, compassion warming her eyes. "You mean, what if you lose him like you lost your husband?"

Did she mean that? She deflected. "And my brother-in-law, though he didn't die, of course. Still, my girls lost the man they considered a second father when he went West." Silas had left to provide, but the provision wasn't enough. Would the same be true of Gilbert?

Mrs. Moller patted Marian's shoulder. "The uncertain future is scary and marriage is for a lifetime. But you know what lasts forever? God's love for you, for Gilbert, for your girls and mother-in-law. You can probably guess how I feel about women's rights, but I also believe that God uses unique ways to provide, especially for widows and the fatherless. Could Gilbert be that for you?"

Could he be the answer to her prayers? But why would God choose the son of the man who hurt them so horribly last year?

"There's a verse coming to mind. Let me find it." Mrs. Moller retrieved a Bible on a nearby shelf, returned to the sofa to page through it. "Here it is. Mark chapter twelve. Jesus is criticizing the religious leaders for 'devouring widows' houses.' If that made Him angry then, do you believe it makes Him angry now? Do you trust God would protect you, the most vulnerable of his children? Perhaps by sending Gilbert to you in your greatest hour of need."

God, I'm placing my life, and the lives of my girls, in Your hands. The prayer settled Marian's doubt and peace filled her heart. The grandfather clock chimed three-quarters of an hour. Marian needed to know one more thing. She gripped Mrs. Moller's wrist. "Would you trust Gilbert with your children?"

Mrs. Moller didn't blink. "Absolutely. I already have, and my daughter is alive today because of it. In fact, she and her husband named their newborn Jonah Gilbert. Did I mention I just became a grandmother? I'm over the moon about it. But we don't have time for me to gush. What have you decided?"

How the woman knew Marian had decided anything she didn't know. Marian herself didn't realize it until Mrs. Moller asked her. If a woman named her child after someone who saved their life, he had to be a good man. The type of man who took a punch to save her would be a man who would protect her girls. That was exactly the kind of man she needed right now.

Marian stood. "Let's find the men and have a wedding." She only wished her girls could be here, too.

With his one good eye, Gilbert watched the pendulum of the grandfather clock swing back and forth while Reverend Moller asked the telephone operator to patch him through to Mr. Burkes. Gilbert slid his palms down his trousers to wipe the sweat off them before he took Marian's hands. Mrs. Moller stood to the side as a witness.

Ten minutes to three. Less than ten minutes to become a husband.

How he wished they had more time. Marian deserved a church ceremony with her girls, her friends, and family—he wasn't even sure how much family she had! And his own mother would be livid when she learned he'd married without her present. Did he dare try to push his boss to extend the deadline in favor of a public ceremony? No. Marian needed provision and protection now. The side of his face ached, but he pushed the pain away.

Marian cocked her head. Had she seen the doubt flash through his eyes? Or his pain? He hoped she saw his determination now. He squeezed her fingers.

"Ah, Mr. Burkes? This is Reverend Moller, Gilbert's—yes, that is why I am calling. Considering the urgent nature of this ceremony, I would like you to remain on the line while I wed Gilbert and—I'm sure you're busy, but the longer you dither about it, the closer we get to your deadline."

Gilbert caught Marian's smile before she tucked her chin.

"Ready?" Reverend Moller took a moment to meet Gilbert's gaze, then Marian's, giving them each one last chance to change their minds. Gilbert squeezed Marian's hands again, he was sure. Then she gripped them back. This was it. Reverend Moller cleared his throat. "Then step closer to the telephone box so our audience can hear clearly. We are gathered here today to join Gilbert Cox and Marian Ward in holy matrimony. Gilbert, repeat after me."

Gilbert dutifully followed Reverend Moller's words, pledging himself in sickness and health, joy and sorrow, but when the vows became a promise, he stepped closer to Marian, wanting her to know he meant what he about to say. "I promise to love you, and to be faithful to you, as long as we both shall live."

Marian sucked in a breath. She understood he meant this promise. The love he'd show her wasn't a dime novel romance kind of feeling, with fluttery hearts and passionate kisses. It was God's love. Sacrificial. Thinking of her before himself. He would fail at times because he was human, but that was the promise he meant. And to be faithful. No matter whether theirs would never be a typical marriage, he would be faithful to her until the end. This was his calling, his ministry, for life.

"Marian?" Reverend Moller prompted her this time. She spoke quietly, but without hesitation. It made Gilbert stand taller. He wouldn't fail her.

The grandfather clock broke into its top-of-the-hour song and Reverend Moller raised his voice. "With the power vested in me, I now pronounce you man and wife." Gilbert's heart did a funny flip. He was married.

Mrs. Moller grabbed the telephone's earpiece as the clock struck the first bell of the hour. "Did you hear that, Mr. Burkes? They're officially wed as requested."

The clock struck the second bell. Reverend Moller leaned closer to the mouthpiece. "You may kiss the bride."

Marian's cheeks turned a brilliant shade of red. Gilbert was sure his had, too. Still, he tugged her closer and pressed a light kiss to her cheek as the clock struck a third time. Gilbert's heart stuttered. Keeping his vow to sacrificially love Marian as she needed might be harder than he realized. A fourth bell. Decades under the same roof with this beautiful woman ...

"Aww." Mrs. Moller sighed before another chime rang in the hall. No one spoke again until the clock fell silent.

"Mr. Burkes would like a word." Reverend Moller motioned Gilbert toward the phone. He'd need to repay the reverend for the long distance bill.

"Sir?" Exhaustion washed over Gilbert, and he realized just how much his cheek throbbed.

"Congratulations on getting hitched just under the wire." Mr. Burkes' gruff voice sounded none too pleased. "What appointments do you have scheduled for tomorrow?"

"Tomorrow?" Gilbert tried to mentally pull up his plan.

"Tomorrow?" Mrs. Moller yanked the earpiece from Gilbert's hand. "You listen here, Mr. Burkes. These two just got married and they're all starry-eyed in love. You expect your man here to work tomorrow while leaving his new bride at home? Hmph. I—"

Reverend Moller took the earpiece from his wife. "I'd apologize, but my wife is right. Surely you can spare your man here until Monday. Good. Here he is."

Again, the earpiece was handed back to Gilbert. He stepped to the phone box. "Yes, sir?"

"I expect impeccable work on Monday, Cox. I want clients calling me with gratitude for you being their accountant. Is that understood?"

Gilbert swallowed. "Yes, sir."

"And any—I mean any—missteps, and you're fired."

Before Gilbert could reply, the phone line clicked with the end of the call.

"Starry-eyed?" Reverend Moller sighed. "My dear wife."

"It's true." She crossed her arms. "I know what I saw."

Before this escalated, Gilbert jumped in. "Thank you both for, well, everything. I should escort Marian back ..." He looked at her, suddenly feeling awkward and unsure what he should do, and too foggy to have a ready answer.

Marian hugged herself. "If you'll drive me back to my truck, I'll go home and ready a room for you. I need to return before the girls are finished with school. And, that way, you can gather your things at your own pace. Perhaps put something cool on your cheek again."

How gracious she was, thinking of him, and yet solidly setting boundaries and expectations. He liked that about her.

"Nonsense." Mrs. Moller hooked her arm around Marian's. "I know full well that Gilbert packed light. One suitcase and he wouldn't let my husband help him with it. If you allow me, I'll be happy to drive your truck back tomorrow and the reverend can bring me home."

The women shared a look that Gilbert didn't understand.

Marian's shoulders relaxed. "Thank you, Mrs. Moller."

"You must call me Jessica." Mrs. Moller lowered her voice to a stage whisper. "Named after a character in a William Shakespeare play, I was."

Laughter broke the last of the tension, and he could have hugged her for it.

Marian leaned back against the car seat, Gilbert's cologne stronger in the closed interior. It was a heady scent. Or maybe that was her own senses swirling from the unexpected day. Her original plan had been to get her mother-in-law's medicine, perhaps see if there happened to be a job opening, then return home. Not get attacked by the men she'd overheard yesterday. And certainly not *get married*!

She glanced over at the man beside her. He was handsome, not that it mattered. His provision and his protection are what did. Women had come a long way in the last several decades—Jessica Moller had helped see to that—but not far enough for her to avoid a marriage of convenience. If only other men she trusted were in town. If only Silas had been able to send enough money from out West. If only she hadn't been in the wrong place to overhear something she didn't understand.

But there was no going back on any of it. Anyway, she strangely didn't mind the idea of having Gilbert around. He gave off a feeling of safety. Odd for the son of the man who put them in this predicament in the first place.

If they were stuck in this situation for … well, life, she might as well try to get to know him. "Mrs. Moller—Jessica—said you saved her daughter?"

"What?" Gilbert glanced at her, then back at the road.

"Sorry." She probably should have started by asking his favorite color or his preferred hobbies. "When I asked if she'd trust you with her children, she said she had and that you now have a namesake."

A grin crinkled the skin around his eyes. "Yeah, baby Jonah. I haven't met him yet since they live in Minnesota. I'm honored, to say the least."

"I sense a good bit of modesty." She had no right to know the story, but her mother's heart wanted to hear it. To sink into the confidence that this man would protect her daughters from the ruffians who cornered her and Gilbert today.

"Not much to tell." He lifted a shoulder. "She's a shy girl, but latched onto me as an older brother from the hours I spent with the Mollers in my youth. One day, she was attacked in an alley near her house. I put an end to it. And that's that."

Marian doubted it. "She named her child after you."

Red colored his neck. "Virginia and I have different perspectives on that day. She considers me a hero. For me, that was the day I chose to become a pacifist."

Unease tightened Marian's belly. "What do you mean, a pacifist?" People who believed that way were against violence. Is that why he took a punch instead of fighting back? Would he actually be able to protect them, or had she just made a huge mistake?

"Somehow, I feel like we should know each other better before we get into such personal beliefs." The edge in his voice caused her heart to pound.

"I don't care about your *personal beliefs*, Mr. Cox. I care about whether you will protect my children if someone tries to harm them. Or will you just stand there and let the thugs knock you out so they can hurt my girls?"

Gilbert swerved the car onto the side of the road. The bridge spanning Crow's Nest Creek, and the only way in or out of town, was just up ahead. She could get out and walk.

But Gilbert caught her wrist before she got the car door open. "Wait."

Marian pursed her lips and glared at the hand he still had on her. He released her immediately.

"Sorry. I'm not proud of what happened that day."

"You saved someone!" This made no sense.

He rubbed his temple, on the good side of his face. "I was so livid to see those older boys cornering Virginia that I jumped in with fists flying. She escaped and didn't see the rest, so she thought my actions incredibly heroic. But I didn't stop beating those boys after she got away. I wanted them to know how it felt to be hurt by someone bigger, stronger than them. It scared me how much I took justice into my own hands."

"Did you ..." She wasn't sure how to ask what happened to those boys, but she wanted to know.

He shook his head. "I came to my senses before they had anything more than broken noses, black eyes, and a few cracked ribs. But I came away changed, too. I realized that I had taken justice into my own hands. From that day forward, I promised myself to use words first. To turn the other cheek. Even while standing up to bullies."

That sounded lovely and all, but ... "What if they physically attack my children?"

He looked her straight in the eye with his open one, a steely determination glinting in its depths. "Then I will do everything in my power to make sure they cannot lay a hand on your girls. No one will touch them. You have my word."

CHAPTER FIVE

With his promise ringing in his ears, Gilbert drove them to the Ward house to check on Marian's mother-in-law before going to pick up her girls.

Only one car sat in the lot as they passed it to park behind the Ward's white farmhouse. Yesterday, when he arrived, he was a stranger. Today he was a husband. He couldn't quite wrap his mind around that drastic of a change. His aching face didn't help him think clearly, either. He wished for something cool to place over his swollen eye.

"Did we do the right thing?" Marian whispered, her fingers tangled in her lap as she sat motionless beside him.

Honestly? Gilbert didn't know. He wouldn't tell her that, however. Instead, he shifted in his seat to face this woman he would now call *wife*. "Can you trust me enough to protect you? And provide? That's why we went through with it."

Marian nodded. "You've convinced me of that, and I thank you." That was a relief, at least.

"Then the rest will work itself out." He hoped.

Marian still didn't move. Why? She worried about something, and he suspected it had to do with them being married. His neck heated. Did she think he'd expect tonight ... Embarrassment pulsed through him. *He* wasn't ready for such things. They hardly knew one another! How could he reassure her when he was too uncomfortable to even broach the topic?

"I've been married, Gil." Her cheeks bloomed red. "I know how these things go. I was so worried about my girls that I pushed the rest of what being married meant out of my mind."

"Marian." He needed to assure her he had no expectations. Though it pinched his pride that she had experience knowing how to navigate a marriage and he did not. His own mother ran from her marriage, so what did he know of being a good husband? His heart twisted. He knew what *not* to do—like manipulate a woman—because he would never be like his father.

"I'm not going back on my vows." Marian turned to him then, her eyes pools of brown. "You can expect dinner when you come home from work. The house will be clean. I'll keep the girls quiet as best I can."

"Wait." Gilbert shook his head free of the physical side of marriage. "What are you talking about?"

Her look of confusion echoed his own.

"Your late husband didn't expect those things, did he?" Had she had a horrible marriage like his mother? His stomach turned. Father had been demanding and unyielding, expecting dinner at certain times, and for his son to be seen and not heard. What had his mother truly endured?

"Oh, no." Marian interrupted his dark thoughts. "Dinner he liked after being in the fields all day, of course, but he loved playing with the girls and made a bigger mess than any of them." Wistfulness colored her voice.

Gilbert pinned his lip between his teeth. She still loved her late husband, who sounded like a good man. He was grateful, yet this niggle of insecurity crept into his mind.

Marian sighed and a look of determination stole over her features. "But since ours isn't a usual arrangement, I want you to know we will make this as easy as we can for you."

"Marian." He didn't want that. "I'm not invading your home."

"And if you'll give me time," her gaze went back to her hands, "I'm sure I'll come around in other, physical areas."

"Oh, Marian, stop." He hated this. "I'm not demanding anything, do you understand? Not dinner, not quiet, not ... physical anything. I'll sleep in the front room, for all that it matters to me."

"For our whole marriage?" Marian glanced at him, a twitch on her lips. Gilbert could have kissed them for shattering the tension building in the car.

Gilbert grinned. "Until I can build onto the side of the house, how about?"

Marian blinked, and a tear slid down her cheek. "Thank you, Gil."

He couldn't help himself, he swiped the tear away with his thumb. "No more of this thinking that you know what I might expect. I'm not here to change things or expect things. I'm here to protect you and your girls, to provide so you are all fed, clothed, and warm. A meal is wonderful, and I'll be grateful for whatever you make, whenever you make it. And, of course, a roof over my head is appreciated, but I'd sleep outside if it made you more comfortable." He stopped himself before he gave voice to the sliver of a wish that rose in his heart. That they might become companionable, even friends. *Or more?* No, he wouldn't wish for that.

"You not sleeping in the house would get people talking for sure, so that's out of the question. We'll figure it out." Marian gave a nod, ending their conversation, then pushed out of the car before he could get her door. "The black Ford out front belongs to Rose Whittlebush.

She stayed with Elaine while I was gone. I want to see how the morning has gone, and ask whether she'd be okay staying until I pick up the girls. Otherwise, you will need to stay. Or I can call Marie Martins."

"I think it's best if I accompany you." He caught up to her, struggling to put their conversation and the feelings it churned up aside. "Perhaps thinking of me in terms of a bodyguard instead of a husband will help." Her and him.

Marian paused on the back step leading into the kitchen. "You have a noble streak, Gilbert Cox."

Did he? He certainly hadn't gotten it from his father. But the thought caused his shoulders to go back. How a pacifist could be a knight in shining armor, he didn't know, but he'd figure it out, as she suggested. Because knights were noble, and he wanted to live up to Marian's opinion of him, prove she could trust him to be what she needed.

He followed her into the house, removing his cap. It was unchanged from yesterday, yet stepping inside held a weight of responsibility. This was his home now. What about his townhouse in Milwaukee? Realization swept through him at what he'd given up. He could never ask Marian to move to Milwaukee, which meant he would live here. Permanently.

What did that mean for his job? His old life? Everything he did from now on would be for Marian and her girls. Panic threatened to steal his breath, and he focused on the smell his quick breaths took in.

"Hello, dear," said an older woman standing by the kitchen stove, stirring a pot of something that smelled of garlic and onions. His stomach growled, and he realized they had never eaten a proper noon meal. Strangely, the thought of something so mundane settled his anxiety, allowing him to study the older woman. She had brown hair like Marian's, but was rounded where Marian was not. Gilbert shook his head. *No noticing Marian's figure.* Especially after the conversation they just had.

"Mrs. Whittlebush, thank you for staying." Marian hurried up to the woman, who wrapped Marian in a hug. "I'm sorry it took so much longer than I anticipated."

"Nonsense. I planned to spend the day and here I am." She peered around Marian. "Who is the young man?"

Marian's cheeks reddened, and she covered her face. Was she ashamed to admit she married him? Mrs. Whittlebush reached for the wooden spoon she'd been using. He wouldn't let Marian give an accounting on her own. A marriage was between two people, not one.

He stepped forward to face Mrs. Whittlebush like a man should. "Marian ran into a bit of trouble in Hawk's River and—"

"And Gilbert protected me." Marian wrapped her arms around her waist. She glanced between him and Mrs. Whittlebush. "We came to an agreement, which is why I was late." An *agreement*?

Mrs. Whittlebush raised her white eyebrow, not relinquishing the spoon as her gaze roved over him, as if she assessed his worth. "And the eye? Your work or someone else's?" Gilbert scrunched his forehead and winced at the pain. What was with women today thinking Marian punched him? And why did they seem to like the idea?

Marian sidled closer to him in an obvious display of support. She thought him noble, which took the sting from Mrs. Whittlebush's words. "He took the blow *for* me, not *from* me."

His shoulders went back again. Yes, he was her knight. And just like when they'd told Jessica Moller about his attempted heroics, respect now shown in Mrs. Whittlebush's eyes. "All right. And?"

Marian gripped Gilbert's wrist. "And the threat is still there." He wanted to turn his hand to capture her fingers in his, show Marian he was on her side, too. But he didn't dare move. Marian had this under control. He could trust her to disclose the situation as she deemed appropriate.

"Another threat? Marian!" Mrs. Whittlebush threw up her arms, concern deepening the wrinkles on her face. "With Silas gone, and Michael O'Connor dealing with what happened up north. David, too. Who can we go to with this? We cannot trust Chief Sebastian, the bloated man. And Mr. Wilson—"

"That is why Gil is here." Marian raised her chin, but there was a tremor in her voice. Gilbert inched closer so that their shoulders touched.

"Gil?" Mrs. Whittlebush narrowed her eyes, and Gilbert had no doubt she saw every unsaid thing between him and Marian.

Marian bit her lip, and Gilbert stepped forward. He didn't know Mrs. Whittlebush's relationship to Marian, nor what she knew of his father's crimes against the Ward family. It didn't matter. Mrs. Whittlebush was a protective mother figure like Jessica Moller, and Gilbert needed to prove to her he could be the husband Marian needed in this moment.

He squared his shoulders in the way he did when he needed to convince a client how to correct a mistake he found in their books. "Ma'am, my name is Gilbert Cox, accountant with Burkes and Dudley."

"Cox! Why you conniving, little ..." Mrs. Whittlebush turned bright red as she advanced on him, wagging the spoon until it nearly hit his sore nose. "You're a relation of Robert Cox's, aren't you?"

Dread pooled in his stomach. Who was Mrs. Whittlebush, and how had his father hurt her? "I'm his son."

She hauled back and slapped his good cheek. "Your father held my niece at gunpoint, sir. He threatened to kill her if she and Silas didn't do as he demanded. How dare you come in here like you can save Marian? What con are you running?"

Gilbert held himself still, though his cheek stung from her strike and emotion caused his chin to wobble, making the other side of his face burn with pain. *Turn the other cheek.* He clung to his basis for being a pacifist while another voice whispered that he deserved Mrs. Whittlebush's anger. A warm hand slid up his back, to his shoulder, then squeezed. Marian. What had he done by marrying her? He thought he was protecting her, doing good as God asked of him, but maybe he'd made everything worse.

"Mrs. Whittlebush." Marian took the spoon from the older lady. She hated seeing the pain Robert Cox caused both Mrs. Whittlebush and Gilbert. She hadn't missed how hard Gilbert was trying to hold himself together, and it broke her heart. And Mrs. Whittlebush ... She needed the whole truth. "I know you're angry, but Gil is not his father. I trust him enough to have married him."

"What?" Mrs. Whittlebush sank to a kitchen chair. "Marian. Why?"

Marian laid the spoon on the counter, then sat kitty-corner to Mrs. Whittlebush and took her gnarled hands in hers. "Because all the men I would normally trust are gone, and I need someone to protect my girls."

"But Robert Cox's son?" Mrs. Whittlebush shook her head, a catch in her voice. "What trouble are you in that you need *his* protection?"

Marian glanced up at Gilbert. He stood rooted to the same spot, expression stoic, but he gave the tiniest shake of his head. He didn't want to draw more people into danger. She turned back to Mrs. Whittlebush. "I don't know exactly, but that's not the whole reason we married. He could have stayed in Silas's old room above the workshop if it was only about protecting us."

"Then what is it, dear?" Mrs. Whittlebush leaned forward, so much concern wrapped up in her features it warmed her heart to know she had such a good woman in her corner.

"It's about Silas." How could she say this? And not hurt Mrs. Whittlebush? "He aimed to provide for us."

"That's why he and Cora went west." The older woman scrunched her nose. "Has he not been able to send you money as he hoped?"

Marian cringed. "Has he been able to send it to you?"

"My dear girl, I told him to support you first. I have my work. I do not need much. Cora supported me while I had a building to maintain and an employee to pay, but now, I have little expense. Sewing will support me fine, or I will take in a border or two. Adaleigh still has her belongings in one of my upstairs rooms." She shook her head. "I am fine and Silas and Cora have not sent me anything but a Christmas gift. But you have your girls and Elaine to look after. Silas is still able to help you, isn't he? Oh, but Cora ..."

Marian nodded. Mrs. Whittlebush had made the connection without Marian having to explain.

Mrs. Whittlebush looked at Gilbert, her expression not quite warm, but no longer hostile either. "My niece Cora and her new husband Silas, who is Marian's brother-in-law, went west for him to find work. Influenza swept their town after Christmas. My dear niece overextended herself helping everyone. She got sick, and with her complicated health situation, she needs more care from both a doctor and Silas in order to recover. Which means less income, and less to share with you, Marian. Why didn't I notice before it came to this? Why didn't you tell me sooner?" Sorrow darkened the brown of Mrs. Whittlebush's eyes.

"Because I know everyone is struggling right now." Marian tightened her hold on Mrs. Whittlebush's hands. "There is precious little to go around. No one has bought anything from the shop since before Silas left. But Gilbert has a good job. He can take care of us."

Mrs. Whittlebush sighed. "I suppose this is why none of your light fixtures have been working lately. I meant to say something, thinking the bulbs had burnt out. But you turned off the electric, didn't you?"

"I can fix that." Gilbert placed a hand on Marian's shoulder, and she found it incredibly comforting. She missed feeling this way, like she had an ally in life. "I'm here to give, Mrs. Whittlebush. To make amends and ask forgiveness. What my father did is inexcusable. If you need anything, with Silas gone, please call on me."

Marian watched as Mrs. Whittlebush studied Gilbert for a long moment. Then the older woman bobbed her head. "Will you stir the soup, young man?"

"Yes, ma'am." Gilbert did as he was asked. With his back to them, Marian had a good look at his broad shoulders. A certain warmth she hadn't felt since Zachariah died inched its way into her chest.

Mrs. Whittlebush leaned close and whispered, "He is rather handsome."

Oh no. Marian and Gilbert may have gotten married, but they were not in love, which gave a matchmaker like Mrs. Whittlebush the perfect scenario in which to work her particular brand of magic.

Mrs. Whittlebush winked, then turned serious. "You need to tell Silas. He will not be happy."

"I know. How do you think Elaine will handle the news?" She hadn't considered the ramifications of marrying a man who wasn't Elaine's son. With her memories all askew, her mother-in-law sometimes thought

Zachariah was still alive. Would she think Marian was cheating on her son?

"It's a complicated situation." Mrs. Whittlebush rose and peered into the pot Gilbert had been stirring. She took the spoon from him and tasted the dish. Marian's stomach rumbled. "It's ready, but the soup can simmer until suppertime."

Marian leaned back to see the wall clock in the hall. "Gil and I need to get the girls. With the danger, I don't want them walking home from school alone. Can you stay with Elaine a little longer?"

"Of course, dear." Mrs. Whittlebush rested a hand on Gilbert's forearm, as if to hold him in place. "She's been sleeping more than not today. I fear this last episode has made her significantly worse." Marian agreed.

"I picked up the medicine Dr. Thompson wants her to take." Would it help?

"Good, good. And while you're gone, I'll make a poultice for your cheek, young man." She patted Gilbert's arm. "We need you seeing clearly out of both eyes if you're to protect our girls."

The non-swollen side of Gilbert's mouth turned up, crinkling the eye on that side. "I'd appreciate that, ma'am. Thank you."

Whatever doubt Marian had left about marrying Gilbert dissipated. Mrs. Whittlebush had offered him a truce, and if she could find peace with the son of the man who nearly killed her niece, then Marian had hope that this was indeed God's answer to her prayers.

Gilbert parked his car near the one-room schoolhouse near Marian's house. "I've never been to Crow's Nest before yesterday." It was a small town, and he was curious to see more of it.

"The girls and I can show you around," Marian said. Ever since their conversation with Mrs. Whittlebush, her shoulders had fully relaxed for the first time since he met her. "In fact, I need to send a telegram, so we can drive down Main Street before we go home."

"I'd like that." Though trepidation rose. He wasn't ashamed to be Marian's husband, but he was already heart-sore at the destruction his father had caused, and wasn't sure he wanted to receive more negative reaction to his presence. A man could only handle so much pain in a day, and he was at his limit.

Marian took a deep breath and let it out slowly. "Ready to tell the girls they have a new father?"

"Marian." He groaned. "I'm not their father. I'm their protector."

"They won't understand the difference." Marian touched his arm. "And from what I saw yesterday, your practice at the orphanage, and the story of the Mollers' daughter, you will be a wonderful protector and, I believe, father."

Gilbert's eyes burned, making his swollen one hurt even worse. He hadn't considered how the girls would view him, that he would take that role in their lives. He crossed his arms and laid them on the steering wheel, lowering his forehead to rest on them. "I don't want to take your late husband's place."

"He's gone, Gil. I've had to come to terms with that over the last two years. My brother-in-law tried to fill his shoes while he was here, but now he's gone, too. It's your turn."

"I—I can't fill his shoes, Marian." He raised his head enough to see her out of his good eye. "My father ... I don't know how."

"No parent knows how to be one, but that has nothing to do with actually being a father to my girls. I suppose I should have made sure you understood I'm a packaged deal before we said our vows."

Gilbert shook his head, bottling the emotion that churned inside. This wasn't about him. "I knew. We got married because of the girls. It's going to be fine, as long as you are comfortable with me being a father figure to them, as the son of Robert Cox."

Marian cocked her head as the school bell rang and youngsters poured from the building. But she said nothing. Instead, Marian exited the car and Gilbert scrambled after her. If he was to be her protector, he needed to make sure there were no threats around her. He searched the area, not seeing much beyond the school yard other than fields and a faraway barn. He heard water, but couldn't tell if it came from the lake or the creek.

"Mama!" Nettie and Essie barreled towards her, a bundle of books bouncing behind Nettie. Marian wrapped them both in her arms. Fierce protectiveness overwhelmed him. They depended on him to keep them safe, fed, and warm. He would do it, if it cost him everything.

"You remember Mr. Gil?" Marian directed the girls toward him.

He knelt at their level. "Hi girls."

"Hi!" Essie skipped over and wrapped her arms round his neck. He sought Marian's gaze. Her brown eyes had turned glassy.

"Can you come home with us and read more of *Anne of Green Gables*?" Nettie sidled closer to him. "We only read a couple chapters yesterday."

Gilbert cupped the little girl's shoulder. "Of course I can."

"Girls." Marian drew near. "Mr. Gil is going to be staying with us. He and I ..."

Gilbert redirected his hand to grasp hers. "Your mama and I decided to get married. That means I can read to you girls every day."

"Yes!" Nettie jumped up and down.

Essie, however, furrowed her little brows. "Are you our daddy?"

Marian squeezed his hand, and he was grateful for the bolstering touch. "If you'd like me to be, yes. Or I can be an uncle, or a friend."

"Mama?" Essie tucked herself within her mother's embrace.

"We have a daddy now?" Nettie's eyes widened with wonder. "Like a real daddy? Can I tell my friends?"

Marian chuckled. "Yes, you may. But this happened quickly, so don't be surprised if other people aren't as happy about it as you are. Okay, sweetie?"

Nettie shrugged, but Essie burrowed closer to her mother. He would have expected Nettie to be angry about a replacement father, but it seemed she just wanted a father figure, no matter who filled it. Essie, however, seemed as if she would need time. She'd been comfortable with him yesterday, so he hoped the rapport they had then would continue.

"I need to send a telegram, then we'll go home to Grandma." Marian redirected the conversation. "Mrs. Whittlebush made us potato soup. I think she made cookies, too."

The girls cheered and dashed for the car. Gilbert leaned closer to Marian. "Cookies?"

She chuckled. "Did you not smell them?"

"The soup took all my attention." He kept his hand over the passenger side car door. "Giving the girls permission to share will spread our news faster than putting it in the newspaper. You're okay with that?"

"It's better than the newspaper." She lowered her voice. "The primary journalist is a smarmy man who was in league with your father. My girls will show everyone this is a good thing. He would twist it to benefit himself."

In league with his father! "Why hasn't he been caught or fired or something?"

"His boss protects him, and he tows the line just this side of legal. But he's on a thin rope. Unfortunately, the people I trust to manage him aren't here."

Gilbert opened the car door, but kept himself in the way of Marian entering for another moment. "What's his name, so I can watch for him?"

"Greg Alistar."

Gilbert filed the name away as Marian gave directions to Main Street. As he drove, Marian provided a running commentary of their favorite places around town. Sweeties, the ice cream shop on the wharf. The Barn, a bakery close enough to the house that Gilbert made a mental note to treat the girls some morning. The Wharfside Cafe where her friend Mindy worked. Even an empty lot where Mrs. Whittlebush's seamstress shop used to be.

"The doctor's office is just across the street there." Marian pointed as they all got out of the car at the telegraph and post office. "The Conglomerate headquarters is just up the street. Come on, girls. Inside we go."

Gilbert searched the few people who walked around nearby. No sign of the pair of ruffians who gave him the black eye. Nettie had grilled him on why he'd gotten it—and every other question he could possibly imagine related to it—in between Marian's tour. Fortunately, exiting the car distracted her from her inquisition.

He held the door for Marian and the girls to enter the telegraph office. The girls chattered beneath a wall of posters. Opposite was a wall of postal boxes. Gilbert stayed close to Marian, not sure what else to do with himself. She smiled at him as she took the pencil to write the telegraph, angling herself toward him as she wrote.

ALL OKAY STOP
MARRIED GILBERT COX

Marian captured her bottom lip between her teeth. "What more can I say? They're going to have questions."

Gilbert leaned close to her ear, where the telegraph operator couldn't hear him. "I'll pay for it. Say whatever you need."

"I don't know ..." her voice trailed off as she raised her chin, bringing her face inches from his. For a moment, he was lost in her brown eyes.

"Is this all, Mrs. Ward?" The telegraph operator interrupted. Gilbert glanced at him, noting the disapproval on the older man's narrow face.

"Mr. Angus, it's not Mrs. Ward anymore." Marian stared at the telegraph, the pencil shaking in her hand.

Gilbert covered it. "I'll finish the note." She nodded and hurried over to her children.

He scratched out Marian's lines and wrote his own:

MARIAN IN DANGER STOP
MARRIED GIL COX STOP
YES COX STOP
WILL PROTECT STOP
LETTER FORTHCOMING

He slid the paper over to the operator, who read it with widening eyes. Gilbert leaned on the counter. "I trust the integrity of this office will maintain Mrs. Cox's privacy?"

"Yes, sir." The man nodded, and Gilbert noted the fear in his eyes. Fear of what? Gilbert's implied threat? Or because Marian was in danger? Was Mr. Angus a victim of Gilbert's father, or did he know something more about the danger Marian faced?

Gilbert tapped his finger. "Do you—"

"Mama, can we go?" Essie whined with an urgency that pulled Gilbert's attention. The little girl tugged on her mother's sleeve, doing a dance he'd seen at the orphanage enough times to recognize the young one had waited too long to attend to her needs.

"Gil?" Marian thumbed toward the door. Asking questions would have to wait.

He slapped the required coins on the counter, making the man behind it jump. Gilbert smiled. "I'll see you later, Mr. Angus. You have a good day now."

CHAPTER SIX

Sunday, January 18

Marian sprinkled flour on the kitchen table, then plopped the dough in the center of the white mess. At one time, she had a host of chickens and a milk cow, but that was before Zachariah's accident. Now she had just enough laying hens to maintain her flock and provide morning eggs for her family. And since Silas left, she'd had to limit their use of milk to just what the girls would drink. So today's biscuits would be a treat.

She smiled at the memory of Gilbert's wide eyes upon meeting her five hens. He rose before dawn with her on Friday and followed her around throughout the day, asking questions about everything she did. Not once did he offer a correction or a better way. It surprised her. And she'd told that to Jessica Moller when she and the reverend delivered the truck—a pretense Jessica created on Thursday to check on Marian's wellbeing. On Saturday, Gilbert cornered the milkman and doubled the milk order, but otherwise, he once again simply observed. And fully won over Mrs. Whittlebush and Mrs. Martins when both stopped by.

Today, she managed to slip out without waking him. He slept in the front room, and for the first two days, seemed to hear everything. She hoped to surprise him with biscuits as a thank you for buying them more milk.

Marian used the heel of her palms to knead the dough. The girls had adapted to Gilbert's presence as if he'd always been a part of their family. Even Elaine hadn't blinked at seeing him around the house. Though, the past two days had been good ones for her. Not only had she joined Marian in the kitchen more than usual, she sat in the front room with Gilbert and the girls, while he continued reading *Anne of Green Gables*.

She snatched her rolling pin and rolled out the dough. Her shoulders hadn't been this light, nor her breathing this easy since her husband died. Maybe even before. She shook her head. That had nothing to do with being married, but everything to do with not having to struggle to provide basic necessities for their family.

Farming was hard, and Zachariah was not a natural farmer. However, he loved the earth, loved creation and creating, and she supported him the best she could. She cut the dough into circles and laid them in a pan. She had to remember these first few days were a blissful period that did not resemble reality. Soon enough trouble would apply pressure. Elaine would have a bad day. A sleepless night would cause irritability. And danger still lurked.

Would their lack of a deep relationship hold up when the tough times came? What foundation did she and Gilbert have to lean on? They both believed in God, both took their vows seriously, but would it be enough? She turned her doubts into a prayer as she finished cutting the dough.

Attending services today would be their first significant outing as a family. Marian checked the woodstove's temperature, then slid the biscuits into the oven. What would people think of her for marrying so quickly? What did that matter? She trusted God had placed Gilbert in their lives, and aimed to thank Him for His provision.

"That smells good already." Gilbert leaned on the doorframe leading into the kitchen. Curly hair askew, shirt untucked from his trousers, suspenders hanging from his hips, he looked entirely too casual to be standing in her kitchen. But it was *their* kitchen. Her heart hiccuped.

She cleared her throat. "To thank you for the extra milk, I made biscuits."

"You have been subsisting on far too little, Marian. If I can ease your burden so it's not such a sacrifice, I aim to do so."

Speechless, Marian pressed her fingers to her chest to ease the uneven patter of her heart.

Gilbert pushed off the doorframe, headed outside for his morning ablutions, but stopped and tapped on the kitchen table she had yet to clean off. "Might I ask a favor?"

"Of course." He'd done so much for them.

"I'd like to visit my mother." Gilbert didn't look Marian in the eye. "I telephoned her on Friday, but ... I'd like her to meet you."

Meet the wife of the man who ruined her family? Or meet the mother of the man she married? Either way, nerves zipped up her arms. She snatched a damp cloth and scrubbed at the table.

"When you're ready." Gilbert tapped the table again, then disappeared outside.

They didn't have another chance to discuss it before Nettie, Essie, and Elaine woke. Gilbert came inside with snow on his shoulders, to the girls' great excitement. Breakfast was a celebratory meal, but Elaine grew more agitated the louder the girls became.

"I don't see what all the fuss is about." Elaine moved her eggs around her plate. "Snow is part of winter."

"But it's the first snow since before Christmas, Grandma!" Nettie bounced in her chair. "Maybe we can make a snowman."

Elaine narrowed her eyes. "I'm not your grandma."

Nettie froze. Marian's gaze went straight to Gilbert. Elaine might have forgotten that her husband and son were dead, but she'd never forgotten her grandchildren before.

"Let's go explore the snow." Gilbert asked silent permission. Marian nodded. The girls and Elaine needed separation before either could inflict hurt. Gilbert pushed to his feet, his breakfast only half finished. "We'll have to get all bundled up. Let's see your hats and scarves and mittens."

Marian tried to capture Elaine's attention away from the commotion of the girls leaving the table. "Would you like more coffee?"

"I've never seen him before." Elaine watched Gilbert. "He is good with those girls. Is he their father?"

Marian's stomach twisted. How could she answer in order to keep Elaine from spiraling?

Gilbert shrugged on his coat. "These girls are sweet ones, aren't they, Mrs. Ward? I hate to leave your company so soon. Perhaps we can visit later."

Elaine smiled. "I'd like that, young man. I'm going to rest now."

"Let me help you." Marian supported Elaine's elbow as the woman struggled to her feet. Her left leg barely worked after her last episode, but it was her mind that drifted further and further away each time. Part of her was glad Zachariah wasn't here to see his mother's decline. Silas, too, though she knew he felt torn about being so far away.

After she settled Elaine in her bed, Marian glanced at the hall clock on the way outside. She donned her worn brown coat, which barely kept out the wind, and stepped onto the back step. There would be no attending services today. She couldn't leave Elaine alone and services would begin in half an hour. As the snow grew heavier, her girls' shrieks grew louder. Gilbert chased them between the workshop and the house, tossing snow at them as they dodged him. Still, Marian couldn't find her smile. The heaviness that had lifted over the last few days returned with this latest development in Elaine's condition. She'd pen a letter to Dr. Nick Matrone tonight to see if there was anything they could do.

Gilbert changed into dry clothes while Marian occupied the girls in the kitchen. Elaine still slept. Was there anything to be done for her condition? He didn't want to overstep, but if there was better medical care, could he afford to provide it? Would Marian, or Silas—being Elaine's next of kin—allow that? It would be just penance.

He rolled his shoulders. The children at the orphanage played as hard as Nettie and Essie, and just like after the orphans chased him around the yard, his back reminded him he sat over a desk most days. Not that his muscles were all that flabby, but the lack of manual labor meant he doubted he came close to Zachariah and Silas Ward's physiques. Did that matter to Marian?

Gilbert snapped up his suspenders. Foolish thoughts. He and Marian didn't have that type of relationship. That type of *marriage*. The problem was, he recognized his attraction for her. This morning, he could barely tear himself away from watching her make biscuits. Spending a lifetime with her would be sweet torture because she could never know his growing feelings for her.

Yeah, feelings. Gilbert sank onto the couch and laid his head against the wooden top. As beautiful as Marian was on the outside, the more he watched her interact with her girls, her mother-in-law, or anyone else, the more time he wanted to spend with her. She was generous and caring, not quick to anger. She had neither a sharp tongue nor a spineless back. He respected her strength and wanted to ease her burdens. Thankfully, she'd allowed him to do a small bit by ordering more milk to be delivered each day. New clothes were next on his list of things to buy them, though he needed to time his suggestion carefully so as not to insult her. But seeing Marian standing outside in the snow, shivering in that brown coat of hers ... he'd barely held back a suggestion to go coat shopping at once.

The day being Sunday helped cool his impulse. He wished they could have gone to services this morning. He missed his church back home, though sitting under Reverend Moller's sermon was equally good. However, he'd wanted to see where Marian went to church, where he would now attend. Again, they had a lifetime for that, for Crow's Nest to become his new home.

He closed his eyes, listened to the icy snow slap against the picture window behind him. It was the largest window in the house, and it overlooked the flat grasses that spread out past the front yard to the barren fields beyond.

Used to the city, the desolate view made him feel tense and isolated. He spent the last few evenings staring out into the dark, unable to see through the inky blackness. How was he supposed to protect Marian and her girls, and Elaine, if he couldn't see the danger? And now, between the snow and Elaine's episode, he felt trapped at the house, unable to whisk his patchwork family away to safety if the need arose. Why had Marian trusted him to protect her? He wasn't brawny enough to make a stand.

Giggles came from the kitchen and Gilbert pushed to his feet, shoving the dark thoughts away in favor of the cheery little voices of Marian's girls. He would return to work tomorrow, and begin his discreet quest for answers, beginning with the telegraph operator, Mr. Angus. As long as he steered clear of Buck Wilson, as the thugs demanded, he hoped to find out the depth of the danger Marian faced. Until then, he aimed to make sure Marian and her girls were as comfortable as possible.

He stopped in the kitchen doorway before the trio noticed his presence. Marian had flour on her cheek, Nettie had some in her hair, and Essie had it powdered all down her apron. Each shaped a chunk of dough in her hands, then set it in a pan.

"Am I doing it right, Mama?" Essie held up her hand, dough precariously balanced on her wide open palm.

"That's it." Marian smiled, her eyes lighting. "Now put it in the pan."

Essie leaned on the table, reaching for the pan just as Nettie plopped her dough ball in with the others. Essie's ball tumbled to the table, rolled with the momentum, and plunked on the floor.

"Essie!" Nettie scolded, doughy hands going to her hips like a miniature mama. Essie's little eyes teared up.

"It's okay." Marian emptied her hands and crouched before her daughter. "Accidents happen, sweetie. We'll sweep it up and give you another piece of dough."

Essie sniffed as she nodded.

Gilbert folded his arms against the rush of emotions in his chest. Marian's patience warmed his heart, sure, but the domestic scene ignited a longing he didn't realize ran so deeply within him. He'd watched Mrs. Moller mother her daughter, or the matron at the orphanage care for the children under her charge, but watching Marian created different feelings in him. Perhaps knowing she was his wife unlocked that which he'd buried. The bittersweet of it was that he would always be on the outside looking in. He'd be present to watch scenes such as this unfold, but he promised Marian theirs would never be a true marriage. The girls might think of him as a father, but he wasn't their daddy.

"Gil!" Marian's surprise dragged him from his internal wrestling. "How long have you been there?"

He blinked, realizing two pairs of blue eyes and one pair of warm chocolate ones stared at him. His mouth dried, and he forced his feet into motion toward the pump at the sink. "A drink," he croaked.

"We're making oatmeal cookies." Nettie followed him, until she stood at his hip, looking up at him with a trust that speared him. "Mama says snow days need treats."

"That they do." Gilbert filled a cup with water, downed it, then squatted beside Nettie so she didn't have to look up at him. "Are oatmeal cookies your favorite treat?"

"Uh huh. Essie, too. But ..." Nettie cast a nervous glance toward Marian, whose attention was on finishing up the cookie dough with Essie. Nettie lowered her voice. "I don't think Mama likes them. She made them at Christmas for me and Essie and wouldn't eat them. I want Mama to have a treat, too."

Sweet girl. Gilbert cupped her little shoulders. "What do you think your mama would like for a treat?" He'd get it for her if he could.

"She used to like chocolate. Before Uncle Silas left. And one time, before daddy left, she made a whole chocolate pie with cream on top." Nettie's wistful tone didn't hide the bittersweetness of the memory. "I remember how happy both my daddy and mama were. Now mama is sad. Can you make my mama happy, Mr. Gil?"

Talk about getting one's heart ripped out. Could he make her mother happy? She was asking for the moon, and heaven help him, he wanted to give this little one everything she desired.

"Cookies are in the oven." Marian said with a forced cheerfulness in her voice. Gilbert met her gaze. How much had she heard? Enough.

Gilbert returned his focus to Nettie, chucked her under the chin. "I know one way to make your mama happy, no matter what. One of your hugs. Go give her one and tell her how much you love her."

Nettie grinned and did just that. Essie copied her sister. Then the pair ran upstairs of their own accord to wait for their treat, shouting over their shoulders that they were getting their dolls for tea.

Marian stared at the empty doorway leading upstairs. "That chocolate pie was the last one we shared together. I can't even recall the reason, if there was one. Zachariah wouldn't hear of skimping on all the ingredients for my favorite dessert. He made sure we could have it at least once a year. I tried to save it for a special occasion, but he'd surprise me with the ingredients on a just-because kind of day."

Gilbert forced his chin not to fall to his chest. How was he supposed to make Marian happy, as Nettie asked? Getting her the ingredients for chocolate pie would only make her sad, and remind her of her husband. The one before Gilbert. The one she loved.

"I'm surprised Nettie remembers." She shook her head. "Oatmeal cookies are inexpensive treats, and the girls like them. I would add chocolate to them, but with pinching pennies and all, I couldn't even take one for myself."

Gilbert did not know what to say ... what did someone like him do in his position?

Marian didn't wait for him to think of a reply, instead she swept to the oven to check on the cookies. "The snow is really coming down."

Grateful to latch onto a safe topic, Gilbert agreed. "It is heavy snow, too. It won't make easy traveling today. Safer we stayed home."

Marian nodded, but squinted out the window. Her shoulders tensed.

Gilbert strode to her side. "What is it?"

"Did you look in the kitchen window while you were outside with the girls?" Marian pointed to a pair of footprints that pointed toward the window, but had not yet been filled in by the falling snow.

"Those are more recent." Gilbert's gut tightened. Someone had been watching Marian and the girls while they made cookies, and Gilbert missed it.

Marian rubbed her arms. "They were watching us. Why?"

Gilbert crossed the kitchen and shrugged into his coat. "I'm going to see if he's still there."

Marian nodded, though she didn't like the idea of him going out there alone. "At least take the rifle." She pointed to the unloaded gun kept tucked on top of the highest cabinet.

"I'll be fine, Marian." He was out the door before she could protest.

Protest. She squeezed her temples. Gilbert was a pacifist. He wouldn't bring a gun to arm himself, even knowing the danger. And here, she sent him outside unarmed and unwilling to defend himself. At least, she thought that's what a pacifist stood for. When he'd first called himself one, she'd panicked, thinking he might not protect her children. Now she knew he would, though she couldn't picture how. She paced the kitchen, tending the cookies, as she waited for him. When he returned safely—because he had to—she'd ask him more about this being a pacifist. She needed to understand his belief in it.

"Mama, where's Mr. Gil?" Nettie appeared in the kitchen, her rag doll under her arm, Essie behind her.

"He went outside for a minute." Marian forced cheer into her voice. "Ready for an oatmeal cookie?"

The girls squealed and bounded to the table. Marian kept glancing out the window, but saw no sign of Gilbert or the stranger. Nor did she hear anything other than the snow. The girls munched their cookies, pretending to feed their dolls. Around the corner, Elaine's door opened and closed. Marian braced, unsure what mood to expect from her mother-in-law. The dementia made her more unpredictable, but with each apoplexy attack, it grew worse, as did her physical limitations.

"Oh good, Marian, you're here." Elaine bustled into the kitchen, her left leg slid instead of stepped. "I'm going to the barn to take inventory and do some cleaning. This snow will keep the customers away, so it's a good day for that type of work."

"It's Sunday, Mom." Marian held up the plate of cookies. "Why don't you join the girls and have one?"

Elaine patted her perfectly coifed gray hair. "It can't be Sunday, silly. I just put myself together."

"Wait, I ..." How could she keep Elaine inside? Away from the possible danger that awaited them outside.

Elaine donned her coat. "Why don't you join me? You know the girls love to play among the furniture."

Where was Gilbert? "That's a good idea. Once the girls are finished with their cookies, we can all go out to the barn together. Wait for us."

"Nonsense. Let them finish and meet me out there." Elaine wrapped a scarf around her hair.

"I'm finished!" Nettie bounced from her chair. "Unless we can have two?"

"Two!" Essie squealed.

"After dinner you can have a second." Marian placed a hand on each head, their joy easing her worry for a moment.

Then the back door swung open, and a gust of snow blew in. Along with Gilbert. Marian barely restrained herself from collapsing into a chair.

"Who are you?" Elaine demanded, looking Gilbert up and down. "And how dare you enter the home of a widow without knocking?"

Gilbert paused in removing his snow-caked hat and glanced at Marian. She hurried forward. "Gil is ... helping us, Mom. He's joining us over at the barn. With Silas gone, we can use Gilbert's muscles."

"Of course." Elaine shrugged. "Good thinking. Now get your coat on already."

Marian stalled as long as she could by making sure the girls were dressed warmly, and then donning her own winter gear. Gilbert sidled up to her as she donned her mittens. "The barn?"

"The curiosity shop." Marian had kept Gilbert away from there all weekend. His father's desk was there, and she was in no hurry to reacquaint Gilbert with it. "Did you see anything outside?"

Gilbert shook his head. "The snow is falling too fast. Are you sure we should take everyone out of the house?"

"Because of the weather? It's fine. And I hope being all together will keep us safe." She swayed closer to him, as if she could borrow from his strength. "We will be safe, won't we?"

Elaine watched them with a critical eye, then ushered the girls outside. Gilbert leaned in as soon as Eliane's back was turned and whispered, "I made a vow, and I intend to keep it." Then he caught up to Elaine and the girls, keeping everyone together as they trudged to the barn. Marian closed up, then hurried to keep pace, but her heart was pounding harder than the exertion demanded. All thanks to the son of the man who ruined them. Now she had to show him the desk that had introduced Elaine to Robert Cox. She drew the shop key from her pocket.

The interior of the barn was dark and stale, and cold. They used to keep a stove going near the front of the store for these winter months, but Marian hadn't opened the shop in over a week. What was the point? If someone was interested, they'd knock at the door. If no one bought anything at Christmas, she doubted they'd have a customer now. She loved the shop, and it hurt to see it floundering. It had been a joy to run with Elaine, to learn the ropes as a newly married woman. Zachariah had been pleased to see her and his mother working so well together.

She shook the thought away and lit several lanterns. Elaine and the girls scattered, leaving her with Gilbert. And the desk.

"This place is impressive." Gilbert let out a low whistle. "How much product do you move in a week?"

"Nothing anymore." The kneehole beast stood five feet away, where it could attract the attention of any customer. It was their best piece.

"Hence the job search." There was no judgment in his tone and the tension in Marian's shoulders eased. "I recognize this desk. My father's, correct?"

Marian cringed, unable to read him this time.

"Marian?" Gilbert reached for her hand and when she didn't respond, he nudged her chin so she would meet his gaze. She didn't expect the compassion she found there. "We don't have to talk about it."

"It's your father's. Don't you want to see it?"

"I'm struggling to forgive my father as it is. Seeing a reminder of the pain he caused won't help. We can look at it again another day." He tugged her hand around his arm. "Why don't you show me the rest?"

For a delightful hour, she gave a tour of the shop. The girls flitted around the barn. Elaine kept busy. The snow was still falling as they made their way back toward the house. Watching her girls run through the inches that had piled up, she nearly missed the tightening grip Gilbert had on her arm.

"Gil, what's the ...?" The back door was open. The one she specifically remembered making sure was shut tight.

CHAPTER SEVEN

Gilbert insisted the women stay outside while he checked the house. He couldn't be sure it was the safest option, but it was all he could think to do. This had happened under his watch.

Room by room, his tension grew. What would he do if he found the intruder? How did one protect while turning the other cheek? Inadequacy warred with conscience as he forced one foot in front of the other. Each moment he expected someone to jump out at him, and then what would he do?

Whoever had been peeping in the window had eluded his original search, then broke into Marian's house as soon as they left for the shop. What if the girls had stayed in the house? Or Elaine? Would the intruder have harmed them while leaving his threat?

No intruder downstairs, Gilbert returned to the kitchen, then upstairs. Two rooms, the girls' and Marian's. Was the intruder hiding here to attack later today? He found no one in the girls' room—a simple space with a single bed covered in a handmade quilt. It fit the girls. Gilbert's palms dampened as he approached Marian's room, but he shoved the embarrassment of entering a woman's room—his wife's room—aside.

A door opened and closed downstairs. Had the intruder returned—or left—while Gilbert was searching the house? Were the women in danger?

He dropped to the floor to check under the bed, then shoved clothes aside to search in Marian's wardrobe, all without seeing signs of an intruder.

He raced down the stairs, fear closing his throat. What would he find? What would he do if Marian, Elaine, or the girls were in danger?

"Anything?" Marian asked as he entered the kitchen, apparently unharmed and entirely too calm.

He stumbled to a stop. Why hadn't she waited outside like he asked? Then he realized she still wore her coat, while Mrs. Ward had already shed hers. Marian had only followed her mother-in-law, likely to make sure she was not in danger. Another moment and the girls tromped in. Essie slammed the door. Tension seeped out of Gilbert. His family was safe, for now. But he—and Marian—would have their hands full protecting these independent women.

"Can we have a cookie?" Nettie wandered to the table, dripping snow off her boots as she went. "Looks like someone left theirs here."

A searing warning shot up his back. "Nettie, that's mine." The lie came too easily, and cut off whatever Marian was about to say. "I think I remember your mother saying you can have a second after dinner. Get dried off and I'll read more of our book until it's ready."

The girls cheered and raced up to their upstairs room. Gilbert earned a raised eyebrow from Marian, until she took a step closer to the table. Color drained from her face.

"I shall do the same." Elaine shuffled through the kitchen, seemingly oblivious to Marian's trembling. "I enjoy listening to a good story."

Once alone with Marian, Gilbert went to her side, wishing they had the type of marriage where he could comfort her with his arms around her. Marian held shaking fingers to her mouth. Gilbert put his hands on his hips as he studied the presentation the intruder had left. The plate of cookies still sat in the middle of the table. Beside it was one cookie, with a single bite taken out of it. Under that cookie was a note.

"Gil." Marian's voice shook. As well it should. Gilbert took her other hand as he picked up the paper.

Keep quiet or die. The accountant can't save you.

"He knows where I live. He's proven he can get inside. My girls." A sob escaped her.

Gilbert tossed the paper down and drew Marian into an embrace. She fit so well. Almost equal in height, he could comfortably wrap his arms around her too-thin waist. Her ear was near his mouth, allowing him to keep his voice quiet even as she cried. "He could have harmed you or the girls today, but chose a threat instead. He's not ready to escalate to violence yet. If we can get ahead of this, take it to the police—"

"No!" Marian pushed him away, swiping at her eyes. "We are keeping this to ourselves. The only officer I trust is out of town, and I'm not sure I'd tell him, anyway. This is my girls' lives we're talking about and I won't risk it. Do you understand, Mr. Cox?"

Gilbert hated the smile that tugged at his lips. But seeing Marian in a full mama-bear fury was a beautifully impressive sight. He sobered. She was right. "The girls' safety, Elaine's, and yours, is my priority, Marian. I won't do anything to compromise that. I promise."

Marian deflated and sank into a chair. "I believe you."

Gilbert sat beside her, unsure of what to say next. There had to be a way to end this threat, to prove to these thugs they had nothing to fear from Marian.

"He was in our house, Gil. He ate one of our cookies." She shivered. "I wish I knew something that could stop them. Other than hearing them talk about Buck, I don't even know what they want to keep from him."

"I wish that mattered." He rested his elbows on his knees. "If you tell Buck you heard someone is keeping something from him, he'll go searching. He'll find out what it is, and who said it. That is a risk to them. And if they get wind of him searching, they could seek revenge before he finds them, and stops them. We still don't know who those two thugs are."

She reached for his sore cheek. The swelling had dissipated, leaving only a purplish-yellow hue in its wake. The coolness of her touch eased the ache that still resided along his cheekbone.

He covered her hand, securing it to his injured side. "I would take another of these many times over if that's what is required to keep you safe. I made a promise, Marian, and I'll see it through."

"I don't doubt that." She wiggled her hand free and clasped her fingers in her lap. "At what cost, Gil? I don't fancy being widowed a second time."

A pang twisted in his chest.

"Ready, Mr. Gil?" Nettie appeared in the kitchen, Essie on her heels, snatching the moment away before Gilbert could understand it. "We're at the part where Anne meets Gilbert Blythe. And he's sooo handsome."

Gilbert scratched his chin. "What do you know of handsome men, Miss Nettie?" Marian chuckled beside him.

"Anne thinks he's handsome. Tells Diana so." Nettie grabbed Gilbert's hand, and dragged him from his chair. "Come see for yourself."

Gilbert glanced over his shoulder as Essie grabbed his other arm. Worry lines marred Marian's forehead, but the indulgent smile warmed his heart.

Instead of getting dinner ready, Marian cleaned away any visible reminders of the intruder before allowing herself to be drawn to the front room, where Gilbert read to the girls. By day, no one would know he bunked on the sofa at night. She should really find a better place for him to sleep. Elaine slept in the first floor bedroom, which could never change. However, with two bedrooms upstairs, Marian could move into her girls' room. They would love to share their bed with her every night, not just thunderstorm nights. But the thought of Gilbert sleeping across the hall from her set an uncomfortable, low simmer in her stomach.

You're married. She reminded herself. These feelings weren't wrong. In fact, they were good, and supposed to be felt between a husband and wife. She knew that from her wonderful years of marriage to Zachariah. Could she allow herself to feel so toward another man? A man she shouldn't trust because of his parentage, yet relied on in ways that eased a burden she hadn't realized weighed so heavily?

She stopped out of sight, letting Gilbert's voice roll over her. As before, in the kitchen, it eased her tight shoulders.

"'That's Gilbert Blythe sitting right across the aisle from you, Anne.'" Gilbert read in a falsetto. The girls giggled. "'Just look at him and see if you don't think he's handsome.'"

He returned to his normal voice as he read the narration that came next. Marian almost had the book memorized since the girls asked to read it so often, but hearing Gilbert's version brought it to life in a new way. He was a gifted storyteller, or at least a practiced one. He spoke slowly, dramatically.

"'He was a tall boy, with curly brown hair, roguish hazel eyes, and a mouth twisted into a teasing smile.'" Gilbert read the description of his namesake. Fitting that the two not only shared a name, but looks as well. Even the roguish wink of the fictional Gilbert seemed like something

Gilbert Cox would have done in his youth. Perhaps he would even now, if danger didn't nip at their heels, stealing their levity.

That thought snatched her from the cocoon Gilbert's voice had recreated. Tempting as it was to continue listening to the story, even on what was supposed to be a day of rest, there were things that needed to be done. Like making dinner. The snow carried on in thick flakes. During the Christmas season, Marian would have thought it a gorgeous sight. Today, it sat like a heavy shawl, nearly smothering her. Who lurked behind the curtain of snow?

Twenty minutes later, the happy feet of her children running toward the kitchen caused her to push away the dark thoughts that had held her captive as she cooked. She would do anything for her girls. She'd married Gilbert to protect and provide for them. The girls took their respective spots at the table, while Elaine went to nap. Gilbert waited for Marian to sit before he took the chair across from her. The chair Zachariah had used, then Silas. Now as she glanced at the man occupying that chair, the warm feeling returned. He helped Essie butter her bread—butter, another treat they had because of Gilbert. He was so good with her girls. She found it undeniable he had spent much time around children with his ease around them.

Yes, after dinner, she determined to change his sleeping arrangements. He deserved an actual bed for all the good he'd brought to their home. No more front room couch. He was part of their home, their family, and it was time to treat him that way.

Once she cleaned up from their late dinner, the girls played in their room as was customary for a Sunday afternoon. Usually Marian would take advantage of the quiet, restful time to sew or read. Today, she used it to ready what would now be her old room for its new occupant. The bed would keep the quilt, but she laid a new bed sheet. The only spare she had, an indulgent purchase Zachariah had given her before Essie was born.

As Marian smoothed the bedsheet, she recalled the day he gave it to her. *To ease the pain in your back,* he'd said, referring to how often she had to launder the large sheets with a toddler learning not to wet the bed. The twinkle in his eye had declared he simply wanted to bless her. Zachariah was like that. From the chocolate pie ingredients to the extra bed sheet, he loved to bring her gifts that made her life easier. How she missed him.

"Marian?" Gilbert called up the stairs. "Might you have a moment?"

She blinked away the emotion, then peeked around the doorframe and down the stairs. "Come up, Gil, and bring your belongings. I have a surprise for you."

Heavy steps on the stairs came too soon for him to have followed her direction. "Marian, what is it? Do you need help? I ..." Red tinged his neck as he reached the top step and stared at her.

Oh goodness, she hadn't considered what he could have thought she meant! "I'm moving into my girls' room so you can have this room. All to yourself."

Breath whooshed out of him. "I'm not displacing you, Marian. I am comfortable downstairs."

"Not as comfortable as you would be in your own room." She waved toward the one she'd readied for him. "All yours, if you'll forgive the flowery water pitcher."

A smile quirked his lips. "I like the flowery water pitcher especially." He turned toward her and she realized how close they stood in the small space that made the second floor landing.

She didn't have to look up at him, as she had Zachariah. It made her feel Gilbert's equal, like they were in this unusual situation together, facing it side-by-side. She touched his upper arm, needing him to know how grateful she was for his sacrifice, for that was what it was. He'd given up his future for her and her girls. "Thank you, Gilbert. For ... for everything you've done for us. I cannot express how much it means to me."

He frowned and eased away from her. "I'm not being kind to get my own room or get in your good graces, Marian. I want to do those things. And I do them without thought of reward or of anything, and I mean anything, you could give me."

"What if I want to do this?" She raised her chin, ignoring the implications Gilbert hinted at. "Because you deserve someone to look after you, too. If nothing else, you return to work tomorrow and need to be at your best. Marrying me allowed you to keep your job, and I won't be the reason you lose it. A good night's rest will allow for a clear mind. If for no other reason, take the room for that reason alone."

Gilbert scrubbed his good cheek. "Thank you, Marian. I'll think about it, okay? Right now, can we talk about tomorrow? I hate leaving you after what happened today, but ..."

"But you have to return to work." She'd miss his presence, too. Because of the security he brought.

"Let's create a plan. Come on." He took her hand and tugged her down the steps.

Obviously, the discussion of the room was over. Had she overstepped by offering it to him? Offended him even?

If it wasn't for the comforting grip he had on her, doubts would have swarmed her. She didn't know how to manage a marriage of convenience. He wasn't a visitor or a houseguest, or even just a bodyguard. This was his home now, and she wanted him to feel welcome. But how? Friendship felt too dangerous to offer him. They were partners, though, so perhaps the best course of action would be to leave the room empty. It was open for when he decided he was ready to claim it.

Monday, January 19

The next morning, Gilbert bundled Nettie and Essie into his car. The snow mounded in thick drifts, nearly blocking their way to the school. Gilbert felt the weight of responsibility on his shoulders as he took the road even slower than he might otherwise. Marian's most precious gifts were in his back seat.

She'd wanted to come along, but someone had to stay with her mother-in-law. This was also the most efficient solution, since he had to drive into Hawk's River to meet with clients and could drop off the girls on his way. Their so-called honeymoon was over.

Other than the intruder, it had been a good few days, Gilbert thought. Getting to know one another. Establishing a routine. In that way, the snow was a blessing. It gave them a whole day extra stuck inside together. Gilbert wished he could be there now. He didn't like leaving Marian without a bodyguard. However, he'd promised provision as much as protection, and knew he had to leave her in God's hands. He still didn't like it.

The girls chatted about school as if he wasn't there to eavesdrop. They'd welcomed him into the family without a second thought. What would his mother think of them? Technically, she would be their grandmother. Would she like that? The girls already had two grandmothers, though Elaine's health robbed the family of her full ability to be one. Gilbert learned Marian's parents worked at the lumber camp where Mrs. Martins's grandsons went for the winter. He wondered what Mr. and Mrs. Nelson would think of him. Would they approve of Marian's choice for a second husband?

Would *his* mother approve of his decision to marry? Not that it mattered now, since they'd already said their vows. Gilbert adjusted his fingers on the steering wheel to ease the ache of gripping it so hard.

He liked being married to Marian. Liked it—her—more than he should. Theirs wasn't a true marriage. It was more like a business partnership, and he certainly didn't hold the same level of fondness for any of his colleagues or clients. Marian created a welcoming home, the likes of which his mother hadn't been able to create thanks to his overbearing father. In Marian's home, Gilbert felt at peace. When he wasn't worried about the danger.

That was one reason he hadn't been sure what to do yesterday when Marian tried to get him to move upstairs. Was she actually ready for him to move from what felt temporary—sleeping on the sofa—to permanent? Not to mention, having a room on the same floor as her felt too close to being truly married. The last thing he wanted was to make her uncomfortable.

The school came into view. "Here we are, girls. Remember, I'll pick you up after school, so don't go anywhere without me, okay?" He parked.

"Okay, Mr. Gil!" The girls said in unison before shoving the back car door open. In an instant, the girls bounded through the snow to join their friends in the schoolyard.

Gilbert hesitated to leave. How did Marian trust others with her girls? He wasn't their father, and yet here he was, stalling. Perhaps the discomfort came from knowing the danger to the family. Yeah. That had to be it. As long as they were at school, they would be safe. Marian was the one alone at home. Why did he have to go all the way to Hawk's River today?

Try as he might, his disquiet grew the longer he was away from Marian. Throughout his meetings, he struggled to stay focused. Fortunately, instead of peeving his clients, they gave him a good ribbing instead. The besotted groom on his first day away from his bride. He let them think that, especially since Marian was the one on his mind.

He finished up with his last client with an hour left before he was due to pick up the girls from school. And since the roads were mostly cleared from the storm, it seemed the perfect opportunity to pay the Mollers a visit. Reverend Moller would help orient him. Perhaps he could even provide Gilbert a perspective on how to protect Marian while not sacrificing his conscience. The thought urged him along as he sidestepped puddles of slush, only to pull up short at the man leaning against his car.

"Mr. Wilson." Gilbert switched his briefcase to his left hand. "To what do I owe the ... pleasure?"

If Wilson detected the sarcasm, the tall man didn't react to it. "I heard congratulations are in order." He appeared relaxed, with his legs crossed at the ankles, hands stuffed in his trouser pockets. But Gilbert could read the tension in the man's shoulders and clenched jaw.

"Indeed." Gilbert halted outside of striking range. Neither made a move to greet the other with a handshake.

"Rather quick moving, aren't you?" It could have been a tease, if not for the hard glint in the man's eye. "What'd you do to convince her?"

"Marian's decisions are her own, Mr. Wilson. Now, kindly move aside so I may be on my way." Gilbert waited a beat for Buck to move, and when he didn't, Gilbert threw a verbal jab. "Don't want to keep the wife waiting, after all."

Buck scowled as he pushed away from the car, coming toe-to-toe with Gilbert. They both wore well-crafted suits and it struck Gilbert then that Marian could have picked either man. Buck stood three inches taller, with a leaner face, whereas Gilbert kept his boyish curls and had his mother's rounder cheeks. Beyond those few looks, what difference was there between him and Buck? Hint of misdeeds followed them both.

"I do not wish to argue with you, Mr. Wilson." Nor speak overlong with him. If the wrong people watched them, it could be disastrous for Marian and her girls. His heart rate picked up. "And I'd ask that you leave Marian alone."

"That wasn't the deal I struck with her brother-in-law." Buck grabbed him by the upper arm, momentarily stunning Gilbert. "I swore to keep my eye on her, to protect her from swindling accountants like you."

"Unhand me, sir." Gilbert yanked himself away. "I think you're confusing me with my father."

"Your father nearly killed me. Why should I think the apple didn't fall far from the tree? He wanted something of the Wards. Is that the reason you manipulated Marian into marrying you? You took all her money, now you take her shop, her house ... *Her*."

Anger roared through Gilbert. "I did not manipulate her. Nor force her to do anything she has not willingly chosen. Trust me, I know what it feels like to be pushed into a corner and I would never, *never*, do that to someone I esteem as highly as I do Marian Ward."

"Esteem? Not love." Buck nearly bumped chests with Gilbert. "And her last name, apparently, is now Cox. As her husband, I'd think you'd remember. How fitting that she bears your father's name?"

"Better than Wilson." Gilbert shouldered past, knowing things would escalate if he didn't remove himself from the conversation. However, getting in his car, he tossed one last admonition over his shoulder. "If you have an ounce of care for her, you'll stay away. Is that clear?"

Buck set a hand on the car hood. "I'll be watching, Cox."

Gilbert slammed the car door. Buck moved away just enough for Gilbert to roar past him.

Esteem? Not love. The words hissed in his ear as he drove to the Mollers. Worse, he'd given Marian the surname of a criminal.

Marian removed Gilbert's frozen shirt from the clothesline that hung between the house and the workshop. She tucked the clothespins into her apron pocket, then gave the shirt a good snap and folded it into the basket. Agitation had her moving quickly, though icy fingers slowed her work.

She removed Essie's stockings from the line. She hadn't realized how insulated she'd felt this past weekend. Adjusting to Gilbert's presence had its own challenges, but nothing compared to his absence. Each plop of snow. Every whistle of wind. She startled at the littlest things, expecting trouble to jump out from every shadow.

Nettie's nightshirt was quickly laid in the basket alongside a pair of Gilbert's socks. Would he be pleased she washed his clothes along with her own family's weekly laundry? He hadn't been receptive to moving from the front room to an actual bed, so what if he hated that she touched his clothes? If she were boldly honest with herself, she enjoyed having Gilbert at the house. He provided a sense of security that even Silas's presence hadn't brought her.

She knew it was unfair to compare her cowboy brother-in-law with her current husband. They couldn't be more different. Moreso, from an outsider's perspective, Gilbert shouldn't give her such a settled feeling. She shouldn't trust him. But she did, and today's jitters proved just how much. She blew out a breath as she removed Elaine's spare housedress from the line.

Less than an hour and all her family would be back under her roof. Then she'd be able to rest.

A car pulled into the drive, causing her fingers to stall on the next clothespin. She didn't expect Mrs. Whittlebush and Mrs. Martins today. While she appreciated all their help with her mother-in-law—who'd slept most of today—they had their own lives, and the snow would keep them home.

She held her breath until Buck Wilson's repaired Ford came into view as he circled past the barn to park in back. She quickly folded her bloomers and tucked them under several layers of clothes. What made Buck think he was welcome to park here as opposed to where customers parked on the other side of the barn? He couldn't be here. If those thugs thought she was talking to him ...

Buck ducked his chin against a gust of wind as he approached. The weather didn't welcome him either. If only she'd recognized his car a few moments earlier, she'd have dashed for the house and locked the doors.

She folded her arms, the wind cutting through her bare coat. A shiver raced through her. "What may I do for you, Mr. Wilson?"

He raised an eyebrow. "I'll cut right to it, Mrs. Ward."

"It's Mrs. Cox."

"Pardon me. I wished to speak with you without Cox being present. May we talk inside?" He nodded toward the house. Its warmth beckoned, but propriety and self-preservation kept her feet still. She needed to send Buck away as quickly as possible.

"What you have to say, you may tell me here." *And then leave, please.* "My husband will be home momentarily."

Buck frowned and shoved his hands into his trouser pockets. "Are you worried about what he might think of me being here?"

"He'd tell you to leave. As you should. I'm a married woman now, Buck. Not a widow. Whatever promise you supposedly made Silas is fulfilled. You may leave now." She glanced around, hoping the thugs were nowhere to be found.

"You're nervous about something, Marian." He took a step closer. "Did Cox force you into this marriage?"

"What?" She whipped around to face him. "It was mutual."

"It was fast."

Why did it feel like someone's eyes bored into her back? Sweat pooled between her shoulder blades, chilling her. She needed Buck to leave.

"Marian." Suddenly Buck was at her side, his hand on her shoulder. "If you're in danger, please tell me. I'll figure out a way to get you away from Cox."

"Away from—Mr. Wilson, we married so Gilbert could protect me. He's not the one I'm scared ..." Marian covered her mouth as she realized her slip. She shouldn't be telling anyone this, let alone Buck Wilson!

Buck inched closer, the intensity in his eyes immobilizing her. "Who are you scared of, Marian, that you would turn to Gilbert Cox for protection?"

Fear strangled her. How she wished Gilbert was here right this moment. Would he put his arms around her like he had when they discovered the intruder? She hadn't felt so safe since her late husband died as she did in Gilbert's embrace.

"Marian?"

She snatched up her laundry basket, leaving a third of the clothes still on the line. "Good day, Mr. Wilson."

"Marian!" Buck trailed her to the house. She slammed the door in his face.

Not her most hospitable moment, but if anyone was watching, she would *not* put her children in danger to placate the head of the Conglomerate. Then again, those thugs said Buck would kill them. What if Buck got angry at her and turned violent?

Finally, she heard his car drive away. She leaned against the door, her legs suddenly shaky.

"What's going on?" Elaine shuffled from her room, her left foot dragging more than usual. "I heard a door slam. Are the girls home?"

Thank God she still remembered Nettie and Essie. Most days. As soon as the weather allowed for someone to stay with Elaine, she'd post her letter to Dr. Matrone. Surely there was more they could do to help her.

"It's fine, Mom." Marian forced a smile, though tears burned her eyes. This all would be hard enough if she didn't have to worry about everyone's safety. She looked to the hall clock. Gilbert should be picking the girls up from school this very moment. She couldn't wait for everyone to be under her roof, safe and sound.

CHAPTER EIGHT

Saturday, January 24

Bright morning light woke Gilbert Saturday morning. Or perhaps it was the squeal of little girls. He shook off his sleep. The week had been slow, and each night became harder to sleep on the sofa, but he couldn't bring himself to take Marian up on the offer to use her spare bedroom upstairs. This marriage was about him making amends, protecting, providing. Getting a private room with a bed on the same floor as Marian felt too privileged, too intimate.

He stretched, and the smell of biscuits wafted from the kitchen. He'd grown up with a cook, and even now had a housekeeper that helped with meals, but nothing tasted as good as Marian's food. His stomach rumbled. He enjoyed seeing how she could take simple, inexpensive ingredients and create the most delicious suppers he'd ever had. This week, he'd felt spoiled. What was he doing for Marian that was worth what she did for him?

After Buck Wilson's visit to both of them on Monday, neither had seen the man since, or any other sign of the thugs threatening Marian. Gilbert didn't enjoy sparring with the man any more than facing the truth the man held up like a mirror. His pride appreciated the fact that Marian had chosen Gilbert, not Buck. Although did she truly have a choice? She hadn't planned to marry until their situations forced the decision. Either way, Gilbert aimed to make sure she never regretted marrying him.

He quickly dressed and wandered down the hall. Marian moved between the stove and the table where her girls played with a pile of dough. Perhaps they were attempting to help their mom, but they were sticking their fingers into their mounds, not shaping it like he'd seen Marian do. It made him smile.

"Morning, Gilbert." Marian smiled at him, and something inside his chest fluttered like a flag in a breeze. "Coffee?"

He nodded, unable to find his voice. She wiped her hands on a towel, then used it to lift the carafe from the stove. She took a cup from the cupboard, poured coffee, then added a splash of cream, just as he liked his morning cup. He didn't deserve Marian. She was too good to him, and for him.

"Here you go." She appeared in front of him, the cup balanced on a saucer she held with one hand. That's when he realized her eyes were brighter than they'd been all week. Her shoulders were a whole inch further away from her ears. Even her movements were more fluid than they'd been, especially towards the end of the past week. "Gil?"

He shook his head and took the cup, tasted a sip. Perfect. "Thank you, Marian."

She smiled again, but didn't spin away like she usually did.

"Everything okay?" He studied her expression, trying to read what she wasn't saying. The girls chattered in the background. Silence came from Elaine's room, so she was likely still asleep. He didn't get the sense that something was wrong, but ...

"I'm glad you're ho—here today." Her cheeks pinked, and she was across the kitchen in another instant. She liked having him here? No, not just here. Home. She liked having him home. Her home. His nose tingled with unaccustomed emotion.

"Can we do something fun today?" Nettie plopped her pile of dough into a bread pan. "The snow is all matted now, so we can't make a snowman."

"I wish Uncle Silas was here." Essie copied her sister. "He made fun stuff in his workshop."

Marian met Gilbert's eye over the girls' heads. "Mrs. Martins is planning to visit Grandma today." She let the thought hang in the air, as if she waited to see what Gilbert thought about doing something as a family. Wait. Did she want him to join them, or even to offer a suggestion?

His mind went blank. "What could we do?"

"You mentioned wanting to visit your mom." Marian busied herself sliding bread pans into the oven. Darling woman.

"Not today." It would be entirely too selfish of him. Yes, his mom had hounded him during his last phone call to her on Thursday, but would Marian and the girls think meeting his mother was *fun*? No, likely not. And today he had the sense that this activity needed to be about the three women in his new family, not his mother. Which gave him an idea. "Does one of the shops in town serve hot cocoa?"

The girls squealed and jumped up and down. "Can we? Can we?"

Marian smiled indulgently at her girls before turning to Gilbert. "Are you sure?"

As long as he had employment, he'd spoil these three as they spoiled him. He set his empty cup on the table. "Of course. After breakfast? Do we drive or walk?"

"Yay!" The girls raced across the floor to wrap their arms around his legs, Nettie adding, "Thank you, Mr. Gil!"

Oh, his heart.

Marian blinked rapidly. "It'll be chilly for a walk, but the Wharfside is just up the boardwalk."

"I did have another idea. Perhaps we can combine them." Three pairs of eyes looked at him expectantly. What would Marian think of his idea? Would she be offended or grateful? His nervousness tangled the words in his mouth.

"Girls, go put on nice dresses so we can leave as soon as Mrs. Martins arrives." Marian urged them towards the stairs. The girls grumbled, but obeyed. As soon as they were gone, Marian closed the distance between him and her. "What was your other idea, Mr. Cox?"

Was she flirting with him? No, of course not. Still, he couldn't stop his hand from cupping her shoulder. "I want to buy you a new coat. A warm one."

Her jaw dropped for a moment, then she was shaking her head. "You're too extravagant, Gil. Cocoa would be fun, but I don't need a coat. Mine is perfectly—"

"Marian, it's not. I see you shiver when you work outside. The wind cuts right through the worn places."

Her chin trembled. "But the girls need clothes more than I do. They're growing so quickly, their dresses are getting too short."

Slowly, in case she rejected his touch, he moved both of his hands from her shoulders, up her neck, until he cupped the sides of her face. "What if I told you I have enough for new dresses *and* a coat?"

"Gil. It's too much."

"Let me provide for you, Marian. During my bachelor days, I didn't know what to do with my excess, so I gave it away. Now I have a personal investment in you and the girls. I want to give that excess to you."

"What if you lose your job? Shouldn't we be saving in case something … happens?"

"Who said I haven't done that, too?" Not as much as he probably should have done. He saw too many widows who could use a bit of help, and the orphanage always had a need or two.

Marian's brown eyes widened, looking so much like her daughters that it gave her a look of childlike wonder. Now he had a widow and two fatherless girls of his own. It made caring for them personal, more than helping neighbors or acquaintances. Sure, he'd still like to help at the orphanage, if Marian was agreeable, but his priority was now here.

"I am well paid, Marian, but if it's the future you're worried about, then let's outfit ourselves now, while we have the funds to do so." He ran his thumbs along her cheekbones. "What is that verse? Where Jesus says the birds are clothed and fed? And yet we are even more important to Him than they?"

She closed her eyes and tilted her head into his touch. "Matthew chapter six. *Take therefore no thought for the morrow: for the morrow shall take thought for the things of itself.*"

He pulled her closer and kissed her forehead. "*Sufficient unto the day is the evil thereof.* If anyone has experienced that these past ten days, it is you. Let's push troubles aside for today, all right?"

She'd barely moved her head in a nod when movement erupted around them. The girls raced down the stairs. Elaine shuffled about in her room. And a car pulled around the back of the house. Their moment was broken, and Marian hurried to the oven to check her bread. But

Gilbert tucked his hands into his pockets as he tucked the past minutes into his heart.

Flummoxed. Marian had been introduced to the word in her youth when an Englishman came to work at her parents' lumber camp. It stuck with her, but had never seemed applicable until now. She tried to push the disconcerting feelings away as she welcomed Marie Martins into her home.

"And Sam, too?" Marian drew the young woman into a hug. "What a surprise to see you."

Samantha blushed and adjusted the box she held under her arm. "I brought something for you, and I figured best to tag along with Grandma today." She peered past Marian's shoulder. Ah, she wanted to meet Gilbert.

"Can we go yet?" Nettie bounced beside Essie. Gilbert placed his hands on their heads, as if that could silence them. Not likely, in Marian's experience.

"How is Elaine today?" Mrs. Martins removed her coat only for Gilbert to take it from her to hang on the hooks along the wall. "Good man."

Samantha pressed her lips together, her eyes tracking Gilbert's movements. Why? Marian pressed her fingers to her forehead, where Gilbert kissed her. What was Mrs. Martins's question?

A comforting arm slipped around her shoulders. Gilbert. "We haven't seen Elaine today, though I heard her moving about her room a few moments ago. Perhaps you can convince her to join us?"

A twinkle lit in Mrs. Martins's eyes. She and Mrs. Whittlebush were one of the few who knew the truth behind Marian and Gilbert's marriage. What matchmaking plans was she thinking up now?

"Gilbert and I are taking the girls out for cocoa." Hopefully she could circumvent any awkward conversation. "Will you be okay alone here with her for a little while?"

"Of course." Mrs. Martins waved the question away. "Since Sam is here with me, you can leave the girls, too."

"No!" the girls whined, Nettie adding, "We want to go with Mr. Gil."

"We have a family outing planned," Gilbert laughed. "Girls, let's get your coats on so we're ready when your mom is."

The girls squealed and effectively broke up the conversation. Mrs. Martins excused herself to greet Elaine, but Samantha followed Marian to the oven. Marian removed the loaves of bread. "What's on your mind, Sam?"

Samantha shifted the box under her arm. "I saw those two thugs again."

Marian straightened. "You didn't speak with them, did you?"

She shook her head. "I took your words to heart, Mrs. War—" She shot a glance at Gilbert.

"It's Mrs. Cox now, but you can call me Marian."

Samantha chewed her lip. "They were watching the Conglomerate building as I left work the past couple days. I don't think they saw me notice them, seeing that they were standing in the alley. And the taller one was smoking a particularly foul smelling cigarette."

Marian thought back to the day the intruder left his note. There had been no hint of cigarette smoke, so the taller one—Hayes, if she remembered right—hadn't been the one to break into her house.

"What do they want? I haven't told Grandma, but I wish Kyle ... No, I wish David was home. And Uncle Mike. I've never been nervous to walk home before."

Marian cocked her head. She was pretty sure Kyle was Samantha's beau. The young man went with David and Patrick Martins to spend the winter working at the lumber camp where her parents lived. "Why not Kyle?"

Samantha wrapped her arms around the box. "He hasn't returned a single letter of mine since Christmas."

"I'm sorry, Sam." The pair were young, and Marian had seen many a lumberjack forget his girl back home during a long winter. Had that happened to Kyle?

"I'm not giving up on him yet." Samantha squared her shoulders. "There are only a few more months until they return home."

David and Detective O'Connor would return home; Marian was sure of that. But whether Kyle would ... Marian kept her doubts to herself. "Do you have someone else who can walk you home?"

Samantha shook her head. "But I'll be okay."

Marian wished she had another option to offer the young woman, but with all the trustworthy men gone, Marian herself had been put in a position to marry Gilbert. And she'd never suggest Samantha talk to Buck Wilson for fear the thugs would target her next. "You'll keep away from those men, won't you?"

"I know. And I figured telling you about them required a bit of subterfuge." Samantha grinned, and shoved the box at Marian. "I brought you a gift as a guise to see you, since I don't usually join my grandma."

"A gift?" Marian took the box. "I cannot accept."

"I hope you will." Pink darkened Samantha's cheeks. "I saw the color and shape of the hat that looked good on you the other day, so I made one for you. It's not perfect, so we can't sell it. But I didn't think you'd mind a few flaws."

"Of course I don't mind. Samantha, I'm honored." Marian opened the box to discover a dark green cloche with a brown lace band. "It's gorgeous."

"You see the round top isn't even, and the brim goes in more on this side than this one." Samantha pointed to the offending areas. "You don't mind that?"

"Not at all." Marian placed the hat on her head. "How does it look?"

Samantha's eyes shown with the pride of someone whose creation was on display. But it was Gilbert who answered Marian's question. "It's stunning, Marian. Now, let's get you a coat to match."

Before Gilbert could suggest driving, the girls took off at a run toward Lake Michigan. Marian slipped her arm around his before he could call them back, or run after them.

"They're fine," Marian said, a smile in her voice. "They know the way."

"But the water." Gilbert fought the urge to hurry Marian along. If the girls' mother wasn't worried, why was he?

"We walk this way any time we go into town. They learned to respect the water early on. And after one of their friends fell in last year and nearly drowned, they haven't forgotten the rules."

"Drowned?" Gilbert choked on the word. They reached the faded boards that ran along the frozen lake where sluggish waves lifted icy chunks of snow against the boardwalk. Stretching out beyond the snowy ice cover, the lake spread out before them in a chilly beauty of white and blue. A shiver had him tugging Marian a little closer to his side, grateful he stood between her and the cold expanse.

"Nearly," Marian continued, seemingly oblivious to his reaction to the lake. "But a stranger saved him. Adaleigh Sirland. Mrs. Martins took her in, and now David is courting her."

"David Martins." So many names for him to remember. People who meant a lot to Marian. But many of whom were not here for her when she needed them, forcing her to rely on—and marry—a man who should be the enemy.

"Girls! Slow down!" Marian called and the girls slowed to a walk. Quickly. "There's often ice on the wharf. What was I saying? Oh. David is a fishing boat captain, and like many of the younger fishermen, he sought winter work. Took his brother and his sister's beau up to the lumber camp where my parents work."

They passed The Barn, a red building that housed the bakery. Gilbert noted the distance so he could treat Marian and the girls one day. "Tell me about your parents?"

"My father is a lifelong lumberjack. Began climbing trees as a boy. Met my mother one summer when he was working with a company near Lake Superior. It's a nomadic life, but my mother loved it, and her ability to cook gave her a permanent spot on the crew."

"You grew up in the camps?" He couldn't quite picture Marian as a girl. Then he spotted Essie skip to catch up to Nettie, her little braids swinging. Transpose the scene from icy boardwalk to vibrant forest, and he knew that's exactly how Marian would have looked.

"As a child I alternately loved it and hated it. I had few friends, and since we moved every so often, I rarely kept them. But I loved the trees." A nostalgic sheen lit Marian's eyes. With her new green hat, brown hair, and brown eyes, she was meant to be surrounded by trees. Not the cold blue of the lake. Snowy pines, yes. Faded buildings, no. But how could Gilbert give her that? He was an accountant, not a lumberjack. And would she even want her girls to grow up in such a place? If she did, wouldn't she have taken them to live with her parents?

"Why not go back?" The question spilled from him.

"Elaine needs me." Marian shrugged, but Gilbert sensed there was more.

"Before Elaine got sick." Dare he voice the thought that nagged him? "Why not return home when your husband died?"

"The girls needed stability." Marian extended her hands in a defensive gesture, but again Gilbert knew there was more to it. Up ahead, the girls turned into an empty, roped-in area. Should he let the matter drop?

Perhaps. Yet he wanted to understand. "What about you, Marian? You stayed for Elaine, for Nettie and Essie. Would you have stayed for you?"

"I don't know. I ... I couldn't go back to the camp after Zachariah died because that's where we met, where we fell in ... Well, where our story began."

An ache Gilbert didn't recognize filled him as they stopped at the corner of the roped area. Inside was the Wharfside Cafe, which the girls had entered. Outside was Martins's Fishing Shanty. He guessed that was David's outfit. Marian looked out toward the horizon.

"Crow's Nest was his home, and it's my girls' home. You know I'd do anything for them."

"But?" Gilbert prompted.

"But the shop isn't the same without Elaine. Without the customers. So if it were just me, there is nothing truly keeping me here. Yet, where else would I go?" A lost expression crossed her face, like a boat suddenly bobbing free of its moorings. Then the look vanished. "No sense wondering. This is my home and the girls are waiting for us. Come on."

Gilbert followed, but their conversation lodged deep. It bumped against Nettie's question, *Can you make my mama happy, Mr. Gil?*

"Marian!" A woman with her blonde hair tied up into a swinging tail hugged her as they entered the Wharfside. "It's so good to see you. The girls already picked their table. They told me hot chocolate is on the menu."

"Indeed it is." Marian laughed, as if she'd shed their conversation like a duck did water. "Mindy, I'd like you to meet my ... husband. Gilbert Cox."

Gilbert pushed away the sting of her hesitation, and reached to shake Mindy's hand. "A pleasure to meet you, Miss ...?"

"Oh, goodness. You are polite. I'm Melinda Zahn, but everyone calls me Mindy." She nudged Marian's shoulder with her own. "I thought it odd you married so quickly when none of us knew the man, but he's a handsome one. No wonder you snatched him up."

Marian blushed and stammered. Gilbert grinned. "I like to think I was the one who swept her off her feet, but I'm no Casanova. In truth, she won me with her strength and love for her girls." As soon as the words left his mouth, he realized just how true they were. When had Marian snuck a piece of his heart?

If possible, Marian turned an even deeper shade of red. Mindy's gaze swung between them. "Huh. For all the gossip I hear in here, no one thought this was a true love match. But—"

Marian grabbed Mindy's arm. "Let's find our table, yes?"

A true love match. Normally Gilbert, the numbers man that he was, would have chalked up such feminine dribble to, well, just that. Except addition was his forte, and math didn't lie. Could their marriage of convenience turn into ... more? A hope he hesitated to trust sprung up as they settled at the table with Nettie and Essie.

The girls chattered, drawing Gilbert's attention away from Marian. However, he remained aware of her the entire time at the Wharfside. Later, as they walked north along the boardwalk to Mrs. Whittlebush's in-home seamstress shop, she allowed him to wrap her hand around his arm again. Hope grew like a weed in spring. Then he remembered that she already had her one true love. The father of her girls. If Gilbert didn't get a handle on his feelings for her, they would be lopsided. Marian would grow uncomfortable as he became a besotted fool.

Unless he could win her affection. Perhaps not a love for the ages, but ... enough?

He mulled the question as he sat on the sofa in Mrs. Whittlebush's front room, listening to the girls' giggles coming across the hall in the older woman's seamstress room. It would be a risk to his heart to allow himself to care for Marian in such a way. But Marian deserved to have someone take care of her the way she cared for those around her, especially her children and mother-in-law. Gilbert had already given up whatever foggy future dreams he had in order to marry her, and marriage was for a lifetime. But if Marian never returned his feelings, if he failed to protect and provide as he promised, the future would look as bleak as the lake did over the cliff beyond Mrs. Whittlebush's house.

Nettie bounded into the room, causing Gilbert to jump to his feet. "I'm getting a new dress!"

"Me, too! Me, too!" Essie ran after her sister and latched onto Gilbert's leg. He knelt. "Mama said to say thank you."

"Thank you, Mr. Gil!" Nettie flung her arms around his neck. Emotion clogged Gilbert's throat as he hugged them both. *Protect and provide.*

"It'll be a few days before I have everything ready." Mrs. Whittlebush joined them, uncertainty in her step. "Marian said to send you the invoice, Mr. Cox?"

Gilbert untangled himself from the girls to approach Mrs. Whittlebush and Marian. "Absolutely. Anything for my girls."

Any reaction to his declaration was interrupted when Mrs. Whittlebush's telephone rang. She held up a finger and dashed down the hall, moving faster than Gilbert would have guessed possible.

"Thank you, Gil. Truly." Marian kept her chin ducked.

"She's making you a warm coat, right? No skimping."

"Mr. Cox?" Mrs. Whittlebush returned. "Marie Martins has a telegram waiting for you. The errand boy who delivered it was instructed to wait for a reply, so she felt it urgent to inform you."

Gilbert exchanged a glance with Marian. Who ...? Had something happened to his mother? "I'll have her read me the telegram, if I may?"

Mrs. Whittlebush led the way to the telephone box hanging on the wall of her kitchen. She asked the operator to put her through, then handed the earcone to Gilbert. When Mrs. Martins answered, Gilbert shared his request.

"It's from a Mr. Burkes and reads, *Call me at once. Urgent.* That's all, Mr. Cox. Shall I reply?"

Gilbert's stomach churned. What could his boss demand of him now?

CHAPTER NINE

Marian had barely herded the girls into the house when Gilbert was asking where to find the telephone. She sent him toward the workshop, then hesitated a few feet from the back door. Cold wind worked itself under her collar and through the threadbare portions of her coat. Yet her feet didn't move. She was stuck between being needed inside and wanting to find out why his boss needed to speak to him so urgently. The last time that happened, the man had instigated a wedding.

"Marian?" Mrs. Martins appeared in the doorway. She looked from the workshop into which Gilbert had disappeared and back to Marian. "Go on, dear. Samantha has already left, but I can stay a while longer."

Though grateful, she was still torn. "The girls might be hungry."

"I made cookies and muffins. They'll be fine." Mrs. Martins shooed her away. "Go be a wife."

Packed snow crunched under Marian's boots as she quick-marched across the space between the house and Silas's workshop. *Go be a wife.* A wife, not a mom. The thought struck her as one she needed to mull over, but now was not the time. She slipped into the unheated workshop and stopped. Across the room, Gilbert was already speaking into the telephone box, his back to her.

"Mr. Burkes, sir, I received your telegram. What may I do for you?"

How could Gilbert speak so respectfully to a man who forced him to marry or lose his job? What if Marian had no pressing need to be married? Where would that have left Gilbert? Guilt churned in her stomach. She was so concerned about being a good mother, had she left off being a good wife? No, she did try. She made sure Gilbert was fed, his clothes laundered, the house clean. She even cleared out a room for him to sleep—not that he'd taken her up on it. And, thank the good Lord he hadn't pressured her to offer herself in a wifely way. But was that all there was to being a good wife? She should know. Zachariah had often called her a good wife. But Zachariah was her one true love. Gilbert was—

"Sir, I'm a newly married man, and it being my day off, I spent it with my wife." The hardness in Gilbert's tone had Marian taking notice, though she didn't know what to make of it. Especially juxtaposed against her own thoughts on being a wife. "I am, sir. Have you received another complaint from one of my clients?"

Marian wrapped her arms around her stomach as the churning turned to full on nausea. A chill worked its way down her back. What if Gilbert lost his job? It'd be because she allowed him to take them for cocoa. The momentary indulgence could cost him more than a few cents. Had they stayed home, they would have been here for Gilbert to receive his boss' call. Maybe they should move the telephone into the house so he would never miss a call again.

"I appreciate that, sir." Gilbert tensed, then slowly turned. He spotted her and met her gaze with one of hardened determination. "Sir, I don't think—"

She was causing Gilbert difficulty. Again. He'd been so good to them, buying them clothes, ordering more milk, reading to the girls, protecting them. Yet she received all the benefits, and Gilbert all the trouble. She thought giving him a room to sleep would be enough, but he hadn't received that gift. What else could she do for him? What else must he sacrifice for her?

"Yes, sir." Gilbert sighed, and Marian knew he would agree to whatever his boss wanted.

She escaped outside, emotion clouding her vision and the cold air seizing her lungs so that she paid no heed to her steps. The gunmetal gray sky above pressed down on her as her feet brought her to the curiosity shop barn. Since they had no customers, she kept it locked up tight, the key hanging from a string around her neck for ease if she needed to get inside. She unlocked the door and slipped into the dusty interior.

Her breath fanned out in a white puff. Old furniture rose up on one side. Dressers and wardrobes that Elaine had found over the years. Shelves and table tops were covered with items from bygone eras. She loved the nostalgia of the shop and it saddened her that no one came to give these things a new home. Moreso that Elaine could no longer maintain the robust operation she'd built with her own hands.

"Marian?" Gilbert's frame blocked the sunlight streaming in through the back door. "Can we talk?"

"Now what is your boss deman—" Marian closed her eyes and turned away. She needed to be supportive, not resentful. Had she completely forgotten how to be a good wife?

"What is my boss demanding?" Gilbert's footsteps sounded closer until she felt his presence behind her. "That's a good word. He is very demanding."

The knot in Marian's stomach eased some. "I'm not causing you more trouble, am I?"

"You?" He tapped his palms on her shoulders, as if testing her reaction. When she didn't move, he closed his fingers around her upper arms. "You are not trouble, Marian."

More tension seeped out of her only to be replaced by a different type of feeling, one she hadn't felt in years. It unsettled her with its mix of foreign and familiar.

"In fact, I highly admire you." Did he move closer to her? "You are strong. Courageous. You'll do anything for your girls. I ... like that about you."

Theirs was supposed to be a marriage of convenience, not a real one. A business arrangement to keep her girls fed, clothed, and safe. Was Gilbert angling for—

"It's what I respect about you, too." He put space between them, leaving Marian with an odd feeling of loss and relief. Why were her emotions so topsy-turvy?

She faced him and was struck by the sadness in his eyes. "What's wrong?"

He shook his head and the look was replaced by a glint of determination. "My boss gave me another ultimatum. Lose my job or work with a client who requested my accounting services."

Something sounded fishy about that. She folded her arms. "Why must you work with this client? And why is your boss forcing you to do so?"

Gilbert stuffed his hands into his trousers pockets, the bottom edge of his coat pooling around his wrists. "The client lives nearby, so it's logical for me to take him on. However, he asked for me specifically and landing this client would make my bosses very happy."

"But it wouldn't make you happy." She pieced together what Gilbert was working up to say. The client who specifically requested him. *Buck Wilson?* Her threadbare coat did nothing to chase the chill that raced through her. Why would Buck request Gil? Not just ask for Gil's help, but go through formal channels so that his boss demanded it.

He rocked back on his heels, his brown eyes locked on hers. "Do you trust me, Marian?"

Panic nearly closed her throat. "Trust? We're strangers, Gil. How can there be trust?" Yet, even as she said those words, she knew it wasn't true. She did trust him. Tears stung. He protected her from the thugs, sacrificed a chance of a love-filled marriage, willingly put himself in harm's way, and bought her a coat to keep her warm. She no longer thought of him as related to Robert Cox, or the son of the man who ruined her family. No, Gil was just ... Gil.

"Marian?"

"The client is Buck Wilson, isn't it?" The implications slammed into her.

If Gil worked with Buck, the thugs would come after her and her girls. The whole reason for this marriage arrangement was to protect against exactly that. Why was Buck interfering? Why wasn't Gilbert fighting this? Why did God allow her to be backed into yet another corner?

Fear, hot and powerful, speared through her and she grabbed Gilbert's lapels. "You can't accept. Those thugs said not to talk to him. If you do, you'll put my girls in danger and you promised, *promised*, to protect them."

"And provide." Gilbert's voice was annoyingly quiet. "I can't do that without a job."

Money. It all came down to money for the Cox men. No, that wasn't fair. Hadn't she just thought the opposite? But nothing made sense and her girls' lives were in danger. Marian's heart pounded against her ribs as if it would escape. Protection was more important than provision. She could work with a lack. She raced to the shop's counter for paper and pencil to make a list, purposefully ignoring Gilbert trailing her. Words tumbled out. "I'll personally visit Mrs. Whittlebush and cancel the clothing order. Hopefully she hasn't started yet. Then I'll reduce our milk order and cancel the electricity. We never should have—"

"Stop. Marian, stop. Please." He covered her hand, trapping the pencil against the paper. The warmth of his touch mixed with the softness of his tone collided with the turmoil churning inside. "I think I should take the job."

"No." Marian pulled away. Not only would her girls be in danger, images of Gilbert suffering injuries worse than a blow to the face, flashed across her mind. "You can't, Gil. Please."

"Wilson is inviting me to have unfettered access to his books. If there's a crime, I'll find it." Gilbert rounded the counter, removing the barrier between them. "We can end the danger and then you'll be safe."

Marian was already shaking her head. "No, then both the thugs *and* Buck will be after us."

"Not if they're arrested."

Stubborn man! "Detective O'Connor isn't here, don't you get it? There isn't another officer I trust. Buck is too connected."

Gilbert sighed and leaned his backside against the counter. "Hear me out. There's a reason Wilson asked for me and I think it's wise to find out what it is. You know I would never do anything to purposefully put you or the girls in jeopardy, right? I truly believe this is an opportunity to end the danger to you. Yes, it's risky. I get that. But I'm also good at assessing investments. Having Buck Wilson as a client gives me work right here in Crow's Nest where I can be close by. It lets me find out more about him and what he's hiding. And it lets me keep providing for you. Let me at least talk to him."

The arguments were good, but ...

"Can you trust me, Marian?" He reached for her without moving, his fingers snagging her own. A gentle tug drew her to him. "You've asked me about how I can protect you while still being a pacifist. I think this is one way for me to do that. Instead of fighting the problem with fists and threats, let me find a solution that will end it for good, at its root. I'm an accountant, which I'm sure everyone in town already knows. So if the thugs wonder why I'm working for Buck, it should be clear it has nothing to do with you. It's just a job. That's the benefit of having my boss make this demand."

"But what if it doesn't matter?" Marian searched Gilbert's face, surprised at the calm assurance he projected. Did nothing rattle him? "What if they think you'll tell Buck what I overheard? Won't they try to stop you?"

"They probably will." His mouth quirked up on his uninjured side. "And that's another reason I want to take this job."

"What?" Marian tried to yank away, but Gilbert not only held fast, he straightened and looped an arm around her waist.

"I want them focused on me because the accountant always knows all the dirty secrets." His gaze bored into hers and she couldn't look away. "I expect they'll try to turn me, and then I'll know exactly what they don't want Buck to know. Money and knowledge are both powerful leverage."

"So is family." She placed her hand over his heart. "They might use us to get to you."

"They won't need to." He wove his fingers between hers, keeping their entwined hands to his chest. "I'm going to do everything they want me to do until I have what I need to bring them down."

"What if they discover your duplicity? They'll ..." She shuddered as her imagination careened out of control. "I told you, I don't want to become a widow again."

"And why is that, Mrs. Cox?" He drew her closer, freezing her thoughts.

"I—" *care about you.*

Gil dipped his head and placed the gentlest of kisses on her lips. "I care about you, too."

"Marian!" Mrs. Martins's shout came from outside.

Gilbert jumped away. Marian stared at him, her brain in a muddle, but she was first to react when Mrs. Martins called for her again. She hurried out the back door. Gilbert on her heels.

Mrs. Martins met them in the middle of the empty space between the buildings, her chest heaving. "It's Elaine. She collapsed and I can't wake her."

The fog from Gilbert's kiss vanished like an illusion. Marian pushed him toward the house. "Distract the girls."

"Yes, ma'am." He ran, bless him.

"Call Dr. Thompson," Marian ordered Mrs. Martins. "I'm sorry. I—"

"Nonsense." Mrs. Martins waved off Marian's guilt. "I'll call Rose, too. Have her telegraph Silas."

"See if she can contact Dr. Matrone, too?"

Mrs. Martins gave a single nod and hurried for the workshop.

Marian took a bolstering breath before picking up her skirt. Urgency pressed against fear. Would she find her mother-in-law alive? She pushed into the kitchen. No Elaine. Gilbert's voice came from the front room accompanied by the giggles of her girls. Marian entered the hall, and then Elaine's room. She lay on the ground beside her bed as if sleeping. A sob slipped up Marian's throat as she knelt beside her mother-in-law. And then, mercy upon mercy, she saw Elaine's chest rise and fall.

He hadn't meant to kiss Marian. Not that he regretted it. It's just that now Gilbert wanted another, and theirs wasn't that type of marriage. Nor should he be thinking about kissing when Elaine lay in a drugged sleep in the other room. She'd woken not long after Dr. Thompson arrived, but her entire left side had ceased to function. Then she became so insistent on seeing her late husband, that Dr. Thompson had no choice but to ease her agitation with a sleeping agent.

Gilbert sighed. Alone on the couch in the front room, the house quiet, his thoughts swirled like the wind blowing the falling snow outside. He'd been trying to rest for an hour, and neither his thoughts nor his body would let him. Marian had taken the girls up to bed soon after supper and he hadn't seen her since, so he hoped she'd fallen asleep. Mrs. Whittlebush took Mrs. Martins's place beside Elaine, leaving him at loose ends.

He swung his feet to the floor, propped his elbows on his knees, and carefully placed his face in his hands. His cheekbone still hurt, though not nearly as badly as it had those first few days. Nevertheless, he'd take a dozen more punches if it meant keeping Marian safe. Was taking the Buck Wilson job really the best idea? If he didn't, Marian would still be in danger *and* he wouldn't be able to provide. A failure all around.

Even still, he wouldn't discount Marian's fear. The idea of her or her girls getting hurt caused a boulder to roll around in his stomach. *Father in Heaven ...* The prayer stalled. If Gilbert's earthly father hadn't swindled the Wards, would Marian even be in this situation? She wouldn't be married to Gil, that was for sure. Silas would still be here, a safe protector for Marian and the girls. He'd be here with his mother, too.

But from their first meeting when Gil was a youth, Reverend Moller had insisted that God wasn't like Gilbert's earthly father. He massaged his forehead with the tips of his fingers.

"Gil?" Marian hugged the door frame as she knocked on the wood.

He leapt to his feet. "Marian."

"I'm sorry it took so long. The girls had question after question. I think they're finally asleep, but I worry they'll wake in the night. They're trying to understand. Especially Nettie."

Gilbert absorbed her words, though he didn't understand why she was telling him all of this. He thought she'd retired along with the girls. Did she think he was waiting for her? Looking for an accounting of some kind?

"Essie said Elaine kept staring as Mrs. Martins read to them until she tumbled off the bed. Mrs. Martins tried to catch her, but it all happened so quickly."

Gilbert stuffed his hands in his trouser pockets to keep from reaching for her. He felt slightly underdressed, being in only his shirtsleeves and suspenders. Even if Marian was his wife, should they have this level of comfort between them? The pain in Marian's voice tugged at him, but he didn't move, still unsure what Marian wanted from him.

"Dr. Thompson doesn't think she'll walk again and suggests sending her to a rest home. But I can't do that. I can't send her away." Marian's volume grew. "And you've heard the horror stories of what happens in a poorhouse. Sure, Dr. Thompson said there are good rest homes, and they're getting better. But are they? The good ones must be overcrowded. And there's no way we could afford it, anyway. But I'm not sending Zachariah's mother to die alone. I won't do it."

Her words ended with a stamp and a sob. Gilbert didn't think twice. He wrapped her in his arms and she cried on his shoulder. The harder her body shook, the tighter he held her. His heart broke for her. For Elaine. For Nettie and Essie. For the way the body decayed even before death, and there was nothing a person could do about it.

Slowly, her crying subsided. He ran his hand over her hair, the woven braid half undone. The silky strands smooth to his touch. He wished he could protect Marian from this pain, but he'd be here for her as she went through it. He promised to show her God's love in sickness and health. Now was his opportunity to put his vows into action.

"I'm sorry." Marian pulled away, tucking her chin and swiping at her cheeks. "Please forgive me. I—"

"Shh." Gilbert tucked a strand of her hair behind her ear. "What good is having a husband if he doesn't comfort you when you need it?"

Her lips tipped into the ghost of a smile. "I'll see your shirt laundered."

He glanced at his shoulder and realized how wet she'd made it. He shrugged. "You do laundry every Monday. It will keep until then."

She sniffed even as she studied him. "You truly didn't mind me unloading all of that onto you?"

"Did Zachariah mind?" He could have kicked himself for bringing up her late husband, but the question popped out.

"No, of course not."

"Then why would I?"

"Because ..." Her words faded, and she cocked her head. "Why don't you mind, Gil? Why aren't you uncomfortable right now?"

How could he express the convoluted feelings swirling around inside? And do so without scaring Marian away? She opened up to him, and that made his spirits soar even while he hated the pain she felt. Would that he could take it away. A sentiment that told him much.

"Gil?" She searched his face.

"I told you, Marian. I care for you." He cleared his throat. "When we married, I promised I would love you as God commands us to love one another, with the kind of love that gives all things, bears all things. But this is no longer about duty. I genuinely care about you. I hate seeing you hurting."

She blinked at the sheen in her eyes. "How are you the son of Robert Cox? He is the opposite of you in every—I'm so sorry! I shouldn't have said that." She clapped a hand over her mouth.

His neck heated. "I'm glad you don't think me like him. Forgiving him is still beyond me, but I want to make his wrongs right. Thankfully I had a good mother, and the Mollers, who showed me a better way than greed and selfishness."

"Then I must meet your mother, to thank her." She placed a cool hand against his good cheek and it soothed his very soul. "You are a good man, Gilbert Cox. I am sorry you are saddled with us, and all our problems. I wish you didn't have to sacrifice having the girl of your dreams, a love for the ages, to be married to me. But I am grateful to have you part of my family."

"Being married to you is not a sacrifice, Marian Ward Cox." Quite the opposite, really.

"What do you get out of it, though?" She stepped back and hugged herself. "What benefit do you have being married to me?"

Benefits? Where could he begin? With the lamp light glow casting flickering shadows across her face, it highlighted a faint row of freckles. "I am a blessed man to have the most beautiful woman in Wisconsin—nay, the world—on my arm."

She scowled. "Be serious."

"I am being serious." He held back a chuckle at her disbelief because he wanted her to know just how much he meant his next words. "Marian, when your eyes glow with the love of a mother. When you stand up for your family against thugs and disease. You are magnificent and I am a tongue-tied fool."

Marian dropped her arms from around her waist. "You exaggerate."

"Not a bit." He moved toward her without conscious thought. "I admire you, Marian. And I'm honored to be your husband."

She pressed her lips together, but it didn't hide the tremor in her chin. Gilbert wanted to wrap her in his arms again, maybe even finish the kiss they started earlier. But now wasn't the time. Not if he wanted to be the man she deserved.

As much as he hated to say it ... "It's late Marian. Mrs. Whittlebush is staying up with Elaine, so you should sleep while you have the chance."

Brown luminous orbs held him captive. "So should you."

"I will." He tore his gaze away, needing to collect himself. Snow left wet streaks on the window, which reflected in the lamp light. He shouldn't be having romantic thoughts about Marian when they needed to make decisions about Buck Wilson and the job, about Elaine and good medical care, about how to keep everyone as safe as possible. It made him long for the wisdom of the Mollers, of his mother's sage advice. "I think I might call my mom. She'll give me what-for, calling at such an indecent hour. But after today, I'd like to hear her voice. Even if she's scolding me."

"Say hello for me?" Marian said, and he turned back to her. "I would like to meet her soon."

"We'll work something out once we know how Elaine is doing." Gilbert cupped Marian's cheek, swiping his thumb against a tear stain. If they were a true married couple, not one of convenience, he would kiss her now. "Now, go sleep."

"Thank you, Gilbert." She pressed lips to his cheek, and then walked away, taking his heart with her.

CHAPTER TEN

Sunday, January 25

Marian sat at the kitchen table, which was so covered in food delivered by the people of Crow's Nest, that she had to hold her cup of coffee in one hand and Silas's telegram in the other. Heat from the oven warmed her back and the smell of Mrs. Martins's freshly baked apple scones wrapped around her like a hug.

She read the yellow paper for the third time:

CANNOT VISIT STOP
TELL MOM I LOVE HER.

Oh, Silas. What pain he must feel, unable to be here for his mother, unable to say goodbye. Dr. Thompson's diagnosis was dire. Resolve strengthened her. She would do the best she could in Silas's place, in Zachariah's place, and then she would write Silas a detailed letter describing the love their community showed his mother in what would likely be her last days.

Since last night, Mrs. Martins and Mrs. Whittlebush had taken up residence as Elaine's personal attendants. Today they also took turns answering the door so Marian did not have to talk to every person who dropped by despite the snow that fell overnight. Even Samantha had come by that morning, sacrificing her day off to keep the girls occupied upstairs. She brought over hat-making supplies and the girls were immediately captivated.

Gilbert hovered nearby. He'd wanted to go to services that morning, hoping to see Buck Wilson in a casual environment that would less likely lead to retaliation by the thugs who threatened her, but one look at Marian's face and he'd changed his mind. She didn't have the energy to do anything but agree to whatever he suggested. Even debating whether he should talk to Buck was too much for her weary mind to consider.

"Here, eat this." Gilbert held out a plate with a warm biscuit, butter melting on top. Her stomach rumbled. "You need to keep up your strength, and Mrs. Martins's biscuits are almost as good as yours."

A laugh jumped out. "That's not true, but thank you."

He shrugged and waggled the plate. "You can't help Silas by reading his telegram over and over. But your girls and Elaine need you to eat."

Another knock at the door, but this one was at the back door.

"I'll get it." Gilbert cleared a place on the table for the plate. "Eat, please."

Marian tucked the telegraph under a platter and took a bite of biscuit as Gilbert opened the door. A whirl of blonde energy entered the kitchen. Mindy Zahan. "Oh, Marian, I came over as soon as I went on break. I only have fifteen minutes—well, five because it took me five minutes to get here and it'll take me five minutes to get back. But I had to visit you so I could hug you." She didn't give Marian a chance to stand, nor set down either the biscuit or coffee cup, before wrapping her arms around her.

Gilbert took the biscuit and cup from her hands and Marian sank into the hug. She wouldn't have called Mindy a particularly close friend. She was David Martins's friend, though the Ward brothers grew up with her, too. But she and Mindy hadn't talked all that much over the years, so this reaction from Mindy surprised her.

"Goodness." Mindy pulled away. "I'm sorry. I was just so overtaken."

Marian stood. "It's okay." What else should she say? Her mind was blank of even common courtesy. Did she invite Mindy in? She was too tired to entertain.

"Thank you for stopping by." Gilbert cupped Mindy's elbow, obviously aiming to escort her from the house. *Thank you, Gil.* He was proving a particularly gallant protector today.

But Mindy dug in her heels. "I, uh, I heard ..." She chewed her cheek and Gilbert released her.

Unease tightened Marian's stomach. Mindy worked at the Wharfside and had firsthand knowledge of most everything that happened in town. People gossiped freely around her, making her a better source of information than the *Crow's Nest Gazette*.

Mindy glanced at Gilbert, then back to Marian. "Can we talk? Alone?"

That didn't bode well. Still, Marian gave Gilbert a nod, and while he didn't look happy about being excluded, he did leave her and Mindy alone in the kitchen. "What's wrong?"

"It's Greg Alistar." Mindy rolled her eyes before concern pinched her features. "He's been sniffing around about your Gilbert. Gilbert is the son of Robert Cox, isn't he?"

Marian nodded. That information was bound to be common knowledge sooner than later, but what Alistar would do with the information was concerning. He knew Robert Cox, and what he'd done. Most only knew the rumors and might not know the name of the person who had swindled Elaine, and put Cora, Silas, and Buck in danger.

"I thought yours was a true love match, but I don't understand why you'd marry Robert Cox's son. Not after what he did to your family." Mindy pressed her fingers to her temples. "My own record with men is horrible. I mean, I let Joe Spelding manipulate me. But what is Gilbert Cox up to? Why would you let him into your life, let alone marry him? You've always struck me as having more common sense than me."

Ouch.

"I mean, don't get me wrong, he's handsome and seems a gentleman. But you've been married before." Mindy toed a crack in the wooden floorboards. "You wouldn't fall for a guy's charms like I have."

Defensiveness rose in Marian, but for all Mindy's accusations, Marian sensed there was more to the question than Mindy let on. Marian's thoughts were sluggish, yet the way Mindy kept comparing herself to Marian sparked something in Marian's mind. But she couldn't grab hold of it.

"Why did you marry him?" Vulnerability filled Mindy's hazel eyes.

"Gil is a good man, Mindy." Marian captured Mindy's shoulders. While she wanted to defend Gilbert, that's not what Mindy needed of her. "He is honorable and sacrificial, and he's most definitely not his father."

"You knew who he was before you married him?"

"I did." Marian considered Mindy. She was maybe a year or two younger, but the naïveté she exuded made her seem much younger. "You're right that I was married before, so I knew what I was entering

into when I agreed to marry Gilbert. I didn't fall for his charms, but ..."
Was she falling for him now? The way he'd comforted her last night, the
way he cared for her today ...

"I might not have the best judgment when it comes to men, but I can
recognize that look." Mindy chuckled. "It may not have begun as a love
match as everyone thought, but it's on its way there, isn't it?"

Heat climbed Marian's neck. She needed to divert Mindy away from
Gilbert, and what better way to do that than to return to the topic
of Greg Alistar, the annoying newspaperman who had dogged David
and Adaleigh, and Silas and Cora. With Gilbert's family history and his
father's connection to the Wards, there was little chance he'd let this story
go. If Mindy became an advocate of Gil, then his reputation could be
saved, no matter how things played out with him working for Buck.
Marian waved Mindy to a seat. "Tell me more about what Mr. Alistar
wants."

"He's asking questions about Gilbert." Mindy obliged, and Marian
returned to her chair. "Like why is Gilbert here in Crow's Nest and
speculating on how he trapped you into marriage. Mr. Alistar makes it
sound noble, but we both know he is anything but."

"No, he is not noble," Marian muttered.

Mindy covered Marian's hand. "If Gilbert has anything bad in his life,
you know Mr. Alistar will find it. And even if he doesn't, Mr. Alistar will
manipulate whatever he thinks he knows to fit his story."

Marian sank back in her chair. "I don't know if we can stop him."
And if Gilbert began working for Buck Wilson, what would Mr. Alistar
make of that? Even if Mindy spread good rumors, who knew what
tales Mr. Alistar would spin. Unless Buck could protect Gilbert from
the newspaperman? Or would a negative reputation help protect them

against the thugs? She rubbed her temples. How could they know the safest path to take?

"Well, my five minutes are well past." Mindy rose, as did Marian, and gave Marian a brief, but strong hug. "I'll keep my ears open for anything more. Tell Mrs. Ward I'm praying for her, too. Prayer is new for me, so I'm not sure how good I am at it, but I aim to do as best I can. Mrs. Ward is a dear lady. So are you, so you take care of yourself, Marian."

An instant later Mindy had swept out the door, leaving questions upon questions in her wake.

"I couldn't help but listen." Gilbert reentered the kitchen, arms crossed. Marian's defenses went down and her shoulders sagged. "You mentioned Greg Alistar that first day we picked up the girls from school together. A newspaperman of questionable ethics."

"Seems he's caught wind of you." Could a person drown on dry land? Because that's how she felt just now.

"That could be a good thing." Gilbert directed her back to her chair.

She stared up at him. He was a handsome man with his stubble and unruly curly hair. In fact, she preferred when he let the curls run wild rather than controlling them as he did when he had an accounting appointment. It was opposite of his usual steady personality. Add that to his rolled up shirt sleeves and the loosened top button of his shirt, and he seemed—

"Think about it." Gilbert grabbed a chair to sit knee-to-knee with Marian, pulling her from her wayward thoughts, and lowered his voice. "He'll damage my reputation, which is exactly what I need if I'm to throw the thugs off what I really aim to do."

"At what cost, Gil?"

"Keeping you safe." He grabbed her hands. Comforting and warm. "My father has already dented my reputation. So long as I have your faith in me, then I have nothing to lose."

The depth of what Gilbert was saying slowly seeped in. What exactly was he willing to risk? And most impactful of all, how she viewed him mattered. He esteemed her that much. It humbled her. "I think Buck might offer you some protection, too. He is not a fan of Greg Alistar."

"You think I should take the job." He rubbed his thumb along her knuckles. "What made you change your mind?"

"I'm not sure I have exactly. Do you think it's true that you can bring an end to these threats? That you can figure out what the thugs are hiding? Maybe find what Detective O'Connor has been searching for? But what if you bring Buck down? You'll be in his sights and we'll have him and the thugs after us." Panic tightened her chest.

"One thing at a time, Marian." Gilbert reached to press his palm against her cheek. "We have to make decisions one step at a time. If we look at the big picture and make plans without knowing all the facts, we will make miscalculations. This requires slow, methodical consideration."

"And you're good at that, aren't you?" She leaned into his touch, which calmed the fear. "You're solid. Not much ruffles you."

"I'm glad you think so. Inside I don't feel so unruffled." He blew out a slow breath. "You ruffle me."

"And you steady me." She covered his hand with hers. Electricity arced between them.

The circuit snapped with another knock at the back door. Gilbert shook his head. "I'll get it." He opened the door and Buck Wilson entered the kitchen.

Heavenly Father ... Again Gilbert's prayer faded. He didn't know what words to pray as Buck Wilson shrugged out of his coat as if planning to stay for a while. Irritation flared. He tamped it down. Now was not the time to explore the emotional connection nor the attraction he was feeling toward Marian.

Wilson handed Gilbert his coat and Gilbert shook the snow onto the rug. He supposed he now had no excuse not to have a conversation with the man. There was much they needed to discuss, man-to-man, before they ever got to business. And doing so under the guise of Wilson visiting Elaine would hopefully be sufficient cover to protect Marian from the thugs. As sure as he was about his plan to work for Buck Wilson, the doubts and Marian's concerns were ever present in his mind. They were all too real and made for serious threats. Still, Gilbert believed that digging the problem out by the root would be the wisest plan. Seemed Marian was coming around to the idea, too.

Of course, Wilson barely acknowledged Gilbert before greeting Marian, reaching both hands out to her. "I'm so sorry to hear about your mother-in-law. How is she doing?"

"About the same." Marian's fingers tangled in her apron instead of placing them in Wilson's.

Gratification momentarily filled Gilbert, before being replaced by guilt at his pride. *Forgive me, Heavenly Father.*

"Her left side is mostly useless," Marian was saying. "The doctor has her propped up so she can swallow without choking, but she can only manage liquids right now."

Elaine hadn't asked for her late husband all morning, so perhaps that was a positive? Though Gilbert hadn't heard her speak at all during his limited moments when asked to help lift her for one reason or another.

"Have you reached Silas?" Wilson shoved his hands in his pockets, pulling up the ends of his coats. It was a move Gilbert used often, one he now didn't want to make again.

Marian nodded, picking up the yellow telegram. "He can't come home."

The implications of that sat heavy on Gilbert's conscience. If his father hadn't spent the money he'd stolen from the Wards, he could have returned it, and maybe Silas wouldn't have had to travel west for work. He'd be here with his mother in what very well might be her final days.

Gilbert's jaw tightened and his fists clenched. He wanted to make amends to the Wards for the damage his father had caused, but this he could not fix. He wasn't poor, but he wasn't wealthy enough to purchase a round trip ticket for two. One even, not that Silas would leave his wife behind. He probably couldn't leave his job, either. Hadn't Marian said Silas had unexpected expenses so he couldn't send money home for her? Gilbert's stomach soured. Then there was no way Silas could come home.

Wilson shifted closer to Marian, showing the back of his shoulder to Gilbert. The man's voice dropped. "And how are you fairing?"

Gilbert barely contained a growl. Yeah, he needed to have words with Buck Wilson.

"Mrs. Martins and Mrs. Whittlebush have been of great help. Even Samantha is entertaining my girls today. I couldn't be more thankful." Her words rushed out.

Gilbert swallowed back his dratted pride. He didn't need Marian to specifically mention him. He'd been helpful, at least, he thought so—and that should be enough.

Buck opened his mouth, likely to point out the matter, but Marian continued. "However, it's Gilbert who has been the rock I can rely on most of all."

So much for pride. Any he had left was swept away by the very unmanly tears that blurred his vision. Marian held out her hand to him, wiggling her fingers, and he rounded the table to her side. A kiss to her cheek brought his mouth close to her ear, and words tumbled out in a whisper. "Thank you, my darling."

Her eyes widened as she shifted her chin to face him. Wonder and question mingled in her brown gaze. How he wished he could kiss her.

Wilson cleared his throat. "Obviously the rumors of this being a love match are true." He didn't sound happy about it.

Gilbert turned on him. "Is that why you requested me specifically? My company is not the only accounting firm, nor am I my company's only accountant." Gilbert kept Marian's hand wrapped in his as he stared Wilson down.

"Partly so." Wilson glanced at Marian. "Perhaps we should have a conversation where we might speak freely."

"You can speak in front of my wife." Gilbert internally rolled his eyes. Could he be any more juvenile? Of course he, too, wanted a private word with Wilson. Not because he didn't want Marian to hear, but because he did not want Wilson to hold back on account of Marian's presence. Yet he couldn't seem to stop himself from pushing Buck Wilson's buttons.

Marian leaned into his side. "Take Buck to the workshop. I need to check on everyone before dinner brings another round of food. Not that I know what to do with all we received this morning." Did she see through him? Probably.

Gilbert gave Marian's hand a squeeze before he and Wilson donned their coats and hats, popped their collars against the icy wind whipping off the lake, and crunched through the snow to the workshop. Neither sat on the two stools tucked under the work table. Instead, they faced each other like two mirror images, frosty breaths filling the stale air between them. Gilbert tried not to shift, to show his discomfort. Did Wilson have a violent streak or did he war with words? Because this felt like high noon, a disconcerting position for a pacifist.

"A week is fast to fall in love." Buck tossed the thought out like the first jab of a boxer in the ring. Words it was, then.

"Marian makes it easy." A weak parry. Anyway, was he really in love with Marian? He told her as much and he supposed it was good to be in love with one's wife, but now wasn't the time to think about it. He narrowed his gaze at Wilson. "Do you have feelings for her?"

Buck snorted. "I don't make it a habit to fall in love with the widows I aim to help. But I am protective of them and I don't trust you."

"I don't trust you." Gilbert crossed his arms. He searched the room for inspiration on how to move this conversation away from unproductive male posturing. His gaze landed on the half-empty wall of tools. Silas must have taken many with him when he left town. He was a carpenter, so it made sense he'd take the tools of his trade with him. Ah, that's the line of questioning he could take with Wilson. "Why did you demand I work for you?"

Wilson rested a hip against the work table. "Because Marian is scared of something and I want to know what it is. It doesn't seem to be you, though that was my first thought."

Gilbert mulled Wilson's words. How much could—should—he tell him without putting Marian in worse danger? Nothing yet. He first needed to discern what type of trouble Buck Wilson was into and the direct approach usually threw off the unsuspecting. "Why is Detective O'Connor investigating you?"

"Heard about that, did you?" Wilson shook his head. "I'm not doing anything illegal or he would have found it already."

"You know I'll find out the truth if you hire me." Gilbert rocked on his heels, poking to see what type of reaction he'd get.

"If?" Wilson raised an eyebrow, then sighed and shifted to rest his whole backside against the table. "Maybe the good detective will listen to you when you tell him I'm clean."

With Wilson seemingly off his guard, Gilbert asked, "Have you ever killed someone?"

The man choked on his own spit, red mottling his clean-shaven face, and Gilbert knew the truth without Wilson saying a word. This suave, put-together businessman had taken a life. But he didn't get *killer* from his eyes. He'd seen those types before. The ones who would murder to keep their financial secrets quiet. Heavens, his own father was nearly one of those. Was Wilson? Or did he regret killing someone, and that's why he looked out for widows with such passion?

Buck still hadn't spoken, so Gilbert asked, "Was it justified?"

"What does that matter?" Wilson set his jaw. "A life is a life."

Huh. He hadn't expected guilt. Something wasn't adding up about Buck Wilson, and Gilbert couldn't figure out the missing equation. "Why would someone be scared of you killing again?"

"These are not the questions I expected ..." Wilson trailed off, then snapped upright. "Wait. Is Marian scared of *me*? Am I the one who scared her into marrying you?"

Gilbert took a step toward him. "Should she be?"

"Cox, just say it already." Wilson flung out his hands. "Enough trying to draw me out, or incriminate myself with something you won't find. What is going on? What is the real reason you married Marian? Because I know full well you didn't love her when you married. You might now, but not when you first met her. You married her for a reason. Why?"

"First, tell me why you want to hire me. I'm sure you have an accountant already." This was the sliver of doubt that had been festering since his boss had made the demand.

Wilson tossed his bowler onto the worktable. "Because Marian trusts you and I don't know why. I want you close so I can figure you out. Are you like your father? I want proof so I can tell Silas that Marian is in good hands."

Wow. Not what Gilbert expected at all.

His thoughts must have splayed across his face because Wilson gave a humorless chuckle. "Obviously you suspected something more sinister. Why?"

"If I tell you, it puts Marian in more danger." Gilbert blew out a breath and scrubbed the non-bruised side of his face, knocking his cap sideways. He dragged it off his head. "Working with you—even talking with you right now—could get her and her girls killed."

"What?" Buck advanced to stick his face in front of Gilbert's. "She's in danger because of me? From whom and why?"

Gilbert held his ground, his cap crumpled in his fist. "If I knew that, I would have gone to the police."

"Not the Crow's Nest police." Buck paced away and back. "Don't do that. Not until O'Connor gets back."

There it was again, that underlying *something* that didn't fit with the data. "Marian said the same, but funny you should trust the detective who is out to get you."

Wilson's shoulders sagged, making him appear nothing like the confident businessman whom thugs feared would kill them. "O'Connor is honest and not full of himself. If he brings me down, then I have crossed a line and deserve it."

"You are not who I thought you were." He didn't mean to say that out loud.

Buck shook his head. "Cox, I'm thinking the same thing about you."

Silence settled for a beat, and then, as if by mutual agreement, they both leaned against the work table. Side by side. Gilbert looked over at Wilson. "So how do we keep Marian and her girls safe? I'd take them back to Milwaukee, but with Elaine's health, we can't move them."

"And no idea who is threatening Marian?"

"Only if you can identify a man based on a fist." Gilbert pointed toward the yellow remnants of the punch to his face. "If I work for you, it's to keep my job, and I'll do *whatever* it takes to keep Marian safe."

Buck shifted to study Gilbert, respect showing in his eyes. "You have a plan in mind. What is it?"

Gilbert gave a chagrined smile. "I don't trust you enough to share it." Yet?

"Fair enough. Then since you'll be digging, there's something else you should know." Buck returned his hands to his pockets. "Someone in my organization was leaking information to your father and your father was in communication with Greg Alistar. I haven't found the leak, but maybe you can."

"Why would they do that?" Gilbert sifted through the little communication he'd had with his father over the past year, but nothing stood out.

"Doesn't it always come down to money?" Buck said. "You're a money man. Find it."

"It's not always money." A pair of brown eyes came to mind. "The people we care about make fine leverage, too."

"You think I'll leverage Marian." It wasn't a question. The man was astute.

"Maybe. Maybe not you, but someone. She married me, a man whom she could have considered an enemy, because she was afraid for the safety of her children. Whoever those thugs are, they broke into Marian's house." His chest tightened. "Needless to say, I won't be sleeping tonight after spending half an hour talking to you."

"Then my next stop is the Wharfside." Buck grabbed his bowler. "I'll enlist Mindy's help extolling your giftedness at numbers, which your boss assured me was fact, and why anyone would be a fool to turn down your accounting services. You might have more work than you can handle by the end of the day."

"Burkes and Dudley will like that." And it made sense too. Of course Buck would choose the best, and if everyone thought Gilbert was the best, the thugs shouldn't blink at this conversation. Still ... "It might not matter. They might want to remove loose ends." And that meant Marian would remain in danger until they rooted out the thugs.

"And you don't know why?"

He wished he did. "Only that they're scared enough of you to threaten Marian with her life."

Buck nodded as if mentally creating a plan of attack. "Tomorrow morning, come down to the Conglomerate headquarters and I'll set you up with every ledger I have."

"It's a deal." Gilbert shook Buck Wilson's hand, praying he hadn't just made a deal with the enemy.

CHAPTER ELEVEN

Marian blinked gritty sleep from her eyes as she set the coffee to heat on the stove. Gilbert had sent Mrs. Martins and Mrs. Whittlebush home last night because he planned to stay up with Elaine. Except Elaine had a difficult night. If Marian hadn't given in to a good cry the other night, she'd indulge in one this morning. Despite the bright sun causing the freshly fallen snow to sparkle like a thousand diamonds, her soul felt dark and heavy.

"It'll be a cold day." Gilbert entered the kitchen, snapping up suspenders. He had his hair controlled with pomade. Looking his best to work for Buck. But Marian still preferred when he let his curls go free. It showed the part of himself that hovered below the professional exterior he kept up for his clients.

Then she spotted a shaving knick that bled along his jaw. She snatched up a clean cloth and held it to the spot. How comfortable had she gotten with him in so short a time that she could approach him so easily?

"I guess I'm not as steady as I want to be today." His lips quirked, but worry swam in his eyes. Her heart hitched.

"The girls will be safe at school and I'm sure I'll have a rotating door of help here. I won't be alone." She lifted the cloth to see if the bleeding had stopped. Not quite. She pressed a clean section to his jaw. "You stay focused on those numbers. We'll be fine."

"I know you're trying to make me feel better." He tugged her hand away from his face. "You don't have to be strong for me."

She stood close enough that she had to tip her chin up just a bit to look him in the eye. Close indeed. Like a husband and wife should be. And the emotion churning in her stomach told her that her care for him had grown exponentially over the last few days.

The charged moment melted like snow before a fire as the girls clomped down the stairs. Marian's senses whooshed in as she smelled the biscuits were overdone and heard the coffee at a furious boil. Flustered, she whirled away. Gilbert's chuckle followed her.

"Morning, Mama, and Mr. Gil." Nettie skipped into the kitchen, hair loose and two blue ribbons in her fist. "I combed my hair."

"Me too, Mama." Essie had several ribbons of varying colors wrapped around her fingers.

The tension—good and bad—fell from her shoulders as she smiled at her girls.

For the next half an hour, Marian could almost believe life was good. Elaine slept soundly for the longest stretch in the last twenty-four hours. Healing sleep, *please, Lord*. The girls laughed at Gilbert's jokes and he cast teasing winks at her. Eggs, biscuits, coffee with cream ... It was a wealth Marian would never take for granted.

It ended when the clock struck the hour. The girls helped clear the table, then gathered their school books. Gilbert had already donned his coat, hat, scarf. Marian stood by the stove, the good feelings of a moment ago washing away as she scrubbed the breakfast dishes.

"It's going to be okay." Gilbert took a plate from her hands and dipped it back into the washbasin. Then he took her wet hands in his, ducking to make sure she looked at him. "Like you said, Mrs. Martins and Mrs. Whittlebush will be here soon. I moved all my appointments in Hawk's River to later this week so I'll be in town all day today."

"Ready!" Nettie stuffed her arms into her coat. Essie pulled her knit hat over her braids.

Gilbert brushed a kiss over her cheek, like a husband might before he left for work. Then he winked. "Alright, gals, who has mittens and hats and scarves?"

"Me!" The girls jumped up and down. Marian knelt to help Nettie and Essie with their winter clothing.

Gilbert opened the back door, and a gust of frigid air blew in. He slammed it shut. "On second thought, let's go out the front door."

Marian jerked her gaze up to meet his, catching the fear in his eyes before he tried to hide it behind a smile.

Gilbert shook his head and herded the girls toward the front of the house. "Stay on the porch girls. I'll pull the car around." The girls tried to scoop the fluffy snow into their hands only for it to fall away like sugar.

"What's wrong?" Marian whispered as soon as she was sure the girls wouldn't hear her.

"Someone left a message on the back step." A muscle ticked in Gilbert's jaw. "And they did it between when we gathered eggs and I opened the back door."

"I was in the kitchen that whole time. I should have heard something." Or worse. They could have entered the kitchen and Marian would have been there all alone. "Do I want to know what it is?"

"Can you trust me not to look? It's … It's another threat."

Her stomach churned. "At least tell me so my imagination doesn't make it worse than it is."

"All right. It's a dead rat. I'm going to clear it away so the girls don't see, then ..." Gilbert tugged his cap lower over his head. A dead rat? "Do I tell Buck everything? Or do I not take the job? It's one or the other, Marian."

Stirring came from Elaine's room. Happy shrieks came from the front porch. Three people depending on Marian and Gilbert to protect them. "I don't know the wisest plan, Gil. What if we chose wrong?"

"Come here." He tugged her into the circle of his arms, his wool coat scratchy against her cheeks. "Heavenly Father, I don't know what to pray. I struggle to know You are good. That You are not like my father ..."

Tears pricked Marian's eyes as Gilbert's voice faltered. She'd been so focused on her own trials, the danger, Elaine's illness, the girls' needs, that she missed Gilbert's struggle.

Gilbert cleared his throat. "We need wisdom and guidance, and Your protection." The doubt that laced his words broke Marian's heart.

"And show us Your goodness, even when everything seems darkest," Marian whispered.

"Amen." Gilbert blew out a breath and kissed the top of her head.

Thursday, January 29

Four days of searching through the ledgers of Crow's Nest Conglomerate, and still Gilbert came up empty. He pinched the bridge of his nose, winced. The bruising on his face was nearly gone, but there were areas that were still sensitive to pressure.

"Take a break." Buck set a mug of coffee in the one open spot on the table and pulled out a chair.

Gilbert breathed in the roasted brew—not burnt, but not weak. Most businessmen he'd visited this week had offered him watered down coffee. Buck still had access to the good stuff, and was willing to share it. "I have only one luncheon appointment tomorrow, so I plan to spend the day sifting through these numbers." He patted one of the few books he hadn't gone through line-by-line. Interrupting his work to visit other Burkes and Dudley clients wasn't his preferred method of conducting an audit, but he had no choice.

"There's someone I want you to meet." Buck leaned back in his chair, arms and ankles crossed. A week of observing the man and Gilbert had come to recognize Wilson's apparent ease hid a keen intensity.

"Are they part of the Conglomerate?" Gilbert sipped the coffee. Lack of sleep wasn't helping him either. He'd sat up with Elaine most nights so Marian could sleep. It also allowed him to keep watch for the thugs. So far they hadn't appeared and it made Gilbert uneasy. What were they waiting for? Everyone knew Gilbert was working for Wilson.

"Definitely not." Buck chuckled, then sobered. "It wouldn't be outside of normal for him to visit Elaine, but I don't wish to escalate the danger. There hasn't been another incident since the rat message, has there?"

"No. But Marian and the girls have stayed in the house and are never alone. Granted, their company is all female."

"But Marie Martins and Rose Whittlebush are formidable women." Buck grinned. "I know better than to cross them. And if these thugs have a wit of sense, they'll know that, too. I don't think even Greg Alistar is willing to print gossip about them. The closest he came was when Mrs. Martins's son was arrested for murder, but Alistar went after David, not her."

"Wait, David's father was arrested for murder?" And Gilbert thought his own father's crimes were bad.

Wilson must have realized the same because he sat forward, finger wagging. "When Martins returns, you and he have more in common than you might think. Estranged fathers and all. And it's his uncle I want you to meet."

Gilbert's eyes widened of their own accord. "Isn't he the detective?"

Buck inclined his head. "I sent him a telegram after the rat incident. And don't worry, I know not to send something like that through Crow's Nest's telegraph office."

Gilbert straightened. He'd also gotten a strange feeling around the Crow's Nest telegraph operator. "What do you mean, not sending it through the office here?"

"Angus, the telegraph operator." Wilson sipped his coffee. "I haven't confirmed whether he maintains the integrity his position requires, or if he can be ... swayed."

"Toward you or someone else?" Gilbert set his mug on the table and made a mental note to search for any evidence of overpaying for telegraphs or other evidence of paying off Angus.

"Touché, Cox." Wilson tipped his cup toward Gilbert. "That's why I like you. Your father deserves prison, if you don't mind me saying, but you're an all right chap. It's why I urged the good detective to return as soon as possible. He's due on the train in Hawk's River within the hour. It's not wise for the three of us to be seen together, especially in Crow's Nest, but—"

"Then I have the place," Gilbert interrupted. He wanted that conversation with the detective. "Reverend Moller of the First Church of Hawk's River."

"Good plan." Buck rose. "We'll leave separately. I'll get word to the detective to meet us there."

Gilbert checked his pocket watch. Still plenty of time before he needed to pick up the girls from school. He packed away the ledgers. Should he bring Marian to Hawk's River, or would that be too obvious to the thugs? Not wanting to break her trust, he drove home.

Home. It sure was beginning to feel that way. The scent of baked goods wrapped around him as he entered the kitchen.

"Gil." Marian looked up from working over a collection of herbs laid out on a cheesecloth. "You're home unexpectedly. Elaine developed sores since she hasn't left her bed, so I'm making a poultice Mrs. Martins suggested. Is everything all right?"

"I have a meeting in Hawk's River." He removed his hat and circled the table, lowering his voice as he leaned close. The smell of lavender mixed with garlic and honey. "I'm meeting Detective O'Connor in Hawk's River at Buck's orchestration. Do you want to go along?"

First fear, then consternation, then gratefulness, and finally wonder crossed her pale face. She shook her head and the emotion cleared. "It's not wise to leave Elaine, even with Mrs. Martins here."

"It's your life, your girls' lives that are at stake." He laid his hand over hers, noting the dark circles under her eyes. He'd tried to take as much as he could from her shoulders, but it wasn't enough. "You need a break."

She pulled away and wrapped up the cheesecloth, tying it closed with twine. "What if Elaine takes a turn for the worse before I return?"

It was a constant worry. But ... "There are no guarantees in life, Marian. You have to make the best decision you can with the information you have. It's why we married the way we did." And Gilbert didn't regret it for one minute.

"Gilbert, hello." Mrs. Martins breezed into the kitchen. "Pardon me for interrupting. I returned for the poultice, but couldn't help overhearing. If I may offer my opinion, Gilbert is right. Go with him to talk to my brother. It will bring you peace, which will be of benefit to your girls and Elaine."

"You think so?" Marian brightened, as if someone gave her permission to smile. Gilbert wished he could have offered her that.

"I do." Mrs. Martins pulled her into a hug. "Anyway, you need some time with your man."

Heat washed through Gilbert. Mrs. Martins knew this wasn't *that* type of marriage. Before he could protest, the older woman winked at him. And then he remembered what Buck Wilson had said about her son. It made him see her from a different perspective. A kinship he didn't expect, nor one he'd wish on anyone else.

"Thank you, ma'am." Gilbert bowed his head, thankful for more than just convincing Marian to go along to Hawk's River.

When was the last time she left the property? Marian couldn't remember. Had it been when she went to Hawk's River and ended up married? No, they went dress shopping on Saturday. That wasn't even a week ago, yet it felt like months.

Her shoulders tensed the farther from Elaine they drove. What if something happened while Marian was gone? What would she tell Silas? That she'd been out galavanting with the son of the man who ruined their family? Oh, that's not who Gilbert was to her anymore, but it fed the guilt that wrapped its thorny vines around her chest.

Crossing into the Hawk's River town limits only increased the tightness. Her mind zipped ahead and yet flashed back to the last time she'd been in Hawk's River. She could see the thugs following her into that drugstore. Gilbert trying to protect her only to get knocked to the floor. And then their wedding. When she'd left to get Elaine's aspirin that day, never would she have guessed she'd return home with a husband.

Yet now he sat beside her, intent on protecting her and including her in his plans. Respect for Gilbert sparked a prayer of thanks, which surprised her. It was difficult to reconcile the God who watched her first husband die in a field with the One who sent His provision in the form of a second husband. She hadn't exactly left her faith after Zachariah died, she'd just been too weary to wrestle with the heartache. The sense of betrayal. Yes, she'd kept praying, going to church, and teaching her children about Jesus. But truly relying on God for herself?

Her prayer the other day, to see God's goodness, had been one of the first times she voiced her struggle, and it came because she'd felt Gilbert's heartache. She wanted to latch onto the sliver of light that prayer had brought her. Perhaps explore whether she could trust God in the darkness. But it required strength she didn't have to spare.

Gilbert parked where he had that fateful day, outside the Moller's parsonage. They hadn't seen the Mollers since they returned her truck and Marian was looking forward to seeing Mrs. Moller—Jessica—again. How long ago it seemed. Months and months. Maybe even a year. And yet, it had only been two weeks to the day since she and Gilbert had become husband and wife.

"Ready?" Gilbert took her hand in his, weaving their fingers together in a way that felt intimate. Like they were a team. Them against all the trouble they faced. She appreciated it more than she could express.

She nodded. Time to find a solution to end the danger to her family.

Jessica Moller welcomed them with hugs before ushering them into the parlor where Buck Wilson already relaxed in one of the upholstered chairs. He raised a plate with a half-eaten pastry. "Whatever this is, it's delicious. I thank you, Mrs. Moller."

"He's charming, that one," Mrs. Moller said under her breath while smiling at Buck. Louder, she added, "The reverend left a moment ago to pick up the detective from the train station. They'll be back shortly."

True to Mrs. Moller's word, Reverend Moller returned as Marian and Gilbert finished their pastries. Detective O'Connor wore his usual large-brimmed hat, which he removed to reveal his stark blue eyes, his gray mustache, and gray hair. He eased into a rocker with a groan that showed his seventy years more than Marian could remember. He worked as a special investigator for the Crow's Nest police. Nearing retirement, he primarily focused on investigating whether the Conglomerate had a criminal element.

"How is David?" Marian asked him as the Mollers settled in upright chairs, closing the circle.

"Ready to return home." Detective O'Connor's mustache bobbed with his words. "They all are, and plan to catch a train within the next week or two."

"Samson will be happy to see you, I'm sure." Marian smiled at the thought of the detective's large Mastiff.

"Samson?" Gilbert leaned forward.

"My dog." Detective O'Connor gave a gravelly chuckle. "He's been annoying my sister—Marie—for the past month. I fully expect to return home to an overfed dog."

"I went by your place after the snowstorm." Buck shifted in his chair. "It looked okay from what I could tell."

Marian toyed with the ribbon on her dress as she watched Buck and the detective. Like two dogs circling each other, testing one another.

"Thanks." Detective O'Connor's eyebrow twitched before he turned his gaze toward Gilbert. "You look just like your father."

Gilbert turned as red as an apple. "I hope that's where the similarities end, sir. The man is a crook." Marian wished to renew their clasped hands, as Gilbert had done in the car, but refrained in case it wasn't welcome.

"We'll see about that." Detective O'Connor reached for his cup and saucer. "The good reverend explained this was a meeting of the minds. Considering the minds in the room, and the insistence on my presence, I believe it's time for an explanation. Wilson, you start. Since you're the one who demanded I return home at once."

"With all due respect, I believe this is Marian's story." Buck inclined his head toward her. "You should tell it."

"I agree." Gilbert found her hand and Marian pulled from his strength, all under Detective O'Connor's all-seeing gaze.

"All right." Marian squared her shoulders. She took a fortifying breath and began at the beginning. "It's been hard since Silas left, but even harder since January began."

Over the next twenty minutes, Marian told of her struggle to pay her bills, to heat their home, to afford medicine for Elaine. She explained about the thugs, what she overheard that day, and how they had threatened her since. She shared how Gilbert first arrived at the house, looking for absolution, and how he ended up becoming her husband, provider, and protector. Finally, she told of Elaine's worsening condition and Buck's request for Gilbert to audit his books.

Marian heaved a sigh. "Each day, I fear the escalating threats will turn into actual harm. Why they haven't acted on their threat since Gilbert has been working with Buck all week, I don't understand. And with Elaine's health deteriorating before my eyes ..." Her voice cracked, and she shook her head, unable to say any more. Gilbert rubbed his thumb over her knuckles.

"Have you found anything in Wilson's books?" Detective O'Connor speared Gilbert with his gaze.

"No, sir." The confidence Gilbert portrayed calmed Marian. "There should be something, and the lack of it is concerning."

The detective's bushy brows furrowed. "Explain."

Gilbert exchanged a look with Buck. "Wilson explained he suspects a mole. There should be evidence of that in the books."

"Unless they're cooked." Detective O'Connor folded his arms, glaring at both men. Marian glanced at the reverend and his wife. What did they think of this story? She couldn't tell. They appeared to listen impartially with neutral expressions. Perhaps that was for the best. Someone who could give an unbiased opinion on what to do next.

"I want that mole." Buck leaned back in his chair, ankles crossed. "Whether I'm crooked or not, I refuse to tolerate a disloyal employee. If you doubt that, then believe me that I will not put Marian's life, or the life of her girls, in danger. I should have proved at least that much when I helped Silas last fall."

Detective O'Connor grumbled, but Marian believed Buck. Whether he hid something criminal or not, or whether he was violent like the thugs suggested, she didn't know. It did make her wonder ... "Do you think the thugs know the mole? The one thug, Hayes, demanded the other man, Parker, keep quiet. In fact, Hayes threatened Parker because they both knew what you, Buck, would do to them." She couldn't bring herself to say *kill* them, though that was their belief. Could Buck really kill someone?

"You said Parker and Hayes?" Buck rested his elbows on his knees, his usual relaxed posture suddenly tight with tension. "They know me well enough to believe I pose a threat, but I don't recall their names."

"Could they be going by a different name?" Gilbert suggested. Had no one caught the fact that Buck glossed over the threat *he* was to the thugs? "I haven't seen those names in the books. So if they're employees, they use an alias."

"Can you describe them?" Buck looked at Marian. Detective O'Connor watched her intently.

She shook her head, her heart pounding at the memory. "The best I can do is that Parker is shorter than Hayes and Hayes appeared to be the leader of the two. Wait. Sam might remember more. She saw them when they followed me into her hat shop."

"My niece, Samantha?" Detective O'Connor demanded. Marian cringed. Should she tell them Samantha had seen the thugs watching the Conglomerate's headquarters?

"Could Parker or Hayes be the mole?" Gilbert still held her hand, and squeezed it now. "They could be a trusted member of the organization, but by going by another name, you wouldn't recognize their falsity."

"I don't think so." Marian shook her head, absolutely sure. "When I saw them, they acted like thugs, not what I picture a mole to be."

"And how do you picture a mole, Mrs. Ward?" Detective O'Connor raised his bushy eyebrow.

"It's Mrs. Cox now, Detective," Marian shot back, then tamped down on her defensiveness. "And it's not a visual image as much as a personality one. Those two men, Hayes especially, were more hammer than chisel. He would smash through an organization, not try to take it down from the inside. If Parker is the mole, then he is under the control of Hayes. I don't think that works either. A mole strikes me as someone directing the espionage, not the goons protecting it. In fact, if I were to guess, I would say Hayes left us the note and ate the cookie, whereas Parker left the dead rat on the porch."

"Where do you think the two are now?" Detective O'Connor slurped his coffee. "Since you say they haven't bothered you all week."

All eyes turned to her and Marian knew her cheeks had bloomed a bright red. She wasn't cut out for police work or spy rings. All she wanted was to make her home a welcoming place for her husband, her children, and any visitor who stopped by. She wanted to make cookies in a well-heated kitchen. She wanted to fill the rooms with sounds of laughter, stories, and love. This ... danger, want, and threat of death weighed down her soul.

"Marian?" Gilbert pulled their clasped hands to his chest, drawing her focus to his eyes where admiration glowed. "You have a keen mind. Share it with us, please."

"Really?" The word popped out. Not that Zachariah hadn't asked for her opinion on things. He'd just been filled with so many ideas, he was compelled to try them all. It left her to manage the house, which she loved, while he tried each new concept that came his way. Now she had a husband who seemed the very opposite of Zachariah. Where Zachariah could be almost flighty, Gilbert was as settled as the ground under their feet. Marian anchored Zachariah, but Gilbert now anchored her.

"I may not speak for everyone, but *I* want to know what you think." Gilbert's tone dared anyone to disagree with him. Marian quickly scanned the room. Buck watched her, like he wanted to hear her thoughts, too. Reverend Moller had a pleased smile, like a father whose child had done right. Jessica Moller had a broad grin, pride beaming from her eyes. And Detective O'Connor's eyebrow twitched as he watched her and Gilbert, undoubtedly taking in every little thing. Gilbert squeezed her hand. "Begin with why you think they have left you alone this week."

"I wonder how scared of Buck they are." Marian tried to bring her thoughts into some sort of cohesive concept. "When a threat didn't stop Gilbert from working with Buck, what if they're scared that Buck will retaliate if something happens to me?"

"They better believe I would," Buck muttered.

"But you have to figure out who they are." The idea grew muscle. "They've been operating in the shadows. Using aliases, working with a mole. They can't risk their cover being blown. And, since you haven't figured out who they are yet, they must think I haven't either or, if I did, that I can't give them away."

"There's another reason." Detective O'Connor set down his cup and saucer, then steepled his fingers. "If they were called away. When was the last time Samantha saw them?"

"She told me about seeing them last on Saturday." And the rat threat came on Monday.

"Are you missing any employees?" Detective O'Connor asked Buck. "Have any requested leave, or have you sent any on a task somewhere?"

Marian didn't realize a man could wash pale, but Buck turned positively white. "Monday night, I sent my two strongest men—Howard and Otto—to escort Joe back to Crow's Nest. They're due back on Saturday."

"Joe Spelding is returning to Crow's Nest?" Detective O'Connor glared at Buck. Marian's stomach turned. Joe Spelding was a leering, manipulative man who preyed on those he thought weaker than himself. David, Adaleigh, and Mindy all had run-ins with him in the past.

"He worked a deal. Got out of prison early." Buck pushed fingers through his hair. "He's a criminal, no doubt about it, but ... he's my brother."

CHAPTER TWELVE

Gilbert's head swam as he drove Marian back to Crow's Nest to pick up the girls before they headed home. Marian sat quietly beside him, and he had to believe her thoughts swirled as much as his. He hadn't expected to walk away from the meeting with an identity to the thugs, nor with a mission from Detective O'Connor to uncover the mole in the Conglomerate organization. Of course Gilbert wanted that, as did Buck, but O'Connor had plans to use it in his investigation.

The debate had been whether to arrest the thugs upon their return with Buck's criminal brother. In the end, Marian had agreed to let them stay free, with the hope the pair could lead them to the mole. Gilbert was against the idea since it kept Marian in danger. But Marian wanted the root of the problem gone so her family would be safe. Gilbert could respect that because he wanted the same thing; it's why he agreed to audit Buck's books in the first place. But putting himself in danger was one thing, having the ability to remove the direct danger from Marian and the girls was totally different.

Buck promised to keep the pair—Hayes and Parker, or Howard and Otto, whatever name they used—occupied so they couldn't act on their threat to Marian. However, Detective O'Connor also insisted they needed evidence to prove those two were behind the threats before an arrest could be made. In both cases, they needed to be careful not to tip off the mole. So Gilbert felt the race against time: find the mole before the threats against his family developed into physical harm.

His family. He glanced over at Marian, who silently stared out the passenger window as they crossed over the bridge into Crow's Nest. He wanted to reach out to her, draw her out of her worry, but what could he say to reassure her? So far, he'd managed to provide food, clothing, and electricity, but his promise to protect ... it weighed on him. Even if his conviction allowed him to punch in a few faces, that wouldn't solve anything other than releasing the frustration building inside. But finding the mole in the pages of the ledger would end the danger. If he could find proof.

Uncomfortable quiet filled the car until they picked up the girls from school and they proceeded to chatter the entire way back to the house. He still considered it the Wards's house, not his, even if Marian now bore his name. They may be married, but he didn't feel as if he belonged here. That was one of the many reasons he hadn't taken the upstairs room yet. Maybe if he did, he'd feel less like a visitor. Marriage was for a lifetime, so why did it seem like his and Marian's agreement would end once she was safe?

"Thank you for including me." Marian broke her long silence as he parked behind the house. The girls tumbled from the car, slamming doors behind them. "Do you think the mole will learn we talked to Detective O'Connor?"

He debated his answer as they emerged from the car. He patted the roof. "Honestly? He shouldn't since we took precautions, but we'll remain vigilant."

She offered a grim smile and they followed after the girls. Gilbert stiffened. A strange man exited the house and the girls ran right for him. Gilbert took an instant to assess the man. No weapons visible. His thin frame hid no braun. Dark hair like Gilbert's. And spectacles. Honestly, the man appeared more bookish than a thug. Was this the mole?

"Marian!" The man jogged toward them, waving. Marian waved back and picked up her speed as her girls wrapped their arms around the stranger's legs. Not a stranger if the girls reacted so warmly to him. But who was he? The newcomer chuckled, hugged the girls, and sent them inside before reaching for Marian. Hands on her shoulders, he drew her in to kiss both cheeks. Heat raced through Gilbert. Who was this man?

"I expected a letter or telegram, not you in person." Worry had drained from Marian's face, leaving a happy glow. It hit Gilbert in the chest. Had he ever caused this type of response in her? Was this the man she should have married? "Where are my manners? Nick, this is Gilbert Cox."

Nick's olive skin darkened as anger flashed in his eyes. Gilbert took an instinctive step back.

"He's not his father." Marian huffed. Gilbert stifled a groan. This stranger had a run-in with his father, too?

"We'll see." Nick muttered, but held out a hand to shake. "Dr. Nick Matrone. Physician and family friend."

"Dr. Matrone." Gilbert carefully repeated the way Nick pronounced his name. *Ma-trone-ay.* Making a positive impression meant removing any barrier possible, including learning how to properly address someone.

Nick gave a nod, but no goodwill eased his expression. Until he turned back to Marian. "When Mrs. Whittlebush sent me the telegraph saying Elaine had taken a turn, I called her for the details. Silas, too. Dr. Thompson stopped the other medication and has her on bedrest and aspirin?"

"Yes, yes." Marian waved her hands. "But that doesn't explain how you're here. Train tickets are expensive."

"True, and my sister joined me. She's with Mrs. Whittlebush, resting after our journey." The man toed the ground. "I would have been here sooner, but packing took longer than anticipated. My partner bought me out. I'm here to stay."

Stay? Gilbert narrowed his eyes. What was this Dr. Matrone after?

"Nick! That's wonderful!" Marian clasped the doctor's hands. "Silas's old room over the workshop is available if you need a place to stay."

Shouldn't Marian ask Gilbert if he minded a strange man—not a stranger, a *friend*—staying on the property?

"Mrs. Whittlebush already has room for us." Nick chuckled. "When Adaleigh returns, I'll need to find alternate arrangements, but I want to make sure my sister is settled first. I'll bring Bella over tomorrow. She'll love meeting you and the girls."

"I'm looking forward to meeting her." Marian tucked her hand around Nick's arm and jealousy, for there was no denying the unwelcome emotion, flared. "Have you been in to see Elaine? Do you have a prognosis?"

The hope in Marian's voice sliced him. Nick could offer Marian what Gilbert could not: good news. And Gilbert hated himself for the self-pity that draped itself over his shoulders like a cloak. Knowing he was poor company, and seeing how happy everyone was to see Nick, Gilbert retreated to the front room. Now, more than ever, he wished he had taken the upstairs room. It would give the impression that he and Marian were truly married as well as being a secluded place to hide. And he wouldn't have to listen to the quiet murmur of voices coming down the hall.

Gilbert removed his coat, draping it over a chair, and collapsed on the sofa, putting his hat over his face as if he were simply taking a nap. It appeared lazy, but Gilbert didn't know what else to do with himself. He tried praying, but as usual, he stalled at the opening words, *Heavenly Father*. It stirred his irritation, at himself, at God, at his father.

"Got a minute?" A man's voice shoved into his mental wrestling match.

Gilbert removed his hat. Nick stood in the doorway. Gilbert sat up. Might as well get this conversation over with. He beckoned Nick to the chair from across the sofa. In the time Gilbert had been in the front room, Nick had removed his coat and rolled up his shirtsleeves, revealing muscles Gilbert wouldn't have expected on the gangly man. He barely refrained from rolling his eyes. Of course the man would be a fine specimen. Another way Gilbert didn't measure up.

"What do you want?" Gilbert didn't bother to hide his grumpiness.

"Marian explained how you two married." Nick rested his elbows on his knees. "My first visit to Crow's Nest, I offered the same arrangement to Cora, Silas's wife. Well, before she became Silas's wife."

Gilbert frowned, surprised by the lack of aggression in Nick's tone. Based on how he'd first reacted to the Cox name, Gilbert wasn't expecting this. "Then you know I don't mean to hurt Marian?"

"I won't lie, it's difficult for me to separate what your father did to this family from you." He pressed his fingertips together. "I was here the day your father kidnapped Cora and Silas. I've put myself between a gun and a patient several times before, but never a family I cared about so deeply. Cora is like a cousin to me, which makes Marian family. And you now, too."

Gilbert's jaw dropped. "How can you accept me so easily?"

"Because I know how it feels to be judged based on another's actions." A shadow crossed the doctor's face and Gilbert wondered at the real reason the man left New York City with no plans to return. "Marian spoke highly of you, so I will make my opinions based on getting to know you."

Not at all what Gilbert expected. "And how is Elaine?"

Nick leaned back in his chair. "As much as Dr. Thompson is stuck in the old ways, the medical field hasn't advanced enough to help her. I believe she has an apoplexy condition that involves blocked arteries or bleeding in the brain. A few years ago, a man named António Egas Moniz experimented by injecting a sodium iodide solution into arteries in order for a better x-ray scan—or angiogram—to be taken, allowing for better diagnosis. But a diagnosis doesn't help Elaine."

That was all beyond Gilbert. He was a practical man who looked at numbers. What did he know of medicine and science?

"Mainly we help patients manage the aftereffects of an episode. With Elaine, I think she recently began having little apoplexy episodes, which contributed to her memory loss. But this last attack seems to have been significant. She has no use of her left side. Dr. Thompson has done what I would have, and I don't think there is much more we can do except make her comfortable. There is great risk of another episode, and if that happens, I fear the worst."

Poor Marian. "Is there any chance at improvement?"

"I've seen some regain movement, but it takes a lot of work." Nick massaged his forehead. "Honestly? I'm not sure Elaine has the spirit for it. That's what concerns me most."

"Silas isn't able to visit either." Gilbert hung his head. "It's my fault, too. I should have done more to stop my father. My family caused so much harm."

"It's not your fault, Cox." Nick's directness brought Gilbert's gaze up. "What your father did caused irreparable damage, yes, but you aren't responsible for his actions. If I lived in the should-haves, I'd be paralyzed as a doctor. All I can do is make one choice at a time with the information I have. Second guessing is a quick way to cost a life."

"I'm not used to making split-second life-and-death decisions, I suppose. I'm an accountant. I analyze numbers, see the errors, and fix them." Gilbert pressed his fingertips to his injured cheek, checking the tenderness level. "Marrying the way we did, that is as spontaneous as I've been since I left home. My father kicked me out, so it wasn't entirely by my choice, I suppose."

Nick listened to Gilbert's ramblings without a word and silence settled between them. How could Gilbert make amends? He couldn't bring Silas home, nor send Elaine to Silas, but ... "Do you think Elaine could make it to the telephone in the workshop if I carried her?"

Nick raised his brows. "A long distance call to Silas? It's a good plan, but it would have to wait until the weekend when he's likely in town with Cora."

Gilbert stood. "I'll talk to Marian." Anyway, he would like to say a few words to Silas before the man more-than-likely said goodbye to his mother.

Friday, January 30

Marian set a casserole into the oven for supper. There was no telling how many people would join them. Of course she, her girls, and Gilbert, but these days, there was always an extra mouth to feed. Though so far today, only Nick had stopped in to check on Elaine, who now slept soundly in her room. They had scheduled a long-distance call with Silas tonight, so she hoped the rest would make it easier on Elaine.

Throughout the day, Marian spotted more traffic driving by. Buck's men, she had no doubt. It didn't ease her mind, though. Being alone in the house for the first time in weeks was disconcerting. She kept the doors locked, especially knowing the thugs were back in town. Would Gilbert be able to find something in the Conglomerate's books to bring them, and the mole, to justice? Assuming the mole was the one who wanted Marian to keep quiet.

She shuddered.

A black car with luggage strapped to the top turned into the drive. Marian wiped her hands on her apron before hanging it on a peg. She donned her threadbare brown coat, as well as an old hat and scarf. Mrs. Whittlebush thought she'd finish her new coat and the girls' clothes this weekend.

The dirty snow piled up against the buildings and left a muddy trail along the most-used paths between. She gingerly avoided the muddiest spots as she made the way to the newcomers. Were they wanting to visit the curiosity shop? Or sell their belongings? Marian hated to turn them away, but she had no money to buy anything new.

An older man in a customary livery suit emerged from the passenger side. He opened the rear door, assisting an elegantly dressed older woman. The plume on her hat bounced up as it cleared the car. Gray hair piled at the base of her head, below the hat brim. Her coat fit her perfect figure like it was tailored to it. She turned then, with movements slow and purposeful. Her face showed no signs of aging, making Marian feel ancient.

She pushed the insecurity away. "How may I help you, ma'am?"

"Is this the home of the Ward family?" The woman's voice was cultured and smooth. She tucked her clutch under her arm. "Are you, perhaps, the new Mrs. Cox?"

Taken aback, Marian stuttered. "I-I am."

A smile changed the woman from elegant to youthful. "Oh, it's such a treat to meet you. From everything Gilbert has shared, he's quite taken with you."

Marian stared. Was this Gilbert's mother? He hadn't mentioned a visit. In fact, with Elaine's illness, he hadn't brought up going to see his mother for days.

"Pardon me." The woman chuckled, her eyes crinkling the way Gilbert's did when he smiled. She took the driver's arm and he helped her traverse the uneven ground until she stood a couple feet away. "I'm Victoria Cox, Gilbert's mother."

Marian snapped out of her trance and extended a hand. "A pleasure to meet you, ma'am. Does, uh, does Gilbert know ..." Why had she asked that so soon? What must this cultured woman think of the bumbling ninny her son married?

"Goodness, no, he doesn't know a thing. After I heard about your other mother-in-law's illness, I packed up his things and we boarded the train. This kindly gentleman helped us find you." She waved toward the car. The older man and driver were loosening the ties around the luggage. "If Gilbert knew I planned to do so, I'm sure he would have protested. He so rarely considers his own needs, someone has to think of that for him. But I'm sure you've seen that side of our Gilbert, haven't you?"

Our Gilbert. Yes, yes she had. Their marriage being the prime example.

"If we might unload the luggage, the driver can return to town. I assume Gilbert is still working?"

Marian nodded, trying to catch up to Mrs. Cox's plans. "You can put it in the workshop and we can sort it out when he arrives home."

"Wonderful. This is Herbert and Myrtle Johnson." She waved first at the older man, then at an older woman emerging from the far side of the car. "They are the only staff I kept when I left my husband."

"Won't you come inside?" What else could Marian say? Herbert carried two carpetbags to the workshop, followed by the driver who carried a small trunk. Myrtle demurely assured her gray hair was tucked under the handkerchief she had tied around her head. She was short and curved in all the motherly places. She caught Marian's eye and winked, then picked up a satchel and followed the men.

"I've wanted to meet you since Gilbert called to say he married you." Mrs. Cox pulled Marian's attention back to her just in time for Marian to see the older woman's chin wobble. "I want to apologize for my husband."

Speechless, Marian studied Mrs. Cox as she regained her composure. This woman had been married to Robert Cox. What kind of life had he allowed her? She left him, so Marian suspected it wasn't the loving marriage she experienced with Zachariah. And Gilbert, how had his parents' relationship shaped his view of marriage?

"My son and I both wish to make amends for my husband's actions." She laid a gloved hand on Marian's forearm. "I'm terribly sorry for all the sorrow he has caused you."

Marian had never really considered whether she forgave Robert Cox. She never met him, never experienced the fear that Silas and Cora had. Even Nick, as he attempted to save Elaine. Marian had been left with the aftereffects, the damage left in Mr. Cox's wake. Similar to Gilbert and Mrs. Cox. Gilbert had considered himself an enemy to the Wards, but he and Marian were more alike in this situation than she had ever imagined. Compassion rose for him and Mrs. Cox.

Marian tossed aside decorum and pulled her into a hug. "I forgive you, Mrs. Cox. And I couldn't be happier to have another mother-in-law."

To say Gilbert was surprised to see his mother would be a gross understatement. But to walk into the kitchen, dusting flurries from his shoulders, to find Marian and his mother sitting at the table sharing a cup of tea? Even Nettie and Essie froze with scarves and mittens half-removed when they realized a stranger was in their house.

"Hi, Mother." Gilbert shed his hat and coat. Had she told him she planned to visit and he forgot? Marian didn't appear upset.

"Nettie and Essie?" Marian rounded the table to tug the girls to her sides. She smiled affectionately at them, then turned the same smile on Gilbert. It made his heart stutter. "This is Mr. Gil's mama."

"You have a mama?" Nettie looked over her shoulder at him with wide eyes.

"I sure do." He tapped Nettie's nose, then kissed his mother's cheek. "This is a surprise, Mother."

"Of course it is." She patted his cheek. "We'll talk later."

"Mrs. Ward is finally resting comfortably." Myrtle Johnson, the housekeeper-turned-cook who had been with his family since before he was born, bustled in. "Oh, Gilbert, what a pleasure. And who are these sweet little girls?"

"Hi ..." Gilbert turned back to his mom, bewilderment muddling his mind. "What is going on?"

"Girls, run up and change out of your school clothes." Marian shooed the girls toward the stairs.

As soon as they were out of hearing, she told of his mother's unexpected arrival, that she'd packed up his belongings, and taken the train to Hawk's River. How she gave Mr. and Mrs. Johnson Silas' old attic room in the workshop and his mother the spare room upstairs. Regret came at that, though he would have had to move back to the sofa if he'd taken Marian up on the room from the beginning.

Mother folded her hands in her lap. "I heard how tired you were over the phone, and can see it with my eyes now. And Marian, too. We're family now, and ... I want to help."

Gilbert scratched his good cheek, unsure what to do with his mother's unusual display of emotion. He glanced at Marian. She had the most beautiful, compassionate smile aimed at his mother, and then she turned to him and her smile softened, capturing him like quicksand.

The clattering of feet broke their gaze apart. Heat washed over him as he caught his mother's knowing look. Yeah, yeah, he was falling for his wife. A good thing if they had a normal marriage. This ... whatever this was, was all backwards and upside down.

In a moment, Mrs. Johnson insisted on getting the girls something to eat, Mother offered to sit with Elaine, and Marian tugged him outside. "Mr. Johnson is waiting for you to direct where to put your things."

"Are you sure you're okay with this?" He closed the back door behind them and popped his collar against the softly falling snow. "My mother, bless her, is used to a certain financial situation, one I couldn't provide. She made do in a rented apartment I found for us, but neither of us could part with the Johnsons. They've been working for her for a long time."

"I don't mind at all." Marian wrapped her hand around his arm. "I like her, and the Johnsons. I'm sorry she had to live with a man like your father."

Gilbert stopped in the middle of the yard. "You're sorry?"

Snow fell around them, catching in Marian's hair. She hadn't put on a hat and still wore that old brown coat. It brought out the protective side of him. The one that would be willing to fight for her, no matter his conviction to turn the other cheek.

"And grateful." Marian leaned into him. "Grateful you're the one who came to my rescue."

He wrapped his arm around her waist to draw her closer. Whatever had caused Marian to lower her guard around him, he liked it. "We're in this together, Marian."

She looked up at him, brown eyes bright in the twilight. He cupped her cheek. When she didn't flinch, he lowered his lips to hers. Sweet heaven! How had God blessed him with this woman as his wife for the rest of his days?

He broke away. "I don't deserve you."

Marian took a shuddering breath. "This was supposed to be a business arrangement."

"Do you …" He closed his eyes, unable to get his words to cooperate with his fractured thoughts. His heart was hers and he'd never get it back, but if that meant loving her from a distance, he'd do it. He had vowed to love and protect her, and now he had even more motivation to do just that.

Someone cleared their throat. "Pardon, sir?" Mr. Johnson stood outside the workshop door, not quite looking at them, though a smirk twitched on his usually stoic face.

Gilbert tried to shake his head clear. "Yes?"

"A Mr. Silas Ward is on the telephone."

"Where has the time gone?" Marian hustled toward the workshop, tossing words over her shoulder. "Can you bring Elaine? She's had a rough afternoon, so you may need Mr. and Mrs. Johnson to help you."

Gilbert obliged, Mr. Johnson trailing him to the house. When the girls heard Uncle Silas was on the telephone, they ran outside. His mom and Mrs. Johnson helped ready Elaine, who rallied when she heard she could speak to her son. Mother didn't say much as she held the door for Gilbert and Mr. Johnson to carry Elaine into the workshop, blankets wrapped around her. She even herded the girls back outside when it was Elaine's turn to speak to Silas.

Gilbert supported Elaine as she stood before the telephone box. It felt intrusive to listen in, but Elaine could not stand up by herself. He could feel how much weight she had lost and sorrow draped over him. She tired quickly, and Gilbert blinked back tears at the goodbye between mother and son. How grateful was he that his own mother was here for him to hug.

He and Mr. Johnson returned Elaine to her bed where Mrs. Johnson fussed over her. Gilbert left quickly. He aimed to have a conversation with Silas, too. He wanted his brother-in-law's forgiveness, and his blessing on his marriage to Marian. Because, Gilbert wanted to win Marian's heart, not only her hand. When he arrived back in the workshop, Marian was explaining to Silas everything Nick had told him about Elaine's condition. She was about to end the call when Gilbert asked for a minute to talk to Silas alone. She furrowed her brow, but handed over the ear cone and left the workshop.

"Silas?" Gilbert rested a hand on the wall beside the telephone box, braced for this conversation. It wouldn't be private, of course, but he had things he needed to say that would be difficult if Marian looked over his shoulder. "It's Gilbert Cox. I wanted a word."

A long pause. "Okay." Not exactly welcoming, but Gilbert deserved it.

"I care about Marian." Gilbert cringed. He hadn't meant to lead with that. "I mean, I'm sorry for everything my father put you through. I'm not my father, but I should have stopped him sooner. I could have prevented the harm he caused. I'm sorry, Ward. Will you forgive me?"

Silence. Gilbert laid his forehead on the fist he rested against the wall. He heard a muffled conversation, then a female voice on the line. "This is Cora. You did nothing wrong, Gilbert. Parents make their own decisions. I know this better than many. Who you are is what matters."

Humbled, Gilbert's words failed him.

"You take care of Marian, okay?" Cora continued. "Here's Silas again."

Gilbert straightened away from the wall. Braced for what the man would say.

The clearing of a voice came over the line before Silas grudgingly said, "I forgive you."

Air left Gilbert's lungs. "Thank you."

"It's difficult for me, you know?" Silas sighed and the gruffness in his voice softened. "Marian seems to think highly of you, and I appreciate you stepping in to care for them when I cannot."

This was Gilbert's opportunity. Sweat beaded on his forehead and he wiped it away. "And I do care for her. More than I did when we married because I've gotten to know her. She's wise and smart and a wonderful mother."

"Do you love her?" Silas' question traveled softly over the telephone line.

Did he? Not the bubbly attraction he'd seen in many girls' eyes over the years. Not that he wasn't attracted to Marian. She was beautiful. No, this emotion ran deeper than any he'd known before. He genuinely cared for her, and would willingly sacrifice everything to see that she had whatever she needed, and more.

"Your silence is telling." Was that a smile in Silas's voice? "I ask again, do you love Marian?"

"I do." And saying it aloud confirmed it, driving the concept deep into his soul. "I'd do anything for her."

"Then take care of her, Cox. Marian and her girls. She deserves it."

Before Gilbert could answer, Mrs. Johnson burst into the room. "Mr. Cox, sir, Mrs. Ward collapsed."

Oh no. "Silas, I need to go. It's your mom." Gilbert hated to end their telephone call like this. "I'll take care of them. You have my word."

CHAPTER THIRTEEN

Sunday, February 1

Marian ran her hands over the black cotton dress. She hadn't worn it in two years and now it hung on her frame, showing how much weight she'd lost since Zachariah's death. There was no time to take in the dress. She twisted her hair and pinned it in place at the back of her head.

"Marian?" Mrs. Cox tapped at the door.

"Come in." Marian turned from the washstand she shared with her girls. Over the past twenty-four hours, she was grateful for the older woman's presence. Her quiet dignity brought calm to the inevitable chaos that surrounded death. She now knew where Gilbert got that steady part of himself.

"Mrs. Johnson has breakfast ready." Mrs. Cox remained by the door, hands clasped at her waist. "You should eat something."

"I'll be down shortly." Marian tried a smile. Between the Johnsons, Mrs. Martins, and Mrs. Whittlebush, the house continued to run smoothly.

Mrs. Cox disappeared and Marian stared at her reflection in the mirror. Sorrow had drawn new lines on her pale face.

With a heavy heart, she descended to the kitchen. Gilbert rose when she entered, the girls leapt from their chairs for hugs. They were full of questions since Marian told them Grandma Ward had gone to see Jesus, but the one that pierced her most was when they asked if Grandma got to see their daddy.

"Come on back to the table girls." Gilbert gently urged them to their seats, then took Marian's hands. "Did you sleep?"

Tears welled at Gilbert's kindness. He pulled her into his arms and she let a couple tears fall. How could she appreciate him to such a strong degree and yet grieve her late husband so strongly? It was confusing and painful.

Gilbert managed to coax her to eat a little breakfast before they left for the church. After services, they would go to Crow's Nest Cemetery for Elaine's burial. From the moment they left the house, the day proved a blur. Sympathies and kindness abounded, for Elaine had loved well and was well-loved. Samantha and Nick's sister Bella helped with the girls, for which Marian was grateful. She barely had a moment in which someone didn't greet her with a story of how they would miss Elaine. Mrs. Cox, Mrs. Martins, and Mrs. Whittlebush managed every detail, including getting them all to the cemetery on time. Detective O'Connor, Nick, and Buck were a consistent presence, drawing away those who talked to her for too long.

Most of all, Gilbert never left her side. His warm hand at her back kept her upright and his whispers of encouragement kept her from breaking down.

The number of people who gave their condolences overwhelmed her. Zachariah and Silas should be here. They should be the ones hearing all the wonderful things people said about their mother. Not Marian, the daughter-in-law. She felt a proxy, a stand-in. It wasn't right.

The weather had been unseasonably warm before the snowstorm a couple weeks ago, allowing them to bury Elaine beside her late husband and Zachariah in the family plot. It was a beautiful, albeit cold service. The gray sky above. A bleak lake to the east. And a chill wind that tried to slip under the collar of Marian's new coat.

As people filtered away—Mrs. Cox taking the girls home—Marian found herself standing alone in front of Zachariah's tombstone. Not alone. Gilbert stood several paces behind her. Giving her support and space at the same time.

"It's time to say goodbye, Zachariah." The thought had hit her last night, keeping her awake as it rolled over and over through her mind. Losing Elaine was like losing her last connection to the Ward family. It wasn't true, of course. Her girls were Wards. Silas and Cora would keep in touch with her and their nieces. But now, there was no reason to stay in Crow's Nest. She could take her girls and go somewhere safe. Somewhere away from the danger from the thugs who had threatened her family.

Would Gilbert go with them? Perhaps it would be best to free him of his obligation. He could return to his rooms in Milwaukee, continue to care for his mother. But where would Marian take her girls? The lumber camp where her parents worked would never do. There was no work for Marian there, and that alone tied her to Gilbert.

She glanced over her shoulder. He stood with feet shoulder-width apart, hands clasped in front of him, head bowed. The elements didn't appear to bother him. Just then, Gilbert raised his chin, his gaze locking onto hers. Her breath caught at the look in his eyes. *Caring* was too tame a word. It was like he could feel her pain and hurt alongside her, for her. If she were honest, it looked like ... love?

Not quite sure what she was doing, she reached out a hand toward him. He took it, drew her to his side. Together they faced Zachariah's plot. "I haven't been back here since we laid him to rest," she told him.

Gilbert tightened his hold around her shoulders.

"His loss was so sudden. We had dreams, plans, a future. It doesn't make sense, but losing Elaine feels like losing him all over again." She looked for his reaction to her words. "This doesn't make you uncomfortable, does it? Talking about my first husband?"

He kissed her temple. "I vowed to love you, remember? Love does not seek its own, but endures all things, bears all things. I would take this pain from you if I could, Marian." Tears glistened in his eyes.

I promise to love you, and to be faithful to you, as long as we both shall live. Those were the words he'd promised her at their wedding. Two strangers agreeing to help one another. Today he was acting on those vows.

Marian glanced at Gilbert, who turned his chin as he rapidly blinked. This was love.

Her gaze roved the cemetery and a Bible story filtered through her mind. When Lazarus died and Jesus saw his dear friends' grief, he wept, too. God allowing or not allowing pain ... she would never understand that, but remembering that Jesus would weep with her? That He felt her pain because He loved her? It wrapped her soul in a warm embrace, like the one Gilbert held her in now.

She rested her head on his shoulder. For the first time, she didn't feel like she needed to hold everything together for anyone. She could simply cry.

Monday, February 2

Ledger numbers swam before Gilbert and he squeezed his eyes closed. He'd tried to convince his boss to give him the day off to stay with Marian, but Mr. Burkes refused. It wasn't Gilbert's mother, or even his mother-in-law, who passed away. So early this morning, he'd met with a client in Hawk's River before coming to the Conglomerate headquarters.

"Knock. Knock." A man with short brownish-blond hair and closely shaved scruff stuck his head into the small office Gilbert had been using. "You Gilbert Cox?"

Gilbert rose. "I am." Most people who came in and out of the headquarters left Gilbert alone. What worried Gilbert most, however, was the predatory gleam that lit the newcomer's eye when Gilbert confirmed his identity.

"It's a pleasure to finally meet you." The man reached for a handshake. Gilbert obliged, but immediately put distance between them again. "I was acquainted with your father."

"Oh?" Was this someone his father harmed, or someone in collusion with his crimes? The eager way the man leaned forward said the latter. "And you are?"

He whipped out a notebook. "Greg Alistar, journalist with the *Crow's Nest Gazette.*"

Heaven help him, this was the man Marian and Miss Mindy warned him about. "If you have any questions, please refer them to my employer." Gilbert conveniently left off details. If this journalist dug, he'd find the information without Gilbert making it easy for him. And Gilbert didn't want him contacting Burkes and Dudley, if at all possible.

"I'm not here about your work." Alistar waved off the idea, but his gaze snapped to the ledgers.

Gilbert moved to block his eyeline. "Then why are you here?"

"To talk about your marriage to Marian Ward." The man spoke as if he laid down a trump card. "I imagine this is quite the coup for you. Your father tried a heavy-handed approach that failed. Your finesse at getting the Ward inheritance is masterful. I'm impressed."

"What?" The bewilderment slipped out before Gilbert could snap his mouth shut.

"Why else would you marry a woman with kids?"

Gilbert clenched the back of the chair. *Do not hit him over the head with it. Turn the other cheek.*

"Have you discovered the treasure your father was after yet? If you give me an exclusive interview, I'll—"

"Stop!" Gilbert exploded. "I want none of your insinuations. Marian is a woman who loves God and loves her family. Leave her alone."

The newspaperman's jaw dropped. "You have feelings for her? What a chump."

"Better a chump than sticking my nose where it doesn't belong. Good day, Mr. Alistar."

The man glared. "This isn't over."

"I think it is." Buck Wilson appeared behind Alistar, looking dapper in a thin pinstripe suit. "I'd like you to leave my accountant alone. And that isn't a suggestion."

Alistar pursed his lips, but left without a word.

Wilson grumbled under his breath, shaking his head. "One of these days, Adaleigh Sirland and I will have the proof we need to make sure

Alistar can't get a newspaper job within a hundred miles of Crow's Nest. He's slippery and balances just enough truth with just enough opinion to stay employed. But he'll slip up one of these days."

Gilbert sank to his chair, rubbing his eyes with his thumb and forefinger.

"You're no good like this, Cox." Buck leaned against the doorjamb. "Go home."

Gilbert crossed his arms, not in the mood to spar. "My boss expects a full day." A waste because he couldn't find an error in the numbers if someone circled it for him.

"I admire your integrity, truly, but I stopped by the office to tell you that you need to go home." Something in Buck's voice raised the hairs on the back of Gilbert's neck. "I'll cover with Burkes, if it comes to that."

Gilbert straightened. "What aren't you telling me?"

"Take the ledgers with you." Buck turned on his heel and left the room.

Something was wrong. As much as he wanted to make Buck explain, the sense of urgency the man ignited had Gilbert quickly packing up the ledgers in their box. Headquarters was unusually quiet, even Buck seemed to have disappeared, and it set Gilbert on edge. He shrugged into his coat, then carried the box out to his car. As he set it in the back seat, he felt a presence behind him. He dropped the box and turned in time to block a punch to the face.

"Who—" A low punch to the stomach doubled him over.

"Stay away from the Conglomerate." The low voice hissed before shoving Gilbert to the ground and running away.

Gilbert curled up next to the wheel of his car trying to drag in a breath against the spasms of his stomach muscles. What just happened? Who was that man? *Marian!* The threats had become physical, which meant she was in danger. Fear propelled him to his feet and he stumbled, nearly plowing into a young woman. Samantha Martins.

She caught him by the arms, her eyes wide. "Are you okay, Mr. Cox?"

"Yeah." He needed to get to Marian.

"I was leaving the hat shop on my lunch when I saw what happened. It was the taller of the thugs who chased Marian."

Another witness, which put her in danger, too. Gilbert opened the passenger side door. "Get in. You're coming with me."

Without question, Samantha scrambled into the car and Gilbert raced around to the driver's side. In the shortest time yet, Gilbert drove home and parked behind the house. Samantha followed him as he ran for the back door.

"Marian?" He burst inside. No answer. In fact, the house was unusually quiet. No sign of his mother or the Johnsons either. His heart pounded.

"Are they here?" Samantha stopped in the doorway, her breath frosty puffs.

"No." Gilbert pulled his hat from his head. Where could they be? "The shop."

Samantha followed him to the barn, but Marian wasn't there, either. "Mr. Cox, listen." Samantha tapped her ear.

He stepped outside with her. And then he heard it. The girls. They were shouting. No, shrieking. But not with fear, with ... laughter? "Come on. I know where they are."

Gilbert jogged around the workshop, willing his heart to slow down. He rounded the corner to find Marian, his mother, and Mrs. Johnson watching as Mr. Johnson pulled the girls in a homemade sled over the ice-crusted snow between the workshop and the boardwalk. Relief threatened to buckle his legs.

"David used to pull me in a sled like that when I was little," Samantha muttered at his side as if Gilbert's world hadn't rocked on its axis the last twenty minutes.

"Mr. Gil!" Nettie waved. She and Essie clambered off the sled and ran for him. He welcomed them into his arms, but his eyes sought Marian's. Her smile quieted his fears. She was safe. All of his girls were safe.

"You're just in time for hot chocolate, Mr. Gil." Mrs. Johnson chuckled. "I'll go whip it up."

An awkward pause descended as the older woman bustled away. Gilbert couldn't take his gaze from Marian. The reality of what it would mean to lose her slammed into him.

"Girls, can you show me your sled?" Samantha took Nettie and Essie's little hands, freeing him from their grip. They eagerly tugged her toward where Mr. Johnson waited by the sled.

Gilbert inclined his head toward the retreating trio. He needed to talk to Marian alone. His mother nodded. "I'll keep an eye on them."

"What brings you home so early?" Marian approached, her cheeks, nose, and lips bright red from the cold. The dark green of her hat and coat highlighting her brown hair. Simply gorgeous. He forced his focus to her eyes, where grief lay tucked in the corners. "Is everything okay?"

He shook his head. "We've been threatened again."

"What? When?"

He took her gloved hands, needing to touch her, to assure himself she was here and safe. He led her around the corner where they could talk without an audience. "I just came from the Conglomerate headquarters. Buck sent me home. I think he knew the threats were escalating."

She inclined her head, worry darkening the brown of her eyes. "Do you think he had something to do with them?"

"I don't know for sure. I don't think so, but I'm just not sure." As he told Marian about what happened, hearing the girls squeal as Mr. Johnson pulled them, Samantha and Mother cheering, a pang struck him. He couldn't lose his family, and if that meant sending them away to keep them safe, he would. "I think you and my mother should take the girls back to Milwaukee. Or maybe you should go west, stay with Silas and Cora. Now that Elaine ..."

She freed a hand to lay against his chest. "What about you?"

He stared at the place where she touched him. How had he come to care for Marian so deeply? He'd meant to care for a widow, to protect and provide, not ... fall in love. Because that's what these feelings were. He couldn't deny it. He'd pledged to love Marian, sure. But that was sacrificial love, not romantic love. What he felt now? The desperation that had sweat beading under his cap? "I want to stay and finish this. End the danger for good. But I need you safe."

Marian chewed her bottom lip. "I had the same thought yesterday. I ... I don't want to leave you. That is, well, if you want to stay with us. Married to me. But if you don't, I would understand."

"Why wouldn't I stay married to you?" Gilbert's heart twisted. Where had her doubt come from? Sending her to safety would be hard enough. To never see her again? His breath came faster. To show her the sacrificial love he swore he would, he needed to ask, "Do you want out of our marriage?"

Marian hugged herself, and Gilbert felt the loss of her touch. "Ours is a marriage born out of necessity. If I leave Crow's Nest, danger won't be a factor, so we won't need protection. As for provision, we can now move to wherever I can find work."

"No." Gilbert was shaking his head. He'd let her go if she demanded it, but it'd break him apart. He needed her to know that. "I meant my promises, Marian. I have no desire to be free of them. I care about you too much."

Insecurity scrunched her features. "Are you sure? This is your chance to go back to your bachelor life. To have a chance at your own happily ever after."

Gilbert cupped her shoulders. "This is my happily ever after, Marian. I admire you and I want to grow old with you. I ... I love you."

Her lips parted and Gilbert kissed them. Struggling to keep his tangle of emotion from turning this into too passionate a kiss, and scaring her. Only, Marian sank into his arms. Gilbert tightened his hold. This is what he wanted more than anything in the world. *Who* he wanted in his life for as long as he lived.

"Marian and Gil—" Mother's voice stopped abruptly. Marian pulled away, but Gilbert tugged her close, not ready to be separated. Mother shook her head, but Gilbert caught her smile. She approved and that made Gilbert's heart soar. "Pardon me. Carry on. I'll bring the girls in for their hot cocoa. I brought chocolate with them in mind, you know."

Marian's cheeks were even more pink than before. "No, no, I'll—"

Gilbert stopped her with another kiss. He loved his wife and he wanted her to know it.

Gilbert's kiss changed nothing, and yet it changed everything. If only Marian could bury her face so no one could see her blushing like a schoolgirl caught kissing a boy. Even if he was her husband. Technically. A gust of cold air cooled her cheeks and she thanked God for her new coat. Thanked God for Gilbert who provided the new coat.

He tucked her arm around his and led her toward the wharf after Mrs. Cox, Mr. Johnson, and Samantha took the girls inside. If danger wasn't hovering so closely, it could almost feel romantic. And that was confusing. She touched her lips, remembering the barely restrained passion of Gilbert's kiss. Her stomach flipped. Did he truly have feelings for her? As a husband?

I love you.

As much as she wanted to rationalize why he'd say such a thing—duty, expectation, even repeating the vows they shared—she couldn't deny that she believed he meant romantic love. Not after that kiss. Gilbert Cox had fallen in love with her. Did she love him?

Panic rose. She needed space. A minute to think. They reached the wharf and she tugged free to grip one of the posts holding up the wooden boardwalk. A snowy ice field spread out twenty feet or more from shore, slowly buckling under sluggish waves. Beyond, icy spray splashed up like geysers. The gray sky hovered low, blending with the grayish blue of the water. Bleak and colorless.

That's how her life felt after Zachariah died, before Gilbert arrived. Now it felt as if a ray of sunshine sliced through the clouds. She hesitated to trust it, to lean into the love Gilbert showed her. It didn't stop Elaine from dying. Danger still encircled them.

She'd gotten married to keep her girls safe, that needed to be her sole focus now. No matter Gilbert's feelings for her, or hers for Gilbert, whatever they were. "I think taking the girls to Silas and Cora's would be wise."

Gilbert had stayed quietly by her side, and at her words, stepped closer. "I'm sure I could convince Mother to go with you."

She looked up at him, realizing how much she relied on his steadiness. "Can we afford such a trip?"

Gilbert stared out across the lake for a moment, lips pressed in a grim line. "Not that many train tickets, no, but the Johnsons could drive you there."

"Drive? Across the country?" Fear struck a chord. "Not without you."

"Oh?" Gilbert faced her, a light in his eye, and Marian realized what she'd said.

She stepped away from him. "I ..." *didn't mean that the way it sounded.* Only. She did. The thought of taking a car miles and miles away from Crow's Nest without Gilbert made her palms sweat and her stomach churn. The dangers they could face without him by their side. No, no, she couldn't do that.

"Hey, hey." Gilbert tugged her to his chest. "Okay. No sending you driving across country without me."

"What can we do?" Why did her voice tremble? She needed to be strong for her girls, yet Gilbert seemed to bring out her weakness. No, not weakness exactly. Trusting someone required vulnerability, a lack of self-reliance, and that's what this was. The realization of how deeply and confidently she trusted Gilbert struck her. Wonder had her putting enough space between them to meet his gaze. "I trust you."

A slow grin spread over Gilbert's handsome face. "That means the world to me, Marian. We're going to get through this. Together.

"How?" It wasn't doubt this time, it was a request to let her help him work through the problem.

Gilbert resumed their stroll, arm in arm. "Wilson sent the ledgers home with me. I'm going to pour over them and find what we're missing. It also means I'm not leaving your side."

"What about your other clients?" When he didn't answer right away, she patted his hand. "Will your boss understand if you request to solely focus on one client?"

"I don't know." His jaw ticked. "I can't sacrifice your safety for this job, Marian. I know you married me to try to save my career, to provide for you, but you are too important to me to risk you getting hurt."

His words warmed her, but instead of replying, she filtered through possible solution after solution, discarding them as quickly as they came. Nick could stay while Gilbert was gone, but it was no longer appropriate since Elaine had passed and they had no need of a physician's presence. She doubted the thugs would see Mr. Johnson as a threat any more than a group of older ladies. And Detective O'Connor's presence would only anger the thugs more.

"What if I didn't solve who is behind the threats?" Gilbert asked quietly.

"What do you mean?" Marian stopped, wanting all her attention on him, not divided by watching for the occasional ice patches they maneuvered around.

He took both of her hands in his. "If we leave, we remove you from being a threat to the thugs. They shouldn't follow us."

"Us. You mean, you, too." Marian tested the idea. On the surface, it seemed to hold water, but ... "Are we sure they'd leave us alone?"

"No." Gilbert blew out a frosty breath. "But distance can be a good deterrent. They'd have to be desperate to follow us across the country, and they haven't shown themselves to be that way. They've stuck to threats, not violence."

Marian raised an eyebrow. "Other than punching you."

"But they haven't harmed you." Determination set in Gilbert's jaw. "I think we should go. All of us. We'll pack up your truck and my car, and drive to Montana. We can leave in the next few days. As soon as we're packed."

"I like the idea, Gilbert." But something didn't sit right. It felt cowardly. "What if we are the ones who can stop them? Don't we have an obligation to help the case?"

"You mean do I have an obligation?" Gilbert looked up at the sky, then back at her. "You are my first priority. There are other accountants O'Connor or Wilson can use. They don't need me. You do."

Marian chewed her lip. She understood. Truly she did. She willingly married the son of the man who ruined them in order to protect her children. "What about Samantha? She knows who the thugs are."

"That was my fear today. But Detective O'Connor will protect her. And won't her brother be home soon, too?"

Marian nodded. "Her beau, too."

"Then she's in good hands." Gilbert brought hers up to his lips. "Will you be able to say goodbye?"

Though he didn't say her late husband's name, Marian knew that's who he meant. "It's time."

Other than leaving the investigation undone, which didn't sit well, all other obligations and responsibilities were fulfilled. There was nothing holding them here. Silas and Cora were out West, her parents would be headed that way this summer, Gilbert's mother could travel with them. Yes, they would need to leave friends, her late husband's home. But leaving the winter of grief for the spring of a new beginning called to her.

"Mr. Gilbert, sir? Mrs. Marian?" Mr. Johnson picked his way toward them, skirting the ice and snow that littered the wharf. "I don't mean to alarm you, but young Miss Essie has taken ill."

"What do you mean?" Marian hiked up her skirt, prepared to run to her daughter no matter the treacherous ground between them.

"She's spiked a fever, ma'am, and is coughing quite seriously." The older man grimaced. "The Mrs. has already called for Dr. Matrone."

Whatever plans she and Gilbert made would have to wait. Her baby needed her, and they weren't going anywhere until Essie was fully healed.

CHAPTER FOURTEEN

Tuesday, February 3

Gilbert poured himself yet another cup of coffee as the hall clock struck three in the morning. He leaned his backside against the counter beside the stove and the aromatic flavor filled his senses. Tonight called for strong coffee, not double-brewed grounds.

Shuffling feet brought Marian down the steps, and into the kitchen. Gilbert wordlessly poured her coffee and held out the cup. Over the past four hours, Essie's fever had risen dangerously high. They cooled her with damp cloths, set a poultice on her little chest, and tried to get her to drink water and the medicine Nick prescribed. Her coughs shook her small body and equally shook Gilbert to his core. If this was parenthood, it was terrifying. There was nothing he could do but watch. Little Essie needed her mama for comfort, didn't need him. And there was no way to *fix* what she battled.

"She's finally resting." Marian sighed and took another long sip of coffee.

"How's Nettie?" They had moved her into the other upstairs room in hopes she wouldn't catch whatever illness Essie had, and Mom took Elaine's old room down here. She retired after Nick left, around midnight, demanding they wake her if they needed an extra set of hands. The Johnsons had stated the same before they returned to the loft room in the workshop.

"Sleeping." Marian's shoulders rounded. "And Essie's fever has leveled to a consistent warmth."

"They're strong girls, Marian," he said, as much for himself as for her.

"You've been working." Marian ran fingers over the ledgers he had spread over the kitchen table. "You should sleep."

He shook his head. "I couldn't if I tried."

Instead, he studied the Conglomerate books in between helping with Essie. He washed, carried, and did anything else that freed Marian to stay by Essie's side. Numbers settled his worry, and studying the ledgers gave him something productive to do. Not that he'd found a way to find the mole. She leaned closer to the books, flipped a page in one of them, then another. Confidentiality said he should stop her perusal of the books, but the futility of his search hit him anew. He scrubbed his face with his free hand. He needed sleep before his spirits dipped even lower.

"These are the dues various businesses have paid. I see ours, Mrs. Whittlebush, David's fishing." She tapped a page. "This is odd."

"What?" Gilbert set his cup on the counter and leaned over Marian's shoulder. A sliver of hope shone through the darkness.

She turned her head, bringing her lips distractingly close. "Why would Dr. Thompson pay dues?"

He leaned away before his weariness overcame his strength, and he kissed her like a desperate husband.

"Sure, Dr. Thompson owns the business. But he has never been at any of the Conglomerate meetings." She gestured with her cup as if using it as a lecture pointer. "He doesn't vote or weigh in on how the Conglomerate is run. Nor does he speak up against the Conglomerate. He's remained completely neutral."

He struggled to follow her logic. "Buck didn't flag it, and it's a rather obvious entry."

She rolled her eyes and planted her free fist on her hips, as if he were a dolt. "I don't doubt that he actually paid dues, but that's just it. Why? He has no competition in town. No need for the protection. He's not a widow or subject to the whims of the fishing market. There's no reason for him to need the Conglomerate."

Perhaps he was a dolt, or at least dense. Maybe simply tired. "If someone thought he didn't treat them right, or if a family is angry he didn't save a loved one like they think he should, wouldn't he need backing?"

She was shaking her head before he finished his question. "No one has ever done such a thing that I know of. And Crow's Nest is a small town.We'd know if that happened. He's been the doctor here since Zachariah and Silas were children, even longer. People trust him. He's the community doctor. Buck, being newer to Crow's Nest, might not even notice something fishy about this, just like you didn't. But I'm telling you, this is a red flag."

"Okay." Who was he to argue against such an impassioned speech? "Do you think the doctor is the mole?"

Marian took a moment to consider. "It might explain why he hasn't wanted to harm anyone. He's still a doctor at heart. However—"

"Mama?" Nettie's voice traveled down the stairs, followed by a rattling cough. "I don't feel so good."

"Coming, sweetheart." Marian's shoulders sagged for a moment before she handed Gilbert her cup. "It was inevitable that both girls caught the same illness. Look into Dr. Thompson."

"I'll get wet towels." Gilbert caught her fingers. "You stay well."

"Mamas always do." She put on a brave smile before hurrying up the stairs.

Twenty minutes later, Nettie was finally resting. Gilbert stirred the pot of herbs Marian had set to brew. A medicinal tea Nick said would bring down a fever and settle a cough, if the girls could keep it down. The sweet peppermint smell wafted through the kitchen, clearing Gilbert's foggy mind. He set the wooden spoon on the spoon rest and resumed his seat at the table.

He worked through the ledgers, making note of every place where Dr. Thompson's name appeared. From dues to services paid. Every few minutes, he stirred the tea, letting what he'd discovered simmer like the tea he monitored. The ledgers went back the decade-plus history of the Conglomerate, to when Perry Baxter began the initiative in 1920. Buck had taken it over two years ago now, and there was no sign that Baxter remained on the books.

Dr. Thompson, however, was one of the original members—odd, then, that he never participated in the meetings. He never missed a payment, which was one of the reasons Gilbert hadn't considered him before. The man seemed a model of consistency and loyalty. In turn, the organization seemed loyal to him. From 1920 until shortly after Buck took over, the Conglomerate used the doctor's services at least once a month. Gilbert stirred the tea, then added up the monthly payments and compared them to the dues the doctor paid.

"Oh wow." Gilbert leaned back in his chair, hands atop his head. Dr. Thompson was easily receiving three or four times the income that he paid in dues. Why would the Conglomerate be paying him so much? Did they pay for medical services for certain members? More concerning was why those payments ended when Buck took over.

The clock chimed five, startling Gilbert into realizing he'd been at these numbers for almost two hours and Marian had never come down to get tea for the girls. He ladled up three cups and quietly ascended the stairs. They'd moved Nettie back to her shared bed with Essie when it became apparent the illness had spread. It was to that room Gilbert went, stopping in the doorway to take in the scene. The girls shifted uneasily beneath their quilt, but they slept. And Marian sat on a chair beside them, her head pillowed on crossed arms she rested on the bed.

Gilbert set the cups on the washstand so he could lay a blanket over Marian's shoulders.

"Mr. Gil?" Essie's little voice came from the far side of the bed.

"What is it, sweetie?" He knelt beside her and placed a hand on her forehead. So warm, it broke his heart.

Essie's blue eyes shimmered in the moonlight peeking in through the window. "Can you tell me a story?"

"Of course." He kept his voice low as he animatedly told the story of The Princess and Pea. Essie giggled at the best places, easing his worry.

"I don't have a pea under my mattress." Essie patted the bed. "If I did, I..."

The poor little girl rolled onto her side as a violent coughing fit rolled through her. Gilbert sat on the bed, rubbing her back and holding her hand as she coughed and coughed. Marian and Nettie woke with the sounds, which set Nettie to coughing, too. After a few minutes, breathing heavy and with a film of perspiration on their faces, the girls finally lay back against their pillows.

"I brought up tea." Gilbert waved toward the cups he brought up, needing to offer something.

"Thank you, Gil." Marian pulled him aside, keeping her voice low. "You don't have to do all of this."

"What do you mean?" He wished there was more he could do. Then, in the last vestiges of the full moon shining through the window, he caught the look in her eye. Tentative, as if she asked too much of him. *Never.* He cupped her shoulders. "There is nowhere else I'd rather be than at your side caring for your girls. *Our* girls, if you'll allow me."

"Oh, Gil." She went into his arms and he held her. His wife, his family. Yes, there was no other place he'd rather be.

❦

Wednesday, February 4

Marian closed her eyes as the sun streamed through the window of Gilbert's car, belying the frigid temperatures outside today. Nearly a full night's sleep wasn't enough to restore her after sitting up all night with her girls the evening before. Not that she would have traded places with anyone. She hated to see her girls ill, and so horribly ill. Fortunately, they'd accepted both tea and soup since yesterday afternoon, and their fevers were down to a manageable warmth, which gave her peace to leave them for a short time in the care of their new grandmother.

A comforting hand wrapped around hers, and her body relaxed. Steadfast Gilbert. How grateful she was for him. He didn't run when things got difficult, or unpleasant. When children grew ill or death visited. His presence never wavered. Even more, he drew closer. He wanted to claim her girls as his own. Not because they were perfect or sweet—though her bias claimed they were. He chose them when they were in the midst of their illness, in the middle of a sleepless night. For

204

better or worse, went their wedding vows. Gilbert had more than fulfilled his.

"You could have stayed with the girls." His thumb gently rubbed her knuckles. "Though I'm glad for your company."

She smiled over at him. He'd canceled his appointments for the week, and his boss nearly fired him for it, until an unnamed client expressed gratitude for not spreading illness. She had no doubt Buck had put in a good word for Gilbert. Though why Buck supported her husband, Marian didn't understand. The man was under investigation, and yet he made sure Gilbert kept his job. More, he invited Gilbert to look into his books. The oxymoron that was Buck Wilson befuddled her.

"Do you think it was wise to have included Buck in this meeting?" she asked Gilbert, the original threat echoing in her mind. There was a reason the thugs didn't want Buck to know whatever they were doing. They were afraid of him. Why?

"With the detective there, I think it's safe enough." Yesterday afternoon, Gilbert had asked Nick to set up a clandestine meeting with Detective O'Connor and Buck to discuss what he'd found in the ledgers after her observation about Dr. Thompson. He tugged his hand free to shift gears as they turned into the tall pines surrounding Detective O'Connor's house, then sought her hand again. "I don't think Wilson is involved in this particular scheme. Not that he's innocent of criminal activity, but in this case, I think he's on our side."

"Do you think he's dirty, then?" So many people mistrusted Buck, and yet they all paid dues into the Conglomerate. It was an incongruity Marian hadn't considered until now.

"If he is, I didn't find proof." Gilbert shrugged. "He's hiding something, though. I'll be glad to hand over the information and put distance between us and the situation. Once the girls are strong enough,

I think we should leave. With Wilson's recommendation, I'm sure I can find accounting work in most any town we decide to settle in."

Anxiety tightened her chest. "Are we really going west?"

Gilbert parked and faced her. "I think it's wise. We can move near Silas and Cora or your parents' lumber camp. But only if you're fully on board."

Before she could answer, Buck parked beside them. Samson, Detective O'Connor's huge mastiff barreled out the cabin door. She got out without waiting for Gilbert and gave the dog's large head a good rub. Samson's tongue lolled, his hot breath thick white puffs, and he closed his eyes, revelling in the scratches.

"That dog is in love with your wife." Buck chuckled behind her.

"I don't blame him. She's an incredible woman." Gilbert's reply slipped into her heart. He loved her, thought her lovable. The other day, when he'd first told her about his feelings, she hadn't been able to say the same. Now, after watching him care for her girls, she recognized the feeling in her chest. It was one she experienced with regards to only one other man, a man she thought she'd spend the rest of her life beside. Now another had taken his place in their home. Was he taking that same place in her heart as well?

"Get in here." Detective O'Connor called from his house. "It's too cold for man and beast. Coffee's on the stove."

Marian followed Samson into the warmth of Detective O'Connor's rustic cabin while Gilbert grabbed the ledgers and Buck brought up the rear. In no time, they were settled around the detective's low table, a slice of tree with rings of varying sizes spreading out from its center. Gilbert sat beside Marian on the sofa. Buck and Detective O'Connor took the chairs opposite. Samson sprawled out before the roaring fire.

"All right, what have you found?" O'Connor steepled his hands, skipping any pretense and small talk. Marian would have preferred to ease into the conversation, but that wasn't Detective O'Connor's way.

Gilbert began with Marian's observation the night her girls were most ill, then shared how he'd tracked Dr. Thompson's financial activity through the ledgers. When he finished, he looked at Buck. "Do you know why payments stopped after you took over?" That's the question Marian most wanted to know.

"I never knew he was being paid." Buck slid Gilbert's findings closer, and studied them with a frown Marian rarely saw on his angular face. This was a side of the polished businessman she guessed he rarely revealed, and it spoke to his investment in this conversation. "There is no reason for him to be on the payroll at all. We don't keep a doctor on retainer, and if we help with medical bills, we reimburse a member, not the doctor himself. I'm not sure I realized he even was a member. He never comes to meetings."

"That's what Marian said." Gilbert bumped her shoulder with his and she appreciated him giving her, a female, her due in front of these men.

"This information gives me license to ask for all your files." Detective O'Connor reached for his coffee mug, which he'd set on the table. "Seems my investigation should extend beyond you to the entire Conglomerate operations."

"I've told you repeatedly I'm not embezzling or doing any criminal behavior." Buck snapped. He waved at Gilbert. "And now I can prove it."

"I can't prove your innocence," Gilbert amended. "But I can't prove your guilt."

"Aren't people innocent until proven guilty?" Marian didn't know why she defended Buck. Then again, he'd been nothing but kind to her and her family. Maybe it was her mother instinct, keeping these men from turning into bickering boys. "Regardless, we're here to talk about Dr. Thompson. What could he want to keep from Buck, and why does he think I'm a threat?"

"You are the one who figured out the ledgers." Gilbert pointed out with a shrug.

"And now you're telling me, which they didn't want you to do." Buck offered as if the threats meant nothing, but they'd terrified her enough to drive her to remarry. Did these men not realize the vulnerability she faced? Buck continued, "I can't understand. What does Perry have to do with any of this? He's not in the picture anymore. Retired back East."

"They were friends back in the day." Detective O'Connor sipped his coffee. "Fishing buddies. About the same age."

"Did Thompson help Perry create the Conglomerate?" Buck's frown deepened as an odd look flashed in his eyes. Not fear, but something disconcerting. Unfortunately it was gone with a shake of his head. "I can't recall Perry ever mentioning Thompson when he recounted the origin of the Conglomerate. Trust me, I asked. I wasn't about to take over an organization without the details."

Detective O'Connor scrunched his bushy brows together. "You haven't told me that before. Just how much do you know about the first years of the Conglomerate? You seemed to snatch the organization right out from under old Perry."

"Back to Dr. Thompson." Marian barely resisted rolling her eyes. These two kept sparring and getting off topic. "Do you think Dr. Thompson is doing something illegal? Or could he be angry that Buck stopped paying him when his friend used to? And why would it cause him to threaten me? They left a dead rat on my porch, for heaven's sake!"

Buck stared at her. The detective's mustache twitched. Gilbert covered her hands with his, as if trying to calm her. Well, she wasn't interested in being calmed or managed. She jumped to her feet. "I want this situation ended and if you can't put your war aside to keep my girls safe, then I'll figure it out myself."

"Marian, wait." Gilbert called after her, but she was too upset to stop. She marched for the front door, Samson scrambling after her.

Grabbing her coat, she let Samson follow her to the porch. The cold smacked into her, freezing her nose and turning the tears that stung her eyes into icy drops. Why did she have to get so emotional? The men would never listen to her now. She'd proved how much of a female she was.

The door opened and closed, then Gilbert stepped up next to her. They stood side by side, silently watching Samson explore the front yard for several minutes. Her heart rate slowed and embarrassment took its place.

"Do you know what first attracted me to you?" Gilbert shot her a look, his ears reddening.

Marian's heart *ker-thumped.*

"Your passion, specifically when you go all mother bear." He toed the porch railing. "I really like that about you."

"You don't think I'm an emotional female?"

"I'm glad you're an emotional female." He glanced at her with a wince. "I'm not going to get whacked for that, am I?"

She folded her arms, trapping her confusion in her chest. "Explain."

Gilbert scratched his cheek. "You're fire and life. You love with everything in your being. You're loyal, too. It's what made me fall in love with you. And, if there was ever a chance that you would stand in my corner the way you protect your girls …” His eyes turned glassy and he blinked as he looked away.

The emotional display from one so steady shot an arrow right to her heart. He craved *her* protection? She'd married him for his. Then she thought of his father. Gilbert's battle to clear his name, to make amends. His desire to be a good man so opposite from the greedy, abusive man who sired him. And she realized Gilbert needed a champion. He needed *her* to be his champion.

“I've been so selfish!” She covered her mouth to hold in a gasp. “All I've considered is what you can do for me”

“No, no!” He grabbed her upper arms. “That's not what I mean at all. You've been anything but selfish, Marian. You've done so much for me.”

“Stop. You're not taking enough credit for all you've done. It's like you not taking the upstairs bedroom. You don't think you deserve it, but you do. You deserve a real marriage, too.”

“Marian."

She put a finger over his mouth. “I'm not ready yet, but …” She lifted on her toes and pressed her cold lips to his. He froze, but only for a moment. Then he hauled her into his arms and warmed her from her lips all the way down to her feet.

Gilbert hadn't planned to kiss her, not that he initiated the kiss. And that's exactly what set his blood racing. The passion he so admired about her drove their kiss. She was telling him something and he'd figure it out later when he could think.

"Should we interrupt?" A chuckling voice broke through his haze. Wilson, the bounder.

"They're not likely to freeze to death at this rate." O'Connor also had humor in his tone.

It was enough for Gilbert to come to senses. If it were him, he wouldn't care what those two curmudgeons saw. However, Marian might not want their kiss on display. So he wrestled his desire back into its box, though he kept Marian in his arms and she kept her face tucked into his shoulder.

"May I help you, gentlemen?" Gilbert grumbled. The two had the audacity to laugh, which brought Samson to the porch.

"We were in the middle of a conversation." O'Connor sipped his ever-present coffee mug. How much coffee did the man drink?

"I think these two are done." Wilson was still chuckling like a dunderhead. Gilbert tightened his hold on Marian, wanting her to know he wasn't ashamed of their kiss or her display.

O'Connor rolled his eyes. "It's not enough for me to bring Thompson in for questions, but I will put in an official request for your files."

"We don't want to spook him." Wilson finally grew serious. "It's better if he doesn't know Marian and Cox put the details together."

"That's why we're thinking about leaving town." Gilbert kissed Marian's temple. "I want my family out of danger."

Marian raised her head, looking from one man to the next. Her cheeks were flushed and her lips red. But deep concern swirled in her brown eyes. "Do you think danger will follow us if we go west?"

"I can't guarantee anything, but it's a smart idea to leave." Detective O'Connor patted Samson's large head.

If Gilbert had his way, they'd leave right now. However, he'd let Marian have the final decision. She'd been willing to marry to keep her girls safe. Could she leave the home she made with her late husband to do the same? Gilbert's fingers tightened around her shoulder. He was her family now. Their patchwork family deserved a fresh beginning where danger wouldn't dog them. It was the right decision.

Marian must have followed his same logic because she firmed her jaw and said, "I'll contact Cora to set the move in motion."

Gilbert drove slowly home, grateful for a few more quiet moments with Marian before returning to a home filled with two adorable little girls, his mother, and a housekeeper and butler they didn't actually need. He basked in the comfortable silence between them. It made him dream of years from now, sitting together on an old front porch, each in their rocking chairs, watching the sun set. He and his wife. The woman he loved with all his heart.

He heard a car rumble behind them and inched his own car closer to the side of the road so the other driver could pass them. He assumed it was Wilson, and Gilbert wasn't in the mood to have the man critiquing his driving.

Only, the car didn't pass. It rammed them from behind. Marian squealed and Gilbert wrestled the steering wheel as they were hit again, sending them down an embankment straight into the pine trees. Gilbert shot an arm out to protect Marian as he jammed his foot on the brake. The car lurched, then slammed into a tree. Gilbert's forehead struck the steering wheel and stars obliterated his vision.

CHAPTER FIFTEEN

Aching pain radiated through Gilbert's body, and a trickle of something wet dripped down his cheek. His right arm rested in Marian's lap. Had he succeeded in saving her from slamming into the dashboard when they crashed? "Marian!"

She stirred, thank God.

"Get them out of the car." A male voice from outside the car tore his attention away from Marian. Who was out there? Who ran them off the road?

"Marian, you need to wake up." He shook her shoulder, grateful to hear her groan. "Sweetheart, please."

"Let's go." A tall man yanked open her car door and grabbed her arm.

No! He lunged, but someone yanked him the other way. Gilbert landed hard on the ground. Marian squealed, and he scrambled to his feet. He had to get to her.

"Don't move." Parker aimed a gun at him and Gilbert froze.

Hayes brought Marian around to their side of the car. She tried to twist away from her captor. *Atta girl!* But Hayes slammed her against the car, trapping her legs where she couldn't kick him. Gilbert reached for her, but the click of Parker's pistol stilled his movement.

"That's right. Don't move." Parker nodded to Hayes. Unable to think of a way out, Gilbert helplessly watched as Hayes tied Marian's hands and feet, then covered Marian's head with a burlap bag. "Your turn, Cox. And if you do anything out of line, I'll shoot your wife."

Marian screamed, and Hayes smacked her through the burlap. "Silence, woman! Or I shoot your husband."

"Take me, but let her go." Gilbert demanded as Parker bound his hands and feet, unwilling to risk Marian's life with a gun pointed at her. "She hasn't done you any harm."

Hayes grunted as he tossed Marian over his shoulder like a sack of wheat. Hayes chuckled. "No. She knows as much as you do. You both are too big a risk to have to loose tonight."

Tonight? What was tonight? The burlap came over his head and his panic clawed at his chest. He hated small dark places. They were tossed into the trunk of a car and Gilbert tried to slide as close as he could to Marian, both to comfort her and receive comfort. The tight space closed in on him. Tears threatened, but now wasn't the time for them. He needed to keep his wits about him, find a way out of this, keep Marian safe, and get them both home to their girls.

Marian's breath stuttered, telling him that her face was in front of his. "What are they going to do to us?"

He reached forward, finding her hands and tangling his fingers with hers. If only he could find his voice.

"It'll be okay," she whispered. How did she know he struggled? All he could do was tighten his hold on her and attempt to picture each turn and straight away. If only he knew Crow's Nest better. He never got the sense they went over a bridge, so he was pretty sure they stayed within city limits. Exactly where they were, however, he could not pinpoint.

When the trunk opened, the sound of waves told him they were by the lake. Hayes and Parker carried them through the biting wind whipping in off the water, and into a building that brought temporary relief. But the place was unheated and a chill breeze circulated. Hayes set Gilbert on his bound feet, barely waiting for Gilbert to find his balance before yanking the sack from his head. Gilbert hauled air into his lungs. The dark room was illuminated by a single lantern that didn't reach to all the corners. He searched for where the men had put Marian. She sat on the edge of a bed, terrified eyes staring at them.

"Good luck." Hayes gave a sloppy salute, then left them alone. He hopped forward, but the slide of a board and the click of a lock stopped his attempt. They were trapped. He'd promised to protect Marian and failed. Failed spectacularly.

"Gil." Marian beckoned him.

Shame demanded he hide from her, but he couldn't desert her. He dropped to his knees and crawled over to her. Pulled himself up on the bed. "Marian, I'm so sorry. So, so sorry." He lifted his bound hands to her face, cupping her cheeks as best he could.

"Gil, I'm fine, but I'm worried about you. You hit your head." She raised fingers to hover over his temple. "I'll clean it as best I can."

Who cared about that? He hooked the rope tying her wrists. "Don't worry about me. Let's get free and find a way out of here."

The knots proved difficult, but they got them loose eventually. Marian insisted on washing his cut, then taking the lantern, they scoured the room for what the thugs had left behind. A wooden bucket of water, an empty tin bucket for waste, and another tin bucket of bread. The bed had a smelly old blanket and the lantern plenty of oil. The chinking in the wall was disintegrating, but otherwise, the logs were sturdy. Door, too. It didn't budge, and its hinges were rusted so that Gilbert couldn't remove them. They were well and truly trapped.

Again the panic struck. How could he get Marian home to her girls? His own mother was with them, but they needed their mother.

"Do you think they'll be back?" Marian sat on the bed, wrapping her arms around herself. Her fear pulled him from his own.

"We'll figure it out, Love." Gilbert sat beside her. She rested her head on his shoulder and he wrapped his arm around her back, loving the feel of her in his arms. How unworthy was he? "I'm sorry I couldn't protect you like I promised."

"You aren't at fault, Gil. These men want something from us. We need to make a plan for when they return. First time they open the door, we need to get out."

"I like your gumption." He kissed her forehead. "And we'll be quickly missed, so people will be searching for us in no time."

Marian nodded, and they fell silent for a few moments. Then Marian whispered, "I'm scared, Gil."

"I know." He lifted her chin, so she had to look him in the eye, needed her to know the depth of his commitment. "I am, too. But I'll do everything I can to get you home to the girls."

Her eyes widened. "Gil, no. You cannot sacrifice yourself. We need to do this together. *Our* girls need us both."

Oh, sweet woman. He rested his forehead against hers. "They need you more."

"I need you, too." Tears turned her eyes to chocolate in the lantern light, and Gilbert brought his lips to hers. There was desperation in their kiss, but it fired his determination to see her get home. And if he also survived, then they'd pack up the girls, his mom, and drive west to Silas and Cora. No more ledgers. No more danger.

First they needed to find a way out. He pushed to his feet, determined to find a weakness in the structure that he could exploit. But daylight dimmed through the cracks in the chinking until only darkness surrounded them. So much for a quick rescue. Or even the return of their captors. Gilbert turned down the lantern so they could conserve oil. He'd gone over the dilapidated structure five times and could find no escape. Plenty of age, mice droppings, and the like, but nothing that could get them out. He even tried using the bed to leverage the door open. It didn't work.

Now Marian huddled on the bed, her teeth chattering. This wasn't how he imagined their first night in the same room would go, but he climbed beside her on the narrow cot, tucking her under his arm. Marian rested her head against his chest and didn't say a word, which worried him. She'd been so positive, so determined all day. Encouraging him in his search. But as the temperature dipped and night fell, her spirits sank.

Gilbert pulled up the smelly blanket to cover them, then leaned his head against the wall, settling in for the night. He planned to stay awake, keep ears open for either a possible rescue or the return of their captors. He aimed to be ready for anything. If only his head didn't pound ... and the bread didn't sit like a rock in his belly. They conserved as much of the water and food as they could, but a fear he refused to voice aloud drummed in his mind. What if neither the thugs nor a rescue ever came?

As Marian's breathing evened into sleep, Gilbert's limbs grew heavy. The vows he made her when they married raced around in his mind. His promise to provide and protect. And what an utter failure he was at keeping them safe. He rested his chin on Marian's head, her hair tickling his neck. If the danger were against only him, he would stick to words. But Marian needed to get home to her girls. How did he defend her and not fight for her?

If—when, *please God*—their captors returned, he couldn't go down like he had at the drugstore before they married. A band wrapped around his chest and he held Marian a little tighter, grateful he'd insisted on buying her a new coat. It might just save her life tonight. She emitted a tiny sigh. He had to give Marian the best chance to escape. There was no other option.

Heavenly Father ... He stalled as usual. His own father had been domineering well before he became a convicted criminal. Greed and power had corrupted him before he took advantage of the Wards. But God wasn't like that. Was He? Gilbert rubbed his belly, the churning worse. Reverend Moller tried to teach him about God's love and mercy, but Gilbert struggled to believe it.

What about Nettie and Essie? The question blew in on the cold wind that slipped through the broken chinking. He shivered. They had no fear of asking Gilbert for anything. Whether to read or tell them stories. Or for another biscuit or to play in the snow. They looked up to him, trusted him to keep them safe. They saw him as a father, as their father. It humbled him. Especially in light of his failure to protect their mother.

Heavenly Father? The prayer emerged more easily this time. Could he see God the way Nettie and Essie saw him? Moreso, could Gilbert now understand how *God* saw *him*? Gilbert had grown to love Nettie and Essie. He would do anything for them, and wished to take away all the evil that could happen to them. Is that how God felt about Gilbert? About Marian and her girls? But didn't God have the power to stop these things from happening? Gilbert would give his life to keep Marian and her girls together.

Didn't Jesus do that?

A cough ripped from his lungs, followed by a body-shaking shiver. No, no, no! He couldn't be getting sick! His lungs convulsed and he carefully lay Marian's head on the mattress before the coughing fit woke her. He stumbled from the bed to the farthest corner of the room. Cough after cough tore through him so that he could hardly catch his breath.

Heat followed, leaving him clammy and shivering. How could he keep Marian safe like this? His weakness mocked him.

He sank against the wall. *Heavenly Father, I know You love Marian and her girls more than I do. Please keep them safe. Reunite them. I'm not asking for myself. For them, please.*

Pressure of a hand rested on his back as he again coughed to the point of breathlessness. He hated for Marian to see him like this. They hadn't shared any intimacies, and yet she saw him now, at his lowest. Cold fingers wiped his blazing forehead.

"It'll be okay, Gil." Marian's voice soothed him and yet caused tears to prick his eyes. Her compassion undid him. With another pat on his shoulder, Marian left his side and he wanted to call her back. Didn't want her to leave him, yet how could he be so selfish when she could catch this illness? Exhaustion swept over him along with a chill. Was this how the girls felt? As miserable as he was, he'd go back and take this from them if he could.

Marian knelt beside him again and held a ladle of water to his lips. "Drink this. Just a sip."

He obeyed. Then she wrapped her arm around his waist and directed him to the bed. She insisted he lay down, and he didn't protest. Though he wanted her beside him, he couldn't risk her getting sick.

"Rest now, Gil." She smoothed his hair away from his forehead with the tenderest of touches. A chill raced through him.

He turned his face away. "You can't catch this."

"If I do, I do." Then she laid a gentle kiss on his cheek. "I'll be right by your side, Gil. I'm not going anywhere."

The words seeped into his soul like rain on parched ground, and he fell asleep with a prayer in his heart.

Heavenly Father, thank you for my wife.

Thursday, February 5

Marian jerked awake at the sound of crunching footsteps outside the cabin. Her breath was frosty in the morning light filtering through the cracks in the walls. A smattering of snowflakes swirled along the dirt floor. She shivered then laid a hand on Gilbert's forehead. Not too warm, thankfully. He stirred slightly at her touch, but remained asleep.

The footsteps outside gave way to the rumbling of voices. She emptied the bread bucket onto the bed, then took up a position beside where the door would open.

"I don't know why the boss wants us to check on them." She recognized Parker's voice. "Just let them die, I say. No fuss in letting nature take its course. They'll run out of food and water eventually."

Marian clamped down on her fear and adjusted her grip on the bucket. This was her opportunity to get them out of this situation.

"Because we can't give them a chance to escape." Hayes growled. "They know too much. They need to be eliminated."

Marian glanced at Gilbert. Her turn to protect him, get them both home safely to their girls. And she would get home to her girls. Failure to do so was not an option.

The door opened. She didn't take note of who stepped through first before she swung. The pail collided with a mass. The man grunted, bent over, and she slammed the pail on the man's head. He fell to the floor. The second man—Hayes—stumbled over the first, but blocked

Marian's swing and yanked the pail from her hands. She lost her balance, her toe catching on the hem of her skirt, and she rolled on the floor.

A gunshot exploded in the room, and dirt sprayed in her face. Panic closed her throat as she scrambled to her feet. Hayes rolled his eyes and cocked his pistol. She raised her hands, a plea for her life tangled on her tongue. He aimed at her chest and she whimpered. *God, please ...*

Gilbert roared up from behind Hayes, slamming the water bucket down on the man's shoulder. Water splashed and Hayes' shot went wide as the man landed on his knees. Gilbert swung again, catching Hayes on the side of the head, dropping him to the ground. Marian jumped forward, stomping her boot on Hayes' hand to pin the gun to the floor. The man yelped, and Gilbert hit him once more, rendering him fully unconscious.

Marian grabbed the gun, pointing it first at one thug, then the other. "What now?" Her breath came in uneven gasps as the reality of the situation sank in. Her legs trembled, but her resolve to get home to her girls strengthened her.

Gilbert, however, sank to a knee, clutching his stomach as he coughed. "We leave them ... locked in here ... while we get help." Did he look nauseous because he broke his conviction on violence or because he was coughing so violently on an empty stomach?

She stepped toward him, but stopped, not wanting to get too close to the two thugs. "Are you okay?"

"Let me drag them away from the door." He set his jaw and did as he intended, with only a few hacking coughs. Marian maintained her distance, keeping the gun trained on Hayes and Parker.

Once the way was clear, they backed into the early morning, locking the cabin behind them as the thugs had done to them. The instant the latch clicked in place, Gilbert collapsed against the cabin wall, doubled over. A chill shook him as another cough scraped from his throat.

Marian pressed the backs of her fingers to his too-warm forehead. "Deep breaths, Gil. The terrain is snowy and rocky, which explains why I'm not seeing Hayes and Parker's car. I'm not sure how far we have to walk to find it or help. Lean on me."

She wished there was more she could do for him, to make getting to town easier, but this would have to do. Which way should they go? Could they find the car? The road? Another cabin? She didn't know the best path to take—didn't know where they were in the first place—so she had to pick a direction and hope it would take them to safety.

Gilbert nodded and rested his arm over her shoulder, letting her support him, lead him. She struggled under his weight, her steps through the snow slow. Clouds obscured the rising sun and its heat, and a brisk wind blew in off the lake. She shivered despite her warm coat. What if she hadn't allowed Gilbert to provide it? She probably would have frozen to death. And didn't that thought send a tremble down her spine.

They headed east, toward the sound of the lake, until they could see the water below. Gray and angry, it churned in frothy fashion, spraying against the snow covered ice shelf. She scanned the coast, attempting to get their bearings. Should they go north or south? There was no sign of a road or car or house. Gilbert couldn't manage long out here, so her decision would mean life or death.

"Do you recognize where we are?" Gilbert asked between a couple coughs and she shook her head, indecision immobilizing her. He pulled her to his chest. "It's all right, Love. We're alive and together."

She tightened her hold around his waist. "You conserve your energy." She buried her face in his shoulder, hoping he hadn't heard her fear. She needed to be strong for him so they could both get home to her girls. No, *their* girls.

"I love you, too, Marian." The smile in Gilbert's voice had her pushing away so she could see his face. His feverish eyes twinkled though his cheeks were drawn. He tugged her closer, then rested cold lips on her forehead. "I want to kiss you, but not until I won't get you sick."

Something cracked in her chest. Her care and concern for him were symptoms of her feelings, sure, but had she fallen in love with her husband? Tears threatened as she ran her gaze over a face that had become dear to her these last few weeks. And it ignited an even deeper fear. "I can't lose another husband."

He cupped her cheek, but didn't promise what was out of his control. "Let's go south."

A weight dropped from her shoulders. She didn't have to make this decision on her own. They shared the responsibility, and the consequences. Sharing the load with a partner made all the difference. She tugged herself under Gil's arm to support him. "Let's go south."

Gilbert's instincts were correct. Not half an hour later, Marian spotted Mrs. Whittlebush's apple orchard. Gilbert hadn't spoken since his suggestion of which direction to take, and Marian focused on putting one foot in front of the other. Thought of getting Gilbert help, and seeing her girls, kept her going as the wind buffeted them. They climbed the white porch steps Silas had painted last fall and Marian knocked, praying someone was home.

"Mamma Mia!" Bella Matrone gasped as she opened the door. "Come in, come in!"

"Is Nick here?" Marian helped Gilbert navigate the doorway. His pale skin and drawn face worried her. Perspiration beaded his forehead. The cut there looked swollen and angry without proper cleaning.

Bella waved them into the front room. "No, he went to the clinic to talk with Dr. Thompson."

Gilbert stiffened beside her, echoing the skipped beat of her heart. "And Mrs. Whittlebush?" Had she succeeded in keeping the tremor out of her voice?

"She walked over to visit Signora Martins." Bella's dark brows drew together. "What is wrong?"

"Marian, no." Gilbert sank to the sofa with another coughing fit, but didn't let go of her hand. How did he know what she was thinking even before the thought fully formed in her mind?

"You need a doctor, Gil." She knelt before him. "And we cannot risk using the telephone. Dr. Thompson or one of his thugs might intercept the call."

"I can call Nick to come home under a ... *finzione*. A false idea." Bella offered, then chewed her lip. "Though he won't know it is urgent. Too bad we do not have a code phrase."

Tempting, but she couldn't risk Dr. Thompson insisting on helping Bella instead of sending Nick. She also refused to put the young woman in harm's way. Instinct demanded Marian run home, gather her girls into her arms. But what if she led Thompson or his men home? A rattling cough turned her attention to Gilbert. The poor man shivered under the blanket Bella had provided. Yet heat rose in waves from his body.

Gilbert needed Nick. She needed her girls. They both needed Detective O'Connor, who could be anywhere in Crow's Nest at this time of day. And the only help at her immediate disposal was Bella Matrone.

Marian couldn't be everywhere at once, which meant trusting others with those she most treasured. She had no choice but to leave Mrs. Cox with her girls a while longer. She would take the danger upon herself, find a way to get Nick's attention without alerting Dr. Thompson to the situation. However, she would also send Bella for help. No one would think twice if Bella went to see Mrs. Martins, especially if Mrs. Whittlebush was already there. In turn, those two older ladies could alert Detective O'Connor and check on her girls without raising suspicion.

Decision made, Marian turned to Bella. "Can you run to the Martins's home with a note?"

"Marian." Gilbert growled.

"You need a doctor, Gil, and we need help. I trust Nick to be both." To prove her point, Gilbert dissolved into another violent coughing fit that left him exhausted. Marian helped him lie on the couch, tucked the blanket closer around him. Then kissed his forehead. "I love you, Gilbert Cox, and I will be back for you."

Before Gilbert could protest, Marian hurried to Mrs. Whittlebush's sewing room, giving Bella instructions as she went. She found the older lady's notepaper and scratched out a note to Detective O'Connor. Mrs. Martins would know where to find him, then either she or Mrs. Whittlebush could check on her girls. Perhaps Gilbert, too. The plan wasn't perfect, but it was the best she could come up with.

Sending Bella on her way, Marian walked to Dr. Thompson's office. Her heart pounded as she considered her options, for she had no intention of alerting Dr. Thompson to her presence. Sticking to the shadows, she worked her way behind the buildings on Main Street until she came upon the clinic. She crept alongside and leaned around the corner. Only a very few people hurried through the cold on morning errands. None looked threatening.

Careful to keep herself mostly out of sight, she peered into the clinic's window. Dr. Thompson and Nick were conversing in the waiting area. She pressed her back against the wall. She needed to draw Nick out.

How? Her gaze fell to a stone near her feet. Surely both men wouldn't investigate if a rock hit their window. She wouldn't throw it hard enough to break it, of course. If Nick emerged, she would get his attention easily. If Dr. Thompson did, she'd circle around to the back door and hope Nick could hear her knock.

She tossed the stone lightly in her hand. *Lord, Thy will be done.* She drew back, but as she released the stone, someone caught her wrist and spun her around. She barely heard the stone tap the window over the pounding of her heart. Dr. Thompson looked down his hawk-like nose at her, disappointment—and something more dangerous—darkening his gaze.

CHAPTER SIXTEEN

As soon as the door closed behind Marian and Bella, Gilbert swung his feet to the floor. He had to wait for his coughing to subside, then to catch his breath. His fever had risen, and he felt utterly awful. However, he refused to stay on the sidelines when the woman he loved—and who loved him in return—walked into danger.

"Father, I need your strength," he prayed aloud, then pushed to his feet. He swayed.

I love you, Gilbert Cox, and I will be back for you. Marian's words galvanized him, but he was too weak to walk all the way to the clinic, leaving the telephone his only mode of getting help. Wisdom agreed with Marian about the risk, but now that Marian was gone, what if Gilbert drew Dr. Thompson here instead? Could Gilbert summon enough strength to detain the doctor until Marian brought help?

A moment of indecision stalled him, then he spotted Mrs. Whittlebush's black Ford sitting on the road in front of the house. The older woman's choice to walk to her neighbor's house despite the frigid temperatures was his—and maybe Marian's—salvation. He found the keys and sped toward the clinic.

As he turned the corner onto Main Street, he spotted Marian tucked into the shadows between the buildings, something in her hand. She reached back, like she was about to throw whatever it was, except someone grabbed her.

"No!" The word exploded from him, along with a cough. He pulled to the side of the road, unable to see as his lungs spasmed. By the time he looked up again, his body aching like he'd been trampled by a horse, Marian and her attacker were gone.

He stared up at the roof of the car. Exhaustion and failure dragging him down. *Heavenly Father, You promise that in my weakness You are strong.* And right now, Gilbert needed both mental and physical strength. He turned his gaze out the front window and spotted the Conglomerate headquarters. The seed of an idea formed, sprouted, infused him with energy. Gilbert was an accountant, a mathematician. He could rely on others with brawn if he first used his mind to outwit Thompson. He'd make a plan that had no choice but for two plus two to equal four. Four men. The idea snapped into place like gears in a watch.

After first searching the street to make sure he did not recognize anyone, he strolled down to the Conglomerate headquarters. He pushed inside, halting a conversation between Buck Wilson and another well-dressed man.

"Cox! How are the girls?" Wilson greeted him with an enthusiasm that put Gilbert on edge. "This is my half-brother, Joe Spelding."

Gilbert greeted the man who the two thugs had retrieved from prison a few days before. Was he in cahoots with Thompson? Was Buck? Could Gilbert trust a man being investigated for illegal activities, who didn't deny killing someone?

"Cox?" Wilson frowned. "You look like death warmed over."

"Thanks a lot." Gilbert might not fully trust Buck Wilson, but the man had never yet put Marian in danger. In fact, he seemed to protect her and her girls. For now, then, their purposes were aligned. He squared his shoulders, waiting out a cough, then infused his gaze with as much meaning as he could. "May I have a private word?"

Wilson relaxed, stuffing his hands into his pockets, but Gilbert had been around him enough now to recognize the seemingly unconcerned air was merely a front. "Joe, we'll talk later?"

Spelding narrowed his eyes as he looked between the two of them before taking his leave. An itchy feeling climbed Gilbert's neck. If that Spelding character stayed in Crow's Nest, he needed to get Marian and the girls far away. He might not fully trust Wilson, but even a penny of trust in Spelding would be a mistake.

"What's going on?" Wilson demanded as soon as the door closed. "You're clearly sick, but that's not why you're here."

"I'm fine." Not true, but he wouldn't waste time explaining that he'd caught the girls' illness. "Marian has been kidnapped."

"What!" Wilson's unaffected air popped like a balloon as he launched upright.

"We both were. Last night after we left the detective's house. But we got away." Gilbert paused to cough. "She was taken again a few minutes ago, outside the doctor's clinic."

"Back up. Last night?" Wilson shook his head. "Surely your mother noticed you were gone. Are the girls all right?"

"I don't know." The thought churned his stomach. Marian planned to have Mrs. Whittlebush or Mrs. Martins check on his mother and the girls, but now more than ever, he wanted to lay eyes on them himself. It's the only way he'd know for sure they were okay.

"Don't worry. I won't give anything away." Wilson strode to his phone box and placed the call.

Gilbert sank into a nearby chair, his strength ebbing. The situation had changed since Marian's decision to stay away from the girls for their safety. Thompson—it had to be him—now knew they'd escaped, which meant he could use the girls against her. Had Bella delivered Marian's message to the older ladies yet?

"Ah, Mrs. Cox." Wilson spoke into the phone. "Heard the girls were sick ... Yes ... Everything is fine? ... You're sure? ... Okay. Goodbye."

Gilbert raised his eyebrows, not liking how that conversation sounded, as Wilson slowly turned. "What did my mother mean, *everything was fine*?" Obviously Marian's message had not arrived yet.

"That's what I want to know, because I don't believe her." Wilson crossed his arms. "She would know you never returned, so either someone lied to her about your whereabouts or she's covering for some reason. I'm assuming you trust your mother."

"Of all the—" Gilbert snapped his mouth shut and chose to use his brain instead of his emotions. "I didn't tell her where we were going yesterday, but she's familiar with Nick. She could have called the clinic. Maybe Thompson made up some story, assured her everything was fine. Or he threatened her."

"My thoughts exactly." Wilson grabbed his hat. "I'm going to the clinic. You stay here."

Not a chance. Gilbert stumbled to his feet with a cough. "I have a plan, Wilson. I simply came here to get you first."

"You sought me out?" Surprise registered.

"Matrone was my next stop. Marian sent Bella to the Martins's residence to have Mrs. Martins contact O'Connor and send someone to check on the girls."

"If your mother doesn't know what happened yet ..."

"Exactly, so in case Bella or the ladies were waylaid, the three of us men are splitting up." Gilbert stepped out into the cold. "One of you is going for O'Connor, one is checking on the ladies, and I'm going home to see my girls. We'll meet there to form a plan to rescue Marian because we have to find her first."

"And if Thompson is in the clinic with Marian?" Buck followed him out the door. "Or at the house?"

"Then we end it right now." Gilbert marched across the street. "If not, we left the two thugs—Hayes and Parker—up at the cabin and they need arresting. I'm sure they have information to share."

"Who has information to share?" A voice not belonging to Wilson brought Gilbert to a halt. Of all the people, they had to run into the newspaperman, Greg Alistar.

"None of your concern." Gilbert shouldered past.

Alistar kept pace. "Have you discovered the location of the treasure your father wanted?"

Gilbert stopped, and Alistar ran into his back. The motion jarred a cough loose.

Wilson stepped between them. "Alistar, go ask your questions somewhere else."

"What are you two hiding?" Alistar scowled. "I will find out."

Gilbert groaned. "Would you leave us alone?"

"Can't you see the man doesn't feel well?' Wilson growled. "I'm dragging him to the doctor and you're in the way. Now unless you want to catch whatever Cox has, I suggest you move out of the way."

Alistar paled and immediately put several feet between them. "Thank you for your time. Uh, feel better." Then he scurried away like the rodent he was.

"I don't like that man." Gilbert muttered, then bent over, hand on the storefront beside him, to cough again. His lungs burned and his back threatened to spasm.

Wilson grabbed his biceps. "You're in no shape to rescue Marian, Cox. Let's get you to the clinic."

Unable to argue, Gilbert let Wilson lead him down the block.

"I was just closing up." Dr. Matrone met them outside the clinic. He squinted at Gilbert through his spectacles. "You caught the girls' flu. What are you doing out of bed?"

"Thompson kidnapped Marian." Okay, Gilbert didn't actually see the doctor abduct her, but he was responsible no matter who actually took Marian.

"Those are strong accusations, Cox." Matrone folded his arms. "Thompson checked on your girls last night, said I deserved a night off. He never mentioned anything about you or Marian."

"That's why my mother doesn't think there's anything wrong." Gilbert groaned. "He lied to her. Marian and I were trapped in a cabin all night."

"What? Nevermind. Come inside." Matrone reopened the clinic. "Thompson left, but before we go track down Marian, you need medicine."

Gilbert and Wilson followed Matrone to an examination room, where Nick instructed Gilbert to remove his shirt. The doctor refused to hear anything more about Marian or Thompson until he listened to Gilbert's lungs.

"If you're not careful, this will turn into pneumonia." Matrone wrapped his stethoscope around his neck. "Running around in this cold weather is not helping. You are also highly infectious right now. My medical opinion is that you should stay in bed."

Gilbert stuffed his arms into his shirtsleeves. "Not happening. Anyway, your sister could be in danger, too." It was a low blow, Gilbert knew, but it gained the darkened expression he wanted from the girl's brother. Gilbert quickly explained his and Marian's abduction last night, how he got sick, and then their escape today.

"And how is my sister involved?" Matrone glared at him.

"Marian tried to keep her out of danger by sending her to the Martins's house. She thought Mrs. Martins could contact Detective O'Connor, and then someone could check on my mother and the girls. They don't know the danger."

"Okay." Matrone folded his arms, showing a surprising number of muscles for a bookish-looking man. "So my sister is not in immediate danger."

"Wilson just called my mother. She doesn't know we were abducted last night, which means no one has told her anything yet." Did Gilbert have to voice his fear that Thompson somehow intercepted the message? Perhaps harming Bella or the ladies to keep Gilbert's mother in the dark?

It took only an extra moment for Matrone's expression to show he'd arrived at the same conclusion. His eyes widened before he growled like a bear. "I'm calling Mrs. Martins. You said you have a plan? What is it?"

"Let's explore the clinic before we get down to details," Wilson interrupted. "Thompson's not here, but he might have left a clue that changes what we should do next. Doctor, do we have your permission?"

"If the door is open, have at it. If not, I'll see if I have the key." Nick poured a syrup into a cup, which he handed to Gilbert. "Drink up. It won't make you drowsy, but it will stop the cough, hopefully until we find Marian."

Matrone called Mrs. Martins to keep them at the Martins's residence, then the three of them tore through the clinic. No clues that anyone called out. Until Gilbert wiggled the door to Thompson's office, getting it to unlatch. He stepped inside and froze at the bottles lining one wall. "Hey, Matrone, can you explain this?"

"What?" Nick joined him, Wilson following.

"Whiskey." Gilbert pointed. Probably a hundred quarter pint bottles, all neatly labeled.

"It's technically legal to prescribe whiskey," Nick explained. "However, a decade or more ago, the American Medical Association changed its view on medicinal alcohol, believing it's not actually good medical practice. They are also in support of Prohibition."

"Then why is Thompson still using it?" Gilbert picked up a bottle, the label declaring it a local Wisconsin brand.

"Because it's not illegal." Nick shoved Thompson's chair at Gilbert, eyeing him until Gilbert obliged and sat down. "Especially if this stash came from before Prohibition began."

"It didn't." Buck turned from a bookcase on the opposite side of the room, a ledger in his hand. "And he might be selling some through legal prescriptions, but that's not all he's doing. He oversaw a shipment last night. A large shipment headed from somewhere up north to Chicago. It came into port here overnight."

"That's why they got Marian and me out of the way." Gilbert rubbed his chest. The medicine had helped stop his coughing, but his torso ached something fierce. "Thompson is a rumrunner."

Matrone leaned on the edge of the desk. "Why would he need to sell liquor if he can prescribe it legally?"

"Money, Matrone." Wilson tucked the ledger under his arm and pulled out another one before walking over. "A lot of money. Cox, you can make better sense of these than me, I'm sure, but these dates go back to before I took over the Conglomerate."

"So you cutting him out wasn't the reason he joined the illegal alcohol trade?" Gilbert accepted the ledger. His tired eyes barely took in the information, but years of practice helped him glean enough. "This is a large operation. He isn't running it. Someone else is. Thompson is simply the Crow's Nest contact."

"What do we do?" Matrone looked from one to the other.

"Find Marian." Gilbert slapped the book down and stood. "But none of this tells us where Thompson would take her."

"And why keep her now that the shipment has come and gone?" Wilson took a third ledger, piling it on the other two without looking at it. "She has no value to him. Except to draw you out."

"Me?" Gilbert pointed to himself and then made the connection, a sinking feeling in his stomach. "Why didn't I see this sooner? I know the ledgers. I figured it out. He needs to eliminate me, and Marian is his leverage. She warned me he would do that, and I didn't believe her. I thought for sure I could manipulate the situation to keep her out of it. Now they know I'm working against them and he can't let that stand."

"Then he'll be in contact with you." Wilson spoke with an authority that said he'd been through this before. Not exactly comforting seeing that Wilson was probably the one *doing* the kidnapping. "My guess is he'll go to the house. More leverage with the girls there."

Gilbert's gut churned.

"What about Bella and the ladies?" Matrone pushed off the desk. "Mrs. Martins's tone suggested they wouldn't stay put for long."

Wilson accepted Matrone's observation with a nod. "Nick will go by the Martins's house before meeting Cox at the Wards's house. It makes sense for you to make your rounds, check on your sister, the girls. I'll get O'Connor. This is as good a reason as any to work with the enemy for once."

Gilbert couldn't argue there. But would Wilson double cross them?

"What are you going to do with the ledgers?" Nick raised his black eyebrow over his spectacles. Obviously, he was thinking the same thing.

"Take them straight to the detective." Wilson tucked them under his arm. "If anyone is rumrunning in this town, it's under my supervision. I won't abide rogue doctors using children and widows as his armor. This ends today."

Gilbert exchanged a glance with Nick. Buck Wilson was a scoundrel, Gilbert had no doubt about that. But there was a noble layer underneath his put-on polish that didn't fit his persona in the least. For now, Gilbert would trust that sliver of goodness and hope it was enough to save his family.

Marian held her girls close as Dr. Thompson paced the front room of their home. He muttered about how Gilbert ruined a perfectly good situation and he'd tell him so when he arrived. What the doctor planned to do after that, Marian didn't know. It couldn't be good. And now her children were in the middle of the danger. Exactly what she hoped to avoid. They quietly cried against her, breaking her heart. Mrs. Cox and the Johnsons were tied up in Elaine's old bedroom. More leverage should Thompson need it.

She watched the doctor pace. If her girls weren't here, she would calculate how to stop him, but with that gun in his hand, she wouldn't risk her girls being injured. Still, she kept watch because, if a sure enough opportunity presented itself, she would end this standoff. No one messed with her family.

"Where is that husband of yours?" Thompson wagged the pistol in her face. He'd sent another of his men to Mrs. Whittlebush's house to retrieve Gilbert. The man had yet to return. "I have a train to catch, but

I have to make sure he won't send the law after me. He knows too much. You know too much. If you would have just left well enough alone, your girls would be safe. I'm not a killer, you know."

"Then let us go." Marian ground out the words, trying desperately to keep her emotion under control. Fear for her girls, worry for Gilbert, it all wrapped an invisible chain around her chest.

"I can't do that." Dr. Thompson waved his arms, his raspy voice grating on her nerves. "You've left me no choice. You understand that, don't you?"

"You always have a choice." Marian kissed each girl's head. *Lord, please deliver us.*

A car rumbled into the yard. Dr. Thompson adjusted his spectacles as he peered over their heads. "That's Whittlebush's car. About time."

Marian's pulse raced, but she forced herself to stay calm. The girls were frightened enough. But Gilbert! He was ill, and needed a doctor to heal him, not harm him. She tugged her girls closer, needing their comfort as much as she gave it. She loved their patchwork family and Dr. Thompson threatened it. How could she save her loved ones?

Loved ones? Yes. Loved ones. The fierce emotion rising in her as the rumble of the car engine stopped told her one thing very clearly. She counted Gilbert as a loved one. She loved him. He was her family. And she'd do everything she could to protect him.

"Gilbert needs a doctor." Marian scooted to the edge of the sofa. "You have an oath to treat him."

"Stop your prattling, woman!" Thompson smacked the back of his hand against her cheek. Her girls whimpered and Marian clenched her teeth to keep from showing pain.

The back door slammed open. "Thompson!" Gilbert shouted, sounding healthy and hale. How? And why wasn't he a captive like the doctor planned?

Thomson aimed his gun down the hall. "I have your little family, Cox. Come down the hall slowly and give yourself up." *No!*

"Hiding behind women and children, doc?" Gilbert's disembodied voice flung itself from the kitchen, not a hint of cough. "If you want me, come face me like a man."

Oh, Gilbert!

Thompson yanked her from the sofa, his grip on her upper arm surprisingly strong. Her girls cried out as he separated them.

"It's okay." She infused her voice with as much confidence as she could. "Mama will meet you at—"

"Shut up." Thompson shoved her in front of him, using her as a shield and forced her toward the kitchen.

Would her girls run for help? She should have just demanded they run, but she hadn't wanted to scare them worse than they already were. That wouldn't have sent them into action. A sob caught in her throat. Her precious girls.

Thompson jabbed the gun into her side as they entered the kitchen. She immediately locked eyes with Gilbert. He stood with the table between them, arms loose at his side, determination in his gaze. A closer look, however, showed pale skin, sunken eyes, and the sheen of fever. Dear man. How long could he maintain a strong front?

"Now you'll do everything I ask, or I'll harm your woman." Dr. Thompson cocked the hammer of his pistol, his stubble scratching Marian's ear. "It's simple. I'll bind all of you, stick you in the bedroom with the others, then let my men set the stove to smoke. It'll be a painless way to die. You'll simply fall asleep. Unless you'd like a morphine shot. I can do that instead."

Marian shivered. How could a medical man, sworn to heal, turn to murder?

"We won't be doing either, Thompson." Gilbert leaned on the table, showing the first sign of weakness. They needed to take Thompson down now, before Gilbert's strength gave out. "You're going to take me and leave my wife alone."

No he was not. Marian looked daggers at her husband. They were in this together. Had been since before they said *I do*.

"I don't think so." Thompson tossed rope on the table. The moment was gone before Marian could act, not that she could get away from the gun pointed at her side. She wouldn't miss her next chance. "Bind up your hands. Let's go."

Gilbert calmly took up the rope, his gaze meeting Marian's with such loving concern it melted her heart. "Have you ever cooked fowl before, Love?"

"Chicken, of course." What an odd question. Shoving the soft feelings away, she narrowed in on her husband. What was he getting at? Gilbert measured the rope Thompson tossed, draping it slowly over his wrists. Complying, and yet ...

"I was thinking about another type of bird." And then he winked. "Like *duck*."

Gilbert disappeared behind the table. Marian dropped, the sudden motion causing her to slip out of Thompson's startled arms. Gilbert pulled her under the table as the back door slammed open. He wrapped her in his arms, putting himself between her and Thompson.

"Drop the gun and put your hands up!" Detective O'Connor ordered as he stormed inside. Marian gasped. Gilbert brought reinforcements.

Gilbert's long exhale ended in a deep, rattling cough. Marian squirmed from Gilbert's grasp as the detective disarmed the doctor. One danger ended, but Gilbert needed medical care immediately. He gasped between each cough, bent double and braced on shaking arms. He'd given everything to save her.

Marian scrambled for a cup of water, then supported him as she helped him drink, confident Detective O'Connor would handle his job.

After a sip, Gilbert shook his head and pulled Marian to his chest. With a wheeze, he whispered, "Are you okay? I had to wait for the signal."

"Yes, yes, I'm fine. But I left the girls in the front room." She needed to get to them. Now. But Gilbert couldn't stand.

"Nick got them out through the front door." He nodded toward Detective O'Connor, who quirked a finger toward the hall. "And here they are."

The girls raced into the kitchen, skidding around the table, and threw themselves into Marian's arms, sending a cascade of relief through her. Tears streamed down Marian's cheeks as she held her little ones close. Gilbert hugged their whole little patchwork family and a piece of Marian's heart healed.

"It's over." Buck Wilson's voice interrupted the wonderful moment. Marian lifted her head to see what was happening. Buck glared at Thompson, who was now shackled and firmly in Detective O'Connor's grip. "I'm ashamed of you, Dr. Thompson. Rumrunning under my nose. You know you'd never have been caught if you told me your business."

Detective O'Connor muttered under his breath. Gilbert shook his head, then rested it on Marian's shoulder. The heat of it shattered the good warmth she'd felt a moment ago. She pressed her wrist to his forehead. He was burning up!

"Buck!" Marian lay Gilbert on the kitchen floor, her girls holding onto each other as they watched with wide eyes. "Get Nick right now. It's Gil."

241

CHAPTER SEVENTEEN

Saturday, February 21

Gilbert hunkered into his wool coat as he traversed the space between the house and the Curiosity Shop.

Two weeks of recovery and he was slowly regaining his strength from the flu that had turned into pneumonia. For a day or so, he'd been closer to death than he liked to admit, and that wasn't from the threat Dr. Thompson presented. His fever had raged so that he remembered little but panicked dreams and the comforting voice of the woman he loved. Marian hadn't left his side. Had nursed him back to health. For her, he fought to hold on. And it was she whom he sought now.

As much as he wanted to hurry, neither his lungs nor his legs would allow that. By the time he reached the barn, he was winded and exhausted. Nick assured him he'd regain his strength eventually. His boss fired him when he couldn't work—having no compassion for Gilbert's illness—but between Nick and Buck, they made sure Gilbert had references to begin his own accounting business. Right now, however, he was simply grateful to be alive. Alive and with the family he adored.

"Marian?" Gilbert slipped into the barn. With their plans to leave soon for Montana, Marian was setting the shop in order. There was much yet to decide, including finding a buyer for the property. However, Gilbert planned to make use of the welcome home celebration this evening to explore those details. The Martins brothers—David and Patrick—and their women were expected on the train this afternoon, and Mrs. Whittlebush invited close friends to her place, which provided a perfect opportunity to present the brothers with an offer.

"In the front," Marian called from the other side of the building.

Gilbert set aside those thoughts as he wove through the furniture and displays, stopping when Marian came into view. She stood behind the counter, bent over a book. Her brown hair was knotted at the back of her head, stray strands framing her face. She tapped a pencil as she nibbled on her lip and his heart gave a lurch. She was beautiful, inside and out. He'd thank God every day for the blessing of a good wife.

He strode forward, circling the counter. Marian looked up with question and surprise. Gilbert didn't give her a chance to speak. He slipped one arm around her waist to draw her close, the other hand he cupped her face to angle it for a kiss. Kisses he'd missed while he was sick. Marian sank into his embrace, and Gilbert held her even closer.

She hadn't left his side when the pneumonia nearly took him. She'd even slept beside him, keeping him warm as the fever chilled his bones. Once he was well enough, their kisses had grown more frequent. But still she held back on offering herself fully to him as husband and wife. He wasn't sure why, but didn't push, determined to assure her of the extent of his feelings for her. He loved her and wanted her to know how much. No matter how long it took.

His chest convulsed, and he broke away to cough. Dratted lungs! He fisted his hand on the counter as he bent over to clear the congestion that lingered. Her touch on his back eased the strained muscles.

"Take easy breaths, Gil." Marian soothed. "We have a lifetime together."

He looked over his shoulder at her, her words striking him. "Is that why ..."

A blush covered her cheeks. She kissed his temple. "Yes. When you're all better, we—"

He didn't let her finish. He had to kiss her again. Only, his lungs hadn't recovered, and the kiss was once again interrupted with a coughing fit. How he hated this! He wanted his wife, especially now that he knew she was ready to be fully his.

Marian raised her eyebrow. "What brought you out here, dear husband?"

Changing the subject was she? He wrapped his arm around her waist. "A kiss isn't a good enough reason?"

She rolled her eyes, and planted her hands on his chest, not pushing away, but keeping him from kissing her again.

He did have a reason for seeking her out here, a reason not high on his priorities at the moment. But since she insisted ... "My mother has the girls enthralled in reading *Anne of Green Gables* for, what, the third time? And the Johnsons are packing up the other books. I made my escape before I got put to work." His gaze strayed toward his father's desk.

"Ah, that's why you came out here." Her voice was soft. He glanced back at her, grateful not to see hurt in her eyes. "Is it because of Greg Alistar's insistence there is a treasure?"

He couldn't meet her gaze. That was an excuse, but not the reason. He didn't care about treasure. He'd found one already. "Before we leave, I want to set that rumor to rest."

She ran her hand down his arm to tangle her fingers with his. "And perhaps make peace with your father?"

Gilbert nodded. How well she knew him already. Leaving Wisconsin meant leaving his father and the past behind, and Gilbert didn't want to bring the hurt with him. Going west was a new beginning for all of them.

Marian tugged him out from behind the counter, bringing him closer to the desk that first connected their families. The desk behind which his father had ruled. Ugly memories surfaced, but one in particular stood out.

Gilbert rested a palm on the dusty surface. "He stood here, fists planted, when he disowned me. He'd shouted and yelled at me before, but that day, he raged. Face red and purple. Called me every ugly name because I refused to help him cover his greed by using my accounting skills. I walked out and didn't look back."

Marian leaned her head against his shoulder.

"If I'd stood up to him, found evidence to convict him, he never would have swindled your family." The guilt still weighed on him. "I'm sorry, Marian. I'm sorry for all the pain my family has caused you."

She pried his hand from the desk and drew him close. "Without that pain, you wouldn't have been brought into my life. My girls have a father again. I have a husband, whom I love."

He blinked, but couldn't stop the tear that leaked down his cheek.

Marian wiped it away, then wrapped her arms around his waist. "Two plus two might equal four in the accounting world, but when God is part of the equation ... what man intended for evil, God can redeem. You came to make amends, but God used you to save us and bring a criminal to justice. And, He gave you a family."

What man intended for evil. Peace washed through him. *God can redeem.* Which meant Gilbert didn't have to, and the striving to do so dropped from his shoulders. Forgiving his father would take time, but he wasn't responsible for the man's actions. He could finally put behind him the damage his father had caused, and look to a future of blessing and hope. Like a winter pansy, blooming amid the icy snow.

Gilbert ran a finger down his wife's cheek, gratefulness surging through him. "I love you, Marian Ward Cox."

"I love you, too." She lifted up on tiptoes to lay a gentle kiss on his lips. "Now, let's see if we can find any other hidden compartments in this massive desk."

An hour later, Marian sat back on her haunches, hands and skirt filthy. Gilbert knew the desk well, but he'd been studying the bottom right drawer for the past ten minutes. She tried suggesting a break, but he wouldn't hear of it.

"There's a false bottom here, I'm sure of it," he muttered. "If I can just figure out …"

She smiled. It was the third time he'd said that. She believed him, though. The proportions of the drawer indicated a secret compartment.

A log shifted in the stove she'd lighted when they began their search. She rose, stirred the embers. Gilbert may not want to pause his search, but she wouldn't let him get chilled.

He'd been so sick, she'd feared she would lose him. Her girls bounced back quickly, but even Nick hadn't been able to hide his concern over Gilbert's condition. When Nick's medicine could do no more, Mrs. Cox, Mrs. Martins, and Mrs. Whittlebush plied Gilbert with every remedy they could. In those dark hours, Marian relived losing Zachariah. And when Gilbert's fever broke, she knew God had given her a second chance, a second love. No more holding back, Gilbert was her husband and she wanted to enjoy every moment God gave them together.

Which is why she indulged his search while also making sure he stayed warm. To see curiosity and determination mingle in his expression, the health returning to his cheeks. She'd watch him add numbers in a ledger, if it gave her the opportunity to just be with him.

A click sounded, and Gilbert gave a sharp inhale that ended in a cough. He gave his chest two pounds before he lifted a cover from the drawer. Marian slid closer to see what his father had hidden in the drawer, and gasped.

"Is that ... money?" Marian stared at her husband.

He turned wide eyes on her, his jaw hanging. He closed his mouth, opened it again, then shook his head. The man was speechless.

She pointed at the bundled bills. "May I?"

He nodded, made room for her next to him.

Marian lifted out six bundles of twenty-dollar bills, awe hushing her voice. "There must be three thousand dollars here."

"It's yours, Marian." Gilbert cleared his throat. "What my father swindled from your family, this repays the debt with interest."

"It doesn't feel right." The money sat between them, and she didn't like it. "Your father took advantage of others, too. We should divide this, give it to them."

"But he didn't threaten them like he did you. Didn't send Silas and Cora to work out West."

Marian pushed the money aside to slide closer to Gilbert. She put her hands on his shoulders. "I don't care about the money, Gil. I don't need it. I want you. And if that money comes between us, then I definitely want nothing to do with it."

His eyes took on a watery sheen.

"You're my husband, Gil. And worth more to me than any amount of money." The truth of that statement burrowed deep in her soul. "I love you."

He pulled her into his arms, wrapping her so tight she could feel his shuddering breath.

The girls interrupted the moment, and Marian quickly gathered up the bills. She'd give them to Detective O'Connor, let him figure out what to do with the money. With that in mind, they left for the Martins's homecoming party earlier than necessary with the hopes of catching the detective before he left home. Mrs. Cox complained of a headache and sent them to the party without her. When they arrived, Samson not only greeted them, but also kept the girls occupied while Marian and Gilbert explained about the money to Detective O'Connor.

"And what does your mother think of the money?" Detective O'Connor raised a bushy eyebrow.

Marian glanced at Gilbert. "I hadn't thought to ask." Should she have?

"It's not ours." Gilbert folded his arms. "When my father sold the desk, he sold everything inside. The desk belongs to Marian."

Detective O'Connor's mustache twitched. "You're married to Marian, so it is still yours."

Gilbert blew out a breath that caused him to cough. Marian rubbed between his shoulder blades and said, "We don't want the money, Detective O'Connor. We're putting that part of our life behind us."

"I heard about your move to Montana." The detective looked from one to the other. "You don't want to use the money to get set up there?"

Marian was already shaking her head. "I don't want that to be the foundation of our marriage, our family. Use it here."

"Are you sure?" Detective O'Connor asked Gilbert, making Marian bristle. Didn't the man hear what she said?

"The money is Marian's to do with as she chooses. I can provide for my family, detective. We might not be rich, but I will make sure all my girls are happy."

Detective O'Connor smiled, causing his eyes to twinkle. He clapped Gilbert on the shoulder. "Right answer, my boy. I'll take care of the money. You have my blessing. Not that you needed it." He winked at Marian. She couldn't help but return his smile, his approval meaning more than she realized it could.

Later that evening, Gilbert sat ensconced in the crook of the sofa in Mrs. Whittlebush's front room. Marian insisted he stay put while people mingled, and with his energy flagging, he happily complied. It gave him an opportunity to watch Marian as she interacted with her friends. Her graciousness, her smile. Were they doing the right thing, moving away from Crow's Nest?

"So you're Marian's new husband." David Martins lowered himself to the sofa beside Gilbert. They'd met earlier, when David, Adaleigh,

Patrick, and Patrick's pregnant wife, Meri, arrived. But in the crush of people, Gilbert had retreated. He was a stranger, and he wasn't sure of his welcome.

"I am." Gilbert braced for David's reaction.

David folded his arms, straining the stitches of his blue knit sweater, and leaned back against the cushion, feet stretched out and ankles crossed. "Silas insisted I give my stamp of approval, since he's not here. We're good friends, you know. Silas and Zachariah and I spent our childhood together."

Gilbert nodded. He wouldn't offer anything until he saw where David was going with this. But his gaze drifted to Marian, where she conversed with Mindy and Adaleigh. Three very different women. Marian with her straight brown hair, her simple beauty tugging at Gilbert. Adaleigh stood regally, even as she leaned slightly forward, her attention shifting to whomever was speaking as if that person held the secret of life. And Mindy, her blonde hair held back by pins, the waves bouncing as she animatedly told a story.

"A good woman is hard to find." David was also looking at the trio. "Hard to feel worthy when your father is a rotten one."

Gilbert zeroed in on the man beside him, suddenly remembering that David had a difficult relationship with his own dad. Gilbert hadn't learned the details, but he didn't need them to recognize someone who carried a similar wound as he did.

"Can we be the men our women deserve when we haven't had a good example?" David continued, whether to Gilbert or himself wasn't clear. He leaned toward Gilbert. "I finally proposed, you know. She said yes."

"Congratulations." It seemed the right thing to say, but David's tone wasn't celebratory.

"I'm equal parts thrilled and terrified. Awed, too. Adaleigh is so smart, sophisticated, beautiful. That she'd take up with a fishing captain ..." He gave a self-depreciating chuckle. "But I aim to give her the best life I can. I love her, and I'd give my own life for her."

The fierceness in David's words reverberated within Gilbert.

"As would I for Marian." As he declared his affirmation, a weight slipped from his shoulders. He didn't have to be enough. Not for Marian or the girls. If he followed God, trusted Him to help him love Marian as sacrificially as he vowed on their wedding day, then he could be the husband Marian deserved. And the father Nettie and Essie needed.

David slapped the back of his hand against Gilbert's thigh. "I'll tell Silas that Marian is in good hands. Once he meets you, he'll think so, too."

"Thanks, Martins." Gilbert shifted uncomfortably at the sudden acceptance. He changed to a less emotional subject. "So when's your wedding?"

"Probably after the fishing season is over, so this fall or winter." David shook his head. "Never expected my little brother to beat me to the altar, not that I was even looking for a wife when Adaleigh arrived in Crow's Nest. Need to get Patrick and Meri settled before the baby comes."

Gilbert smiled at David's protectiveness. "Think they'd like their own house?"

"Marian's?" David raised an eyebrow, looking very much like a younger version of his uncle, the detective. "Like I said, Silas filled me in. So did my grandmother."

"Your grandmother is an amazing woman." Gilbert rubbed his chest, where his lungs were still sore from coughing. "I might not have survived pneumonia without her and Mrs. Whittlebush. And Nick."

David laughed. "Yeah, Nick. The man arrives just when you don't want him, and yet exactly when you need him."

Gilbert couldn't agree more. Though bookish, with his spectacles and lanky frame, Nick set women at ease. Women of all ages, considering he currently had a captive audience in Mrs. Whittlebush, Mindy, and Essie, leaving Marian and Adaleigh to converse alone.

David stood and waved his brother over. Patrick escorted his wife across the room and Gilbert made room beside him on the sofa. They helped her sit, an awkward enterprise, and she rested a hand on her belly, which was large with child.

"Only another two months, I think." She smiled at Gilbert. Her green eyes glowing despite the weary lines surrounding them. "Thank you for letting me join you. I can't stand for too long these days."

Patrick folded his arms, standing guard over his wife, looking tough with his blonde scruff shading his jaw. From what Gilbert gathered, Patrick had been rebellious and irresponsible before he left with David for the lumber camp. Now he returned with a wife expecting a child. The math didn't quite add up, so there was a story there. Gilbert wanted to ask, but etiquette held his tongue.

Instead, he broached the topic of the newlyweds buying the farm.

"A home of my own? Land that we own?" A tear slipped down Meri's cheek and Patrick immediately knelt before her. "Can we afford it?"

"We can work out a plan." Gilbert jumped in. How could he not? Any woman, especially a mother, who expressed such emotion over having her own home demanded his sympathies. "I'm an accountant. We'll figure out a way."

"A way for what?" Marian joined them, a special smile just for Gilbert.

He rose, waving her to take his place, but snagged her fingers before she sat. "A way for Patrick and Meri to buy our home." His heart pounded. Would Marian approve? It wasn't his property, not really. It belonged to Marian and her late first husband's family. Had he overstepped, and would Meri be crushed?

He shouldn't have worried. Marian lit up like the very sun itself. She planted a kiss on his cheek. "That's a fabulous idea! Oh, Meri, I would love for you to live in our home." She dropped to the sofa beside Meri, took the young mother's hands in hers.

"Truly?" Meri beamed. Patrick tightened his hold on her knee as a telltale glimmer shown in his eye. David nudged Gilbert's shoulder with his own, offering a simple nod of approval.

"Oh yes. I couldn't choose better." Marian dashed a tear from her cheek. "I know we haven't seen each other in years, but to think the little girl I used to watch over while my mama cooked for the lumberjacks is now a grown woman, a wife, a mother ... Of course you should have my home. I can think of no one better."

The women hugged, and Gilbert couldn't help but smile. He hadn't forgotten Marian grew up in a lumber camp, but that she knew Meri from childhood was news to him. However, it only made his idea sweeter. And Marian and Meri were happy, which is what counted.

"I'm loath to break up such a happy moment." Adaleigh stepped into the group, tucking an arm around David's. She leaned around her fiancé to see Gilbert. "Might I have a private word with Mr. Cox?"

They all exchanged glances filled with curiosity. At Marian's nod, Gilbert followed Adaleigh into Mrs. Whittlebush's seamstress parlor, hoping he wouldn't need to submit to another third degree.

Marian watched Gilbert until he disappeared into the other room, not liking the uneasy feeling in her stomach. She wanted her friends to approve of her husband, not judge him for the identity of his father.

"What do you think that's about?" Meri asked the question burning in Marian's mind.

Marian tamped down on the protectiveness surging through her. Gilbert could take care of himself. And Adaleigh was a kind soul. It had been years since Marian had seen Meri, and she'd like to hear Meri and Patrick's story. Though, from a glance at Meri's large belly, their conversation might be best over tea between the two of them. Mother to mother.

She glanced at David, caught his frown. If David worried, too, then that decided it. Marian stood. "Care to join them?"

David didn't need to be asked twice. As they took their leave of Patrick and Meri, Marian checked the location of her girls. Nick and Mindy held their complete attention. Marian cocked her head at the scene, struck by how comfortable the four looked together, but David escorted her into the hall before a thought fully formed. Detective O'Connor's distinctive laugh came from the kitchen, along with Mrs. Martins's scolding and Bella Matrone's giggle. Where had Mrs. Whittlebush and Samantha gotten to, then?

"Oh, good. I knew you'd join us," Adaleigh announced as Marian and David entered the sewing room. Gilbert rested his hands on his hips, his gaze immediately going to Marian's, assuring her all was well. Then why was Samantha chewing her lip as Mrs. Whittlebush fussed over her?

"What's going on?" Suspicion laced David's tone. He looked from one person to the next, his feet shifting, but he stayed by Marian. Rarely had she seen the man indecisive, and he certainly took every chance to be close to Adaleigh.

Adaleigh tipped her chin toward Sam. "I told her what Kyle said before we left camp."

David groaned. "It couldn't wait until—"

"Of course it couldn't wait!" Sam shouted at her brother, her chin wobbling. "Of course I noticed he didn't come back to Crow's Nest with you. And of course I asked Adaleigh why. He was the first person I looked for when you walked in the door. He didn't even have the decency to tell me he wasn't returning to Crow's Nest himself. A letter. A telegram. Anything."

Oh, poor girl. Marian's heart broke for her. She glanced at Gilbert, expecting a sympathetic response, but he avoided her gaze this time. What was that about? What did Adaleigh tell him before Marian and David arrived?

"I'm sorry, Sam." David reached for her, but Sam backed into Mrs. Whittlebush's embrace. The older woman clucked over her like a mother hen, effectively keeping David away. David's arms flopped back at his sides. "I tried to convince him to return, Sam. Honest. With him gone, I need a new first mate."

"All about work for you, isn't it?" Sam lost the battle with her tears. "It's always about work for all of you."

David stared at the ceiling and blew out a breath.

"I have a solution." Adaleigh stepped into the center of the room, between the siblings. "Actually, Mr. Cox turned my idea into a practical one, after I assured myself of his integrity. Naturally."

Marian bristled. Gilbert bowed his head. "I already did that," David grumbled. Adaleigh simply grinned at her fiancé and David shook his head, but the smile he tried to hide betrayed his affection.

Determined to show support to her husband, Marian skirted the room and slipped her arm around Gilbert's. He leaned close to her ear,

"I'm sorry I couldn't confer with you first." She patted his arm. She trusted him. He squeezed her fingers.

"Since Kyle decided not to return, and with Marian and Gilbert traveling west," Adaleigh acknowledged them, but returned her focus to David. "Sam would like to travel with the Cox family."

"What?" David stared first at his fiancée, then at his sister, who ducked her head into Mrs. Whittlebush's shoulder. "Leave Crow's Nest? Leave … us?"

"David." Adaleigh put a hand on his chest, but spoke as much to him as to the room. "Marian's parents are moving with the lumber camp out West. Kyle is going with them. Sending Sam moves her closer to Kyle."

"Chasing a boy?" David folded his arms, trapping Adaleigh's hand.

"Helping a mother, or two." Adaleigh waved at Marian. "You know if Cora has children, she'll need an extra hand with the way her health has been."

"And Sam will be a great help as my apprentice." Mrs. Whittlebush spoke up for the first time.

"Wait, what?" Marian interrupted. How could Sam be an apprentice if Mrs. Whittlebush remained in Crow's Nest?

The older lady smiled. "I miss Cora. Gilbert was kind enough to suggest this as a perfect opportunity to join the caravan. We can all go west together."

"Oh, Gil." Marian hugged her husband's arm. What a blessing to have Mrs. Whittlebush join them! Not just for Cora's sake, but Marian's as well. She loved Mrs. Whittlebush like a second mother, and with the loss of her own mother-in-law, it warmed her heart to think she wouldn't be leaving everyone behind when they left.

"You're still leaving Crow's Nest." David directed the statement at Sam, the forlorn words bringing Adaleigh to wrap an arm around his waist.

Mrs. Whittlebush gave Sam a nudge. The young woman wiped at her tears, then pushed her black hair away from her damp cheeks. "It's not the only reason to go west, David. One of the reasons Mr. Cox is taking Marian to Silas and Cora's is because of the danger she faced. I saw the thugs, too, remember? If it's safer for Marian to leave Crow's Nest, then it's wise for me to do so, too. If it brings me closer to Kyle ... If he didn't even send me a letter to tell me he wasn't returning, then we might not have a future anyway. I need to make my own path. You and Patrick will be settled here, you'll be with Grandma."

"Does she know?" David's voice choked.

Sam nodded. "She's the one who first planted the idea. Both as Mrs. Whittlebush's apprentice and for my safety. When Adaleigh told me about Kyle, she pulled Mr. Cox to see whether the idea was even possible."

"And I think it is." Gilbert straightened, as if a soldier accepting his commission. "I'll look out for her like she was my own sister. I'll bring her safely to Silas, and I know you trust him to care for her. Between Marian, Cora, and Mrs. Whittlebush, Sam will be well."

Marian rested her head on Gilbert's shoulder, her heart bursting with respect and love for her husband.

"Is this what you want?" David asked Sam.

She nodded. "If the Cox family will have me."

"Absolutely." Marian had no hesitation. Gilbert nodded.

David crossed to Gilbert, and Marian stepped away to let the men have their moment. David gripped Gilbert's free shoulder. "I'm relying on you to take care of my sister."

Gilbert reached to shake David's free hand, accepting the responsibility. "You can trust me. Marian and I will take Sam under our wing."

David sighed. "All right then."

Sam squealed and hugged her brother's back. Adaleigh and Mrs. Whittlebush exchanged smiles.

Marian, however, hooked her arm around Gilbert, drawing him into a hug. She rose up on her toes. "You're a good man, Gilbert Cox, and I'm proud to be your wife."

EPILOGUE

Easter Sunday, April 5
Blue Spruce, Montana

Marian set the lamb roast on the new table, her heart full. Their first Easter in Montana was cause for celebration. Not only because of the reason for the holiday, but because her whole family was here together. Her husband, her children, her new mother-in-law ... Even her parents had arrived yesterday. Silas, who'd built them the table, and Cora, who was indeed expecting their first child and worried whether she'd even be able to eat the meal. Samantha Martins and Mrs. Whittlebush, too. Marian wanted to wrap her arms around the whole gathering and hold them close while she could.

"It smells delicious, Love." Gilbert grinned, then tugged her arm, drawing her lips to his for a quick kiss.

"Eww!" Nettie stuck out her tongue. "You kiss too much."

All three men laughed, and Marian patted her warm cheeks. Gilbert tweaked Nettie's nose. "I love your mama, sweetie. I want everyone to know it."

Marian took her seat across from Gilbert, not missing the sadness dampening Sam's eyes. She'd hoped Kyle would travel with Marian's parents when they relocated to Montana in advance of Aleric Lumber's move from Wisconsin. But Kyle had stayed behind, planning to come with the equipment this summer. Sam still hadn't received a letter or any word from Kyle, and Marian's mother had expressed her sympathies over not having better news for the young woman. For some unknown reason, Kyle had to find his own way right now.

Nevertheless, Sam had thrown herself wholeheartedly into becoming an accomplished seamstress. She and Mrs. Whittlebush set up shop in the little town of Blue Spruce. Sam's presence brought many a cowboy looking for new duds, but her flirtatious ways had dampened since leaving Crow's Nest.

Marian took Sam's and Essie's hands as the table joined hands to pray for the meal. Gratefulness welled within Marian. She missed Crow's Nest, but those she loved most sat around this table. Between the women seated here, there was no want for help with Nettie and Essie. Unlike Sam, the girls had blossomed since arriving in Blue Spruce, Nettie especially. They loved their new school, the horses Silas let them ride, and chatting with anyone who walked by their new little house.

Gilbert's prayer brought Marian out of her thoughts, but only doubled her gratefulness as he thanked God for giving His Son. Easter, a time of new beginnings, of fresh starts, of God providing a way for everlasting life. Again, Marian reflected that what man had meant for evil—killing the Messiah—God used to redeem all of mankind. *Thank you, Jesus.*

As *amens* echoed around the table, Marian attempted to surreptitiously swipe at the tear that trickled down her cheek. Of course her new mother-in-law noticed as she passed the spring peas Cora had provided. The understanding smile she gave Marian caused another tear to slip free.

Mrs. Cox was a different woman than Elaine Ward, and a different mother-in-law as well. Instead of being a nurturing second mother, Mrs. Cox pushed Marian toward her strengths. The woman had a backbone of steel, and after living with a man like her husband, Mrs. Cox flourished in her independence. With the help of Mr. and Mrs. Johnson, Mrs. Cox established a boarding house for women. With so few women in the area, having a safe, reputable place for the unmarried ones to stay opened up more opportunities for them. Sam and Blue Spruce's teacher were her first residents.

"I have an announcement." Silas plopped a spoonful of potatoes on his plate and winked at Cora. "We have an announcement."

Chatter erupted around the table. It couldn't be about the baby because Cora had already confided that wonderful news, seeking Marian's advice. Cora's health had improved since her days in Crow's Nest. Except for the nausea, but Marian attributed that to being in the family way. Like Mrs. Cox, Cora seemed fitted to the wide open spaces, albeit in a very different way. Mrs. Cox rarely left Blue Spruce, while Cora was always finding ways to explore. Most recently, she had befriended the women living in the nearby Blackfeet Indian Reservation, learning their language and recording their stories.

Cora chuckled, her expression full of love for her husband. "Don't keep them in suspense, now. Share your news."

Silas grinned. "My boss is retiring, which was behind his big push to get me to return to Crooked Tooth Ranch. I'm now the new foreman." Congratulations spread around the table, but Silas spoke over everyone. "The best part is that I get the foreman's house, which means my family will now live on the ranch with me."

Marian clapped. After months living apart because Silas's position did not allow for him to have a wife on the ranch, this was wonderful news indeed! "I'm so happy for both of you." Marian shared an especially large smile with Cora. The former archaeologist would make the perfect ranch foreman's wife, with her love of the outdoors.

"And I'm officially hiring Cox as our accountant." Silas pointed his fork at Gilbert. "My boss handled the books, but with Gil in the family, it's a task I can delegate. Old Man Orson demands the best, you know. His spread survived the winter of '86, and has only grown since, when others have failed. I won't let him down now."

"He still owns the place?" Gilbert rested a forearm on the table. "How active is he in running it?"

"He and his wife are both well into their eighties, and both still participate in the day-to-day." Silas smiled at his wife. "If Cora and I can have half the love they still show after sixty years, I will be one blessed man."

Gilbert cast a similar look at Marian, one that promised more when they were alone. She ducked her head as heat climbed her cheeks.

Ever since Dr. Thompson kidnapped them, and Gilbert survived his bout with pneumonia, he'd been anything but shy about showing his love for her, no matter their audience. In fact, he seemed to enjoy flaunting propriety to make sure everyone knew just how much he loved his wife. Despite her almost permanent blush, she didn't mind at all. Not even one little bit.

Finally the house was empty, the girls were asleep, and the last rays of daylight were fading. Gilbert rested his palms on the porch railing of their little home on the outskirts of Blue Spruce and breathed deeply of the clean mountain air. It had been a delightful day, but he couldn't wait to get his wife alone.

"There you are." Marian emerged, the front screen slapping shut behind her. Her skirts rustled over the dusty porch as she came to stand beside him. Their new home was a cozy place, albeit smaller than the home they'd had in Crow's Nest. Still, Gilbert loved it because it housed his family. "It's chilly tonight."

He tucked her in front of him, her back to his chest, so he could wrap his arms around her. "Not so cold when I have you," he said into her ear. She chuckled, and Gilbert grinned. He loved that sound.

She rested her hands over his. "Are you happy, Gil?"

"Happy is too mild a word, Love." He kissed her hair. "I am the most blessed man."

She raised her chin, bringing her cheek to his chin. "Even here? On the edges of the wilderness and far away from Wisconsin?"

He turned her so he could see her face. He searched her expression, trying to understand. "Where's this coming from?"

"You moved away from your home." She shrugged, but it belied how much his answer would mean to her. "You've done so much for us, providing and protecting. You gave up your comfortable bachelor life to become an instant husband and father. Are you sure you have no regrets?"

Regrets? The idea was laughable, but expressing any humor would not portray the correct message. Instead, he cupped Marian's face in his hands. "How could I regret being married to you? You are my world.

Our girls are precious treasures. Life with you is all I could ever ask for, and as long as we are together, I could live on the top of a mountain."

Her chocolate eyes shimmered in the fading light and Gilbert wanted to kiss her, but he held back, knowing he needed to ask one more question. A question that cinched his heart.

He summoned his bravery. "And what about you, Love? You had to remarry. And not just any man, someone you could consider the enemy. You had to leave your husband's grave, the house you lived in together. Are *you* happy?"

She ran her hands up his chest to circle around his neck. "I'm very happy, Gil. I never thought I'd find love again after Zachariah died. I had no plans to even look for it, let alone hope it would come to pass. And yet, here you are. I couldn't have asked for a better man to rely on, Gilbert Cox. I love you more than words can say."

"And I love you." He kissed her then. There on the front porch for all the world to see. And not a chaste kiss either. No, not for his wife. He held her close and deepened it, not allowing even a breath of the cool breeze to squeeze between them. How he adored this woman. And she had it right: words couldn't express how much he loved her, which left only actions.

He edged them toward the house, knowing where he wanted this kiss to go. But as he reached for the screen door, it smacked him in the back.

"Eww, you're kissing again!" Nettie announced. Gilbert groaned.

Marian pulled away, covering her mouth with a hand, her cheeks flamed red, but her eyes danced. "What do you need, sweetie?"

"We're hungry." Nettie grabbed her mother's hand, dragging her to the kitchen where Essie waited with a blanket clutched in her fist. Essie raised her arms to Gilbert, and when he lifted her, she laid her head on his shoulder. His heart melted.

"I'll cut you both a slice of bread, then back to bed." Marian went to the sideboard with graceful movements, as if she hadn't been caught kissing him. He admired her motherly ways. What would it be like to have more children together? With Marian, he couldn't imagine a better gift than a house full of family.

Nettie tugged on Gilbert's trousers' pocket, bringing him back to the kitchen. "Can you tell us a story?"

Marian glanced over her shoulder, her smile reaching to his soul. Oh, he'd do anything for these three. He tapped Nettie's nose. "Of course, sweetie. How about we finish *Anne of Green Gables*?" Nettie bounced her agreement, and Essie snuggled deeper into his shoulder.

In a few minutes, they had the girls tucked into their bed on the second floor, each nibbling a slice of bread. Marian raised the lantern flame and held it so Gilbert could see enough to read. She rested a hand on the chair back behind him, her hip leaning into him.

Gilbert cracked open the pages, reading where they'd left off until the girls finished their bread and he came to the final chapter. "'I didn't think you and Gilbert Blythe were such good friends that you'd stand for half an hour at the gate talking to him,' said Marilla with a dry smile. 'We haven't been—we've been good enemies. But we have decided that it will be much more sensible to be good friends in the future.'"

Marian laid a kiss on his head, the quiet snores of the girls filling the silence. Marian turned down the lantern and he closed the book. Snagging Marian's hand in the darkness, Anne Shirley's last words from the story filtered through his mind. *God's in his heaven, all's right with the world.*

Gilbert couldn't agree more. Marian closed the door, leaving their sleeping girls nestled in their bed. Gilbert pulled Marian into his arms. Yes, all was right indeed.

Continue the series in ...
Sheltered by the Doctor
Read on for an excerpt.

Sheltered by the Doctor

Friday, June 5, 1931
Crow's Nest, Wisconsin

A certain smiling blonde waitress had nothing to do with why Dr. Nick Matrone detoured to The Wharfside Cafe that morning. He needed coffee before seeing his first patient. The cantankerous Mrs. Bindle. An older widow who came into the clinic at least once a week complaining of one malady or another. However, in his professional medical opinion, Nick believed the woman was simply lonely. He could relate.

The sun glared off the glassy water to his left as his shoes clumped on the wooden boards of the wharf. The fishing boats were all out on Lake Michigan at this time of the morning. He'd learned enough from rooming with David Martins, a fishing captain, that such calm conditions made for poor fishing. He whispered a prayer for his friend. The man was engaged and needed the income during these lean times. Not that God listened. Nick just couldn't shake the habit of bringing every worry to Him.

He turned his face away from the brightness as his mood darkened. He tightened his grip on his satchel. Beginning a day in a grouchy mood never ended well. His patients needed him to be positive, encouraging, to foster healing. A perspective that had been increasingly difficult over the last six months. Today's newspaper headline only added to the problem.

Coffee.

Nick plowed through the empty outdoor seating and pulled open the door to the Wharfside. He spotted several of the retired captains sitting at a table in the middle of the room and promptly spun around. He didn't want to talk. Didn't want to be jovial. The gregarious Italian. He barely restrained a muttered Italian phrase that would have had his mamma crossing herself.

Sometimes he wished his skin tone was several shades lighter. His nose, not so straight. His hair, not so black. Then people would see him as a doctor. Not as someone related to Al Capone, whose indictment for tax evasion dominated the front page of today's *Crow's Nest Gazette*. Just because Nick was also Italian. No matter that he had never been to Chicago, except to travel through on his way from New York City.

Yes. He needed coffee. Lots of it.

"Dr. Matrone?" Melinda "Mindy" Zahn stepped out of the Wharfside door wearing a serviceable gray dress and white apron, her blonde hair in her usual ponytail. A beautiful, albeit questioning, smile on her fair face. She always said his name correctly, with the emphasis on the first part and the *ay* at the end. It tripped off her tongue in a lilting way he could listen to all day.

"Uh, hi." He shook his head. Being attracted to someone like Mindy wouldn't end well. A guy who looked like him didn't marry a girl who looked like her. He cleared his throat and dredged up his professional voice. "Might I get a cup of coffee while I sit out here?"

"Certainly." Her smile grew. "I'll be back in a moment."

Nick set his satchel down beside a chair and unbuttoned his suit coat. A warm breeze slipped underneath. It promised to be one of the warmest days yet, as expected, seeing that summer would officially arrive in a couple weeks.

"Did you pick a seat?" Mindy returned with a cup balanced on a saucer.

"This okay?" He waved at the table he'd chosen and tucked his thumbs into his vest pockets.

"It's a beautiful morning." She set the coffee cup on the table, then shielded her eyes as she looked out across the water. "I love early summer days. The sun feels like a warm hug, and the warmth is welcome after the winter. It's like a sheep shedding its winter coat. All the weight is gone. It's delightful."

Nick watched her, as he'd done since he met her. She was rarely static. Though she didn't talk with her hands like Nick's mother and sister, her whole body swayed as she talked, her eyes animated with her expressions. If he had a thousand years, he doubted he could read her fully. However, he loved to read.

"What is your favorite season?" She turned her wide hazel eyes on him.

"Can't say as I have one." Certainly not like she did. "New York winters are full of dirty slush. Summers, the heat is trapped in overpopulated apartments. Central Park is pretty in the fall. I never really noticed spring."

She cocked her head, her ponytail swishing over her shoulder. "I don't think I could live in a big city if that's the way the seasons went. It doesn't sound as if there is any fresh air to—Oh no." Her fingers wrapped around the edge of her apron.

Nick followed her gaze, and his stomach knotted. Joe Spelding. A chore of a man who made it his mission to seduce Mindy, or any other woman gullible enough to fall for his charms while he waited for Mindy to come around. Not that Mindy ever would. Nick had heard of their first run-in last summer, knew Mindy wanted to keep as far away from the man as she could. However, Nick knew men like Spelding. Knew they wouldn't give up easily, that their snake-oil words could weave an enchantment over the strongest of people.

"I best ..." Mindy thumbed toward the door, her hand trembling.

"Mindy." Nick stepped toward her. He hated that there seemed no solution, that Spelding didn't take a hint—or an obvious rejection. "What can I do?"

"Nothing." She grazed her fingers along his arm, so lightly he could barely feel her touch through his coat sleeve. It strengthened his resolve to do whatever he could to protect her from the scoundrel. "I avoid him when I can. When he's a customer ..."

She shrugged and slipped away. Nick worked his jaw as his mind sorted through scenarios. He'd bring it up to David tonight. There had to be something they could do. No woman should feel unsafe like this in her own community.

"Morning, Matrone." Spelding turned into the outdoor seating of the Wharfside. The man had the decency to mostly say Nick's surname as it was meant, just with the hard *n* sound at the end. Like how most people said his name. "You come here for the food or the scenery?"

Nick closed his fist at the innuendo in Spelding's voice. *Uno, due, tre* ... "Coffee."

Spelding laughed.

"If you'll excuse me." Without waiting for a response, Nick dropped into his chair and lifted his satchel to his lap. He didn't plan to look over patient files while drinking his coffee, but he needed a physical barrier to keep people—Spelding—from talking to him.

Spelding's chuckling finally ended as the door closed behind him.

Nick removed his glasses and rubbed the bridge of his nose. He was tired. So very tired. The weariness dragged his shoulders down. Even the coffee couldn't infuse his body with energy. How was he going to be kind to Mrs. Bindle with this grouchy feeling stealing any lightness inside? The sun was shining, summer was coming, he was away from the dirty city. Hope should buoy him up. Why couldn't he find his life raft?

A small figure caught his attention. A young girl in a dirty tan dress that came to her knees. Beat up shoes. Messy blonde hair. She walked almost like a ghost. Wandering. Meandering. Nick shifted, ready to react if she went too close to the edge of the wharf and the water. Instead, she turned into the cafe seating area, dragging a carpet bag behind her. Her gaze passed over him to the sign above the doorway, yet she stayed still. Strangely still.

Nick searched the wharf for anyone connected to this child. She couldn't be over eight years old. Surely there was a parent nearby. Or other relative. However, the wharf maintained its early morning quiet.

Slowly, so as not to startle the child, Nick rose from his table. Five careful steps brought him to her and he knelt. "Hi. My name is Dr. Matrone. What's your name?"

She cocked her head, reminding him so much of Mindy.

Nick's pulse picked up. "Where are your parents?"

One thin shoulder rose and fell.

"Are you looking for someone?" Nick's medical training pounded in his ears. The girl's gaunt face, questioning gaze, overly thin frame ... and the fact she showed no signs of desiring to talk ... he shoved his medical instincts aside. For the moment. He needed to find her people. He followed his suspicions. "Are you looking for Mindy?"

The little girl's eyes brightened. He eased out the breath that wanted to whoosh out. This child was connected to Mindy. Somehow.

"Can I help you find Mindy?" Nick held out a hand. She laid bony fingers, pale against his dark skin, in his palm. His heart constricted with a fierce protectiveness.

Mindy straightened her spine as she brought Joe Spelding his fish sandwich. He'd been back in Crow's Nest for several months now, and she managed to avoid him. Except when he came into the Wharfside.

"Here is your meal." She tried to keep a pleasant tone, not just because her boss expected it, but because she didn't want Joe to know how much his presence affected her.

"Thank you, doll." Joe winked, sending a shudder down Mindy's spine. She stepped out of reach in case he tried to grab her hand or attempt any other type of inappropriate touch, which he always tried to get away with. She hated it. Hated that she'd agreed to let him take her out on a date last summer. He thought that gave him a license she didn't want him to have.

Not that he was the only man to think that because she was a waitress, she was an easy woman. If only she didn't need this job to support her family.

"Will that be all?" she asked Joe as she gathered bowls from the table beside his.

The light in his eye warned that something lascivious was about to come out of his mouth. Mindy braced, praying her pale cheeks wouldn't turn red. Then the door opened. A murmured prayer wisped up from her heart.

Nick Matrone didn't look like the knights in shining armor that she imagined as a little girl, with his dark hair, glasses, and general bookish appearance. In this moment, she could almost image his lanky frame covered in chain mail instead of a suit, and a shield on his arm instead of a … her gaze caught sight of the little girl clasping Nick's hand.

"Mabel?" She set the bowls on a table with an unceremonious clatter and rushed forward. She dropped to her knees in front of her baby sister. "What's wrong? Where are Mother and Father?"

Her sister looked back at her with bright blue eyes. Mindy willed her to finally speak. Yet, Mabel's lips didn't move. Then she realized Mabel's little hand was still in Nick's larger one. Her gaze ran up his arm to connect with his. She found question there, and concern. But no judgment.

"Can you come outside?" He nodded toward the door.

Mindy glanced over her shoulder and realized the entire cafe was staring at them. Heat flared up her neck, and she pushed to her feet, desperately needing to get her sister away from so many prying eyes. Her toe caught on her skirt, and Nick caught her elbow. The touch went straight to her heart. It was respectful, protective. He held the door as he ushered them outside.

"Mabel arrived alone?" Mindy searched the wharf for any sign of her parents. Her pulse pounded in her throat. Where were they? Had Mabel wandered so far from the farm? She barely left the house.

"She came with a carpetbag." He pointed to the flowered bag, which sat on the ground beside his satchel.

Mindy pressed a hand to her chest, a bad feeling welling inside. Mabel tugged Nick toward her bag, opened it, and pulled out a folded paper.

She turned her wide eyes toward Mindy and held it out. Mindy took the paper, stared, unseeing, at it. Her heart hammered. Her ears filled with rushing. Then Nick was beside her, leading her toward a chair. He pressed fingers to her wrist, then raised her chin to look into her eyes. She latched onto their brown depths as if they could pull her from the spinning world.

"Sit here while I get Mabel settled." Nick ordered in his doctor tone, except he trailed his thumb along her jaw before he stepped away. It grounded her, made her feel the hard chair, the firm ground.

Yet worry sank deep as she watched Nick return from inside with a muffin for Mabel and a coffee for Mindy. How Mindy wished her sister would speak. Could speak. Never had her sweet little sister uttered a single word. Her parents refused to investigate why. Was it her hearing, her shyness, something else? Mindy would have paid for a doctor's visit herself, if only her father allowed it. Instead, her parents kept Mabel sequestered away on the farm. Hidden from the world as if she would shame the family. It broke Mindy's heart.

So how did Mabel get here, alone, and with baggage? Where were their parents? The paper crinkled in her fingers, and she caught sight of her mother's script. Father didn't approve of Mindy having a job, said the unwelcome male attention she received was because she worked as a waitress. Yet farming didn't bring enough money when her father bought bootlegged whiskey. Not a drunk like David Martin's father, he still overindulged during the slower seasons. Of course, Father would never hear of Mindy sending them money, so she secreted it to Mother. How Mother explained the money, she didn't know, though Mother gratefully made it stretch as needed.

Nick slid a chair beside her. "Do you want me to read it aloud?"

She turned away from him, so he wouldn't learn her secret. Even her mother didn't know. David did. He was the only one. Shame washed over her. If only the words didn't jump all over the page as she tried to read. She could decipher enough to get by ... however, to read a letter in front of Nick?

Continue reading
Sheltered by the Doctor
daniellegrandinetti.com/sheltered-by-the-doctor

HISTORICAL NOTE

The snowstorm that kept Gilbert and Marian home their first weekend together is a true historical event. On January 18, 1931 was the first big snowfall of the year. According to local newspapers at the time, it was a twenty-four-hour snowfall dropping six inches of blinding snow followed by cold weather.

Like other industries, the medical field went through dramatic growth between the World Wars. However, much is still being learned about conditions like stroke. I attempted to show the effects of what we now call a transient ischemic attack (TIA) and ischemic stroke through the lens of the 1930s, including the diagnosis and treatment. For example, the angiogram was first developed in 1927, but it would not have been available to someone in Elaine's position.

With the economic trouble of the early 1930s, the elderly, especially those with health issues like Elaine Ward, were among the most vulnerable. As part of the New Deal, the government began the Old Age Assistance program in 1935.

What about medicinal whisky? As Nick explained to Gilbert and Buck, doctors were allowed to prescribe it in 1930; however, the medical board had already denounced alcohol as a medical remedy. Nevertheless, pharmacies and doctors prescribing, supplying, and creating medical whiskey was a major loophole during prohibition.

One last historical note. Marian's attempt to garner employment at the beginning of the story was a common struggle for women, especially married women, during the Depression. During WWI, women were allowed jobs previously denied them because the men were fighting the war. However, when the men returned and jobs disappeared, women were often the first to be pushed out in the belief that they were stealing jobs from the men. Sadly, much of the progress made due to the women's rights movement of the early 1900s and the passing of the 19th Amendment was undone during the Depression. Until war again opened non-traditional roles to women on the home-front.

FROM THE AUTHOR

Dear Reader,

Thank you for reading Marian and Gilbert's story. Marriage of convenience is my favorite trope, so I was thrilled for this opportunity to write one. I hope you enjoyed it!

As I delved into an unconventional marriage, my prayer was to portray a healthy romance as it developed between two potential enemies. I welcomed the opportunity to portray Marian's strength. As a mother, and then her journey into love as her care for her new husband grew. She was a fighter, a survivor, and during a bleak winter as the Great Depression strengthened its grip, that spirit was much needed. And it's a spirit found in so many mothers today.

Then there's Gilbert. Yes, I borrowed a bit from *Anne of Green Gables*. As the son of a criminal, I wanted to garner an immediate soft spot for him. Who better than the dashing hero of Anne Shirley's story? With his pacifist leanings, Gilbert is not a typical alpha male. But his self-sacrificing love—what I picture when I read of Christ's love for the Church—endeared him to me from the start. I hope it did that for you, too.

The Harbored in Crow's Nest series continues in *Sheltered by the Doctor*. Mindy Zahn and Dr. Nick Matrone will face a fake relationship, an unwelcome suitor, and hearts in need of healing. You can find out more on my website: daniellegrandinetti.com/sheltered-by-the-doctor.

Discover the origin of Crooked Tooth Ranch in *Heart of Beauty*, a 1870s western retelling of *Beauty and the Beast*. Find more details at daniellegrandinetti.com/heart-of-beauty.

In the meantime, I'd love to keep in touch. The best way is via my weekly Fireside News email. As a thank-you, new subscribers receive a complimentary ebook. Sign up here: daniellegrandinetti.com/fsn.

If you enjoyed *Relying on the Enemy* (or even if you didn't), would you take a moment to leave a review on your preferred retail site? It is a wonderful way to support an author by helping new readers decide whether to pick up a copy of this book.

Thank you again for joining me for Marian and Gilbert's story!

Danielle Grandinetti

Join my Fireside News

Grab a spot on my virtual hearth and receive a weekly email filled with bookish content. As a thank you for subscribing, you'll receive a digital copy of my historical romance novelette: *Fire and Water*.

Subscribe Here

HARBORED IN CROW'S NEST

Welcome to Crow's Nest,
where danger and romance meet at the water's edge.
daniellegrandinetti.com/harbored-in-crows-nest

Confessions to a Stranger

HARBORED IN CROW'S NEST, #1
She's lost her future. He's sacrificed his.
Now they have a chance to reclaim it—together.

Refuge for the Archaeologist

HARBORED IN CROW'S NEST, #2
Will uncovering the truth set them free
or destroy what they hold most dear?

Escape with the Prodigal

HARBORED IN CROW'S NEST, #3
Only a Christmas miracle will save
an unwed mother and the lumberjack protecting her.

Relying on the Enemy

Harbored in Crow's Nest, #4
She's protecting her children.
He's redeeming his past.

Sheltered by the Doctor

Harbored in Crow's Nest, #5
A fake relationship might keep her safe,
but will it break their hearts?

Investigation of a Journalist

Harbored in Crow's Nest, #6
A second chance to set the record straight,
and rekindle a lost love.

Fairytale Retellings

Heart of Beauty

stand-alone origin novella

Discover the origin of Crooked Tooth Ranch in this 1870s western retelling of Beauty and the Beast.

daniellegrandinetti.com/heart-of-beauty

His Boss's Little Sister

stand-alone novella in the Apron Strings Tea Tale
multi-author series

A touch of fairy tale, a spoonful of history, and a teacup of hope ... a 1930s historical romance retelling of Hansel and Gretel.

daniellegrandinetti.com/his-bosss-little-sister

UNDERCOVER WISH
stand-alone novella, part of the Di Stasio Giornaliste
Agency series

*A Di Stasio Giornaliste Agency origin story and a retelling of Aladdin
and the Magic Lamp.*

daniellegrandinetti.com/heart-of-beauty

Di Stasio Giornaliste Agency

La Verità con Integrità. Truth with Integrity.
The Legacy of a (Girl) Stunt Reporter.
daniellegrandinetti.com/di-stasio-giornaliste-agency

Undercover Wish

Di Stasio Giornaliste Agency, #0
Alessandra Di Stasio
Chicago World's Fair: World's Columbian Exposition

Eyewitness Sketch

Di Stasio Giornaliste Agency, #1
Gabriella Salatino
Prohibition

Sabotage Games

Di Stasio Giornaliste Agency, #2
Emma Hancock
Summer & Winter Olympics: Lake Placid & L.A.

Shrouded Trail

Fraudulent Progress

Pursuing Dust

Hostile Ally

OUR HOUSE NOVELLAS

As the world marches toward what will become WWII, visit Our House as we join the resistance.

The Italian Musician's Sanctuary

Romance, history and intrigue at Our House on Sycamore Street.

Hunted by one man, can she open her heart to another?

Eden Cove, England, 1931—Margherita Vicienzo flees Italy pursued by her former fiancé, a member of Mussolini's Blackshirt. Smuggled illegally into England, Margherita is a foreigner at the mercy of strangers. Her limp from an improperly healed broken leg means she has nothing to offer the Ferryman family, who offer her sanctuary, and nothing to appease their son who resents her presence.

Luke Ferryman needs a wife. He wants to marry for love, but carries the weight of his family's generations-old expectations on his shoulders. Though he inherited the role of both baker and ferryman, he knows he can't fulfill both needs once his aging grandparents retire. A wife would help, but not an illegal one like the refugee his matchmaking grandmother is harboring.

As opposite as night and day, Luke and Margherita forge a tentative friendship that grows despite the constant threat of Margherita's discovery. But when strangers appear in the close-knit seaside town, threatening Luke's livelihood and Margherita's safety, the choice between justice and mercy becomes harder. And sacrifice proves the only answer.

The Recluse's Vindication
Rumors, Monsters, and Second Chances at Our House
on Heather Wynd

The Loch Ness Monster isn't the only recluse seeking a Scottish haven.
Bieldfell, Scotland, 1933—Falsely accused of murder sixteen years ago, American cowboy Benjamin Ford has chosen to hide out in the Scottish Highlands. Reclusive and not afraid to die, he rescues children out of an increasingly dangerous Germany. When his childhood best friend appears at his door, he's not the boy she remembers.

Eleanor Finch's life ended sixteen years ago. In one horrible day, she lost her dreams, her reputation, and her heart. However, she never gives up the hope of finding her friend, so when she learns of Ben's whereabouts, she leaves all that is familiar to convince him to return home.

But Eleanor isn't the only person searching for Ben. Hunters follow her trail. The thin veil of gossip and rumor may be their only chance of a future ... unless the Loch Ness Monster is real after all.

daniellegrandinetti.com/our-house

Christmas Cabin Series

One cabin in the Northwoods ... a decade of Christmas miracles.
daniellegrandinetti.com/christmas-cabin-series

The Sheriff and the Outlaw

Christmas Cabin, prequel

**Discover the beginning of the Christmas Cabin series
in this Christmas suspense short story.**

The Baby and the Guardian

Christmas Cabin, #1

**A baby in danger, a man in turmoil,
and a woman determined to save them both.**

The Neighbor and the Gifts

Christmas Cabin, #2

**Twelve days. Twelve gifts.
One unlikely hero.**

The Robber and the Witness

Christmas Cabin, #3
**A simple favor, a best friend's promise,
and the end of the line.
Releasing July 2026**

About the Author

Danielle Grandinetti is an award-winning author of 1930s historical romance, where mystery and suspense intertwine with hope. Her work has received recognition including a Distinguished Faith in Writing Award, two National Excellence in Storytelling Awards, and finalist honors in the FHLCW Reader's Choice, Selah, and Daphne du Maurier contests.

A second-generation Italian-American rooted in Midwest traditions, Danielle draws inspiration from tea, books, and the creative beauty of nature. Holding a master's in communication and culture, and driven by a lifelong love of stories, she crafts tales that celebrate resilience, diversity, and belonging. Danielle lives along Wisconsin's Lake

Michigan shoreline with her husband and two sons. Find her online at daniellegrandinetti.com.